PAUL CARR

A veteran of the U.S. Navy, Paul Carr spent his months at sea reading classic mystery and detective novels. He studied economics at Mercer University and worked in financial and computer-related positions before authoring six crime novels, including four Sam Mackenzie thrillers and two Detective Michael Dalton Florida Keys mysteries. He lives with his wife, Elaine, on a lake in Georgia, where he is busy on his next novel.

LONG WAY DOWN

PAUL CARR

W🌐RLDWIDE

TORONTO • NEW YORK • LONDON
AMSTERDAM • PARIS • SYDNEY • HAMBURG
STOCKHOLM • ATHENS • TOKYO • MILAN
MADRID • WARSAW • BUDAPEST • AUCKLAND

For Elaine

WORLDWIDE™

ISBN-13: 978-1-335-14711-0

Long Way Down

First published in 2009 by Paul Carr.
This edition published in 2020.

Recycling programs
for this product may
not exist in your area.

This edition published by arrangement with Harlequin Books S.A.

For questions and comments about the quality of this book,
please contact us at CustomerService@Harlequin.com.

Harlequin Enterprises ULC
22 Adelaide St. West, 40th Floor
Toronto, Ontario M5H 4E3, Canada
www.ReaderService.com

Printed in U.S.A.

LONG WAY DOWN

ACKNOWLEDGMENTS

I wish to thank my friends in the writing community for their invaluable critiques.

ONE

THE WOMAN IN the black jumpsuit walked under the dock lights and stepped onto the deck of *Slipstream*, Sam Mackenzie's forty-foot cruiser. Sam watched her from the shadows of the stern, a cold beer in hand. She was attractive, her hair long, silky, and black as ink. A tingle ran across the back of his neck when he spotted the gun in her hand. It looked like a .22, a weapon of choice for assassins: light and easy to conceal.

A bead of perspiration rolled down his cheek into his shirt. He took a long drink of beer, set it onto the deck, and crept down the other side of the cabin, his pulse drumming in his ears.

When he rounded the corner, she turned to run. He lunged for her, and they fell to the deck. Straddling her on his knees, he twisted the gun from her hand and stuck the tip of the barrel to her chest.

"Hey, get off me!" Panic gripped her voice.

Sam thumbed the hammer on the pistol. "Who are you?"

"I could ask you the same question."

"This is my boat, and you've got about two seconds to tell me why I shouldn't pull the trigger on this little gun."

"You're Mackenzie?" She blew hair from her eyes.

"That's right." Though he still couldn't see her face clearly, the eyes looked nice.

She drew a deep breath and let it out. "Somebody's trying to kill me. I need your help."

"People looking for help usually call or knock on the door."

"Tommy Shoes mentioned your name."

Tommy Shoes? He hadn't thought about him in a long time. Sam and Tommy had crossed paths in Chicago when they were younger, and Sam had forgotten about him until a couple of years ago when a friend said he was in Miami.

"What did Tommy tell you?"

"He said you're the kind of person who can get me out of this mess."

Sam glanced at the gun in his hand.

"What were you planning to do with this?"

"Like I said, somebody's trying to kill me. How about letting me up?"

Sam got to his feet and reached for her hand. "Let's go inside."

She took quick breaths, as if she might be hurt.

He opened the cabin door, flipped on the light switch and moved aside for the woman to enter. She stepped into the lounge and turned as if to say something, but her face went blank, her eyes rolled up, and she dropped to the deck. Sam stepped in and closed the door behind him. She lay on the floor, her face covered with perspiration.

He laid the gun on a table next to the sofa, got a damp paper towel from the galley, and mopped beads of moisture from her face. Her skin was pale, flawless, and appeared translucent in the light of the lounge.

The side above her hip was wet with what looked like blood, so he unzipped the suit to the waist and lifted the fabric. She wore nothing underneath, as if she had dressed in a hurry. There was a crimson smudge on her skin the size of a saucer, with a hole in the center. The bullet, if that's what it was, probably had gone straight through. He checked her pulse: barely fifty beats per minute.

After searching her pockets and finding them empty, he picked up the gun from the table and checked it out. It smelled as if it had been fired recently and the clip was missing several rounds.

Sam looked down at her; she was quite beautiful, and right now she needed to go to a hospital, but he knew what would happen if she did. There would be a lot of questions, probably more than she'd want to answer, and he didn't need that kind of attention any more than she did. He ran his fingers through his hair and sighed.

Sam went to his stateroom closet, lifted a door in the deck where he kept cash, and removed several of the green stacks, and stuffed them into a bag. Back in the lounge, he opened the door and glanced up the dock to see if anyone was watching. No one was around, but good watchers didn't let you see them. He picked the woman up and carried her to his car. It was warm for an April night, and he was perspiring from the effort.

He put her in the back seat and drove inland to Highway 441. Turning north, he went several miles until he neared Miami Gardens. A turn down a winding drive led to a large stucco building. It had a tile roof, and might have been a country inn, except it had no windows. It was nearly hidden behind a lush growth of palms.

Officially, this was Carling Research, a company

that dissected cadavers and produced study aids to be used in medical schools. Unofficially, it was an emergency medical facility for the few who knew about it. All payments were expected in cash. He suspected that the lion's share of the company income was derived from services to practitioners in the Miami crime industry.

Sam drove to the rear of the building where a large Mercedes was parked near the entrance. He pulled in next to it, got out of the car and walked to the door. A camera mounted high on the wall trained on his face. He spoke his name into a microphone below the camera and told about the wounded woman.

The door swung open and two men rolled a gurney to the car. They lifted the woman out of the seat, strapped her to the apparatus and rolled her inside. Sam followed them down a long hall to what appeared to be an operating room.

Another man and a woman entered the room, wearing hospital scrubs and rubber gloves. "You need to wait outside, sir," the man said.

Sam turned to leave and almost bumped into a tall blonde woman in the doorway.

"I need to talk to you," she said. "Follow me."

She led him down the hall to an office, pointed to a chair, and sat down behind the desk.

"Care for a smoke?"

Sam shook his head.

The blonde shrugged, pulled a long cigarette from a pack, lit it up, and blew a ring his way. Leaning back in the chair, she crossed her legs and stared at him. He pegged her to be about thirty-five, and she had the looks of a movie star. Her skirt was short, exposing long, shapely legs.

The office might have been decorated by the same people who do motels, with a sofa and coffee table at one end and inexpensive paintings on the wall. Security monitors next to the desk displayed the building entrances and the driveway.

"Nice setup," Sam said.

The woman blew more smoke and smiled, showing flawless white teeth. She wore bright red lipstick.

"We expect a ten-thousand-dollar deposit."

Sam nodded, pulled the stacks of cash from the bag and laid them on the desk. She leafed through the bills and dropped them into a desk drawer.

"I remember you," she said, "you came in a year or so ago. Had a couple of bullet holes big enough to stick your thumb in."

Sam didn't remember ever seeing her, but that visit was a blur after losing so much blood. His shoulder still ached at the mention of the wounds.

"How's Mr. Craft these days?" she said.

Jackson Craft had a boat in the same marina where Sam berthed *Slipstream*. He was a confidence man, and he was responsible for getting Sam's bullet holes patched up at Carling Research.

"You know Jack?"

The woman nodded, blew a smoke ring in the air. "He did a bit of consulting for us."

Sam couldn't imagine what kind of consulting Jack might have done for her, but unlike most business deals people undertake with Jack, Sam was pretty sure this woman knew what she was getting for her money.

"I'll tell him you asked about him."

She smiled. "I'm Carling. He'll remember."

I'm sure he will.

"We added a medevac a couple of months ago."

She laid her cigarette in an ashtray on the corner of the desk, pulled a card from under the desk blotter, and held it out for Sam to read.

"Remember the number. We can deploy a chopper in five minutes."

Sam suspected the cost would be high, but when you're dying, who cares. He made a mental note, just in case.

"You can wait in the lounge to hear what the doctor says about her. And let me know if you want a cup of coffee, or maybe something stronger."

Sam thanked her and walked out of the office.

A large man in a suit sat in the corner of the lounge talking on a cell phone. His hair looked like wet paint, glossy-black, and he spoke with a street-wise accent. He glanced up as Sam entered the room, mumbled something into the phone, and closed it. Sam took a seat and picked up a magazine.

A few minutes passed, and a man who appeared to be a doctor with blood on the front of his smock walked into the room. He glanced at Sam and headed toward the man in the corner. The man in the corner looked up and squinted his eyes, as if in anticipation of bad news.

"He didn't make it," the doctor said, "too much damage."

The man scratched the side of his face.

"Melba's gonna be pissed."

"I'm sorry, we did all we could."

"Can you...you know, get rid of the body?" The man had dropped his voice, but Sam could still hear.

The doctor shrugged. "Sure."

"Okay, I'll tell Melba he left town. Here's something for your trouble."

The man pulled several bills that looked like hundreds from his suit and handed them to the doctor. The doctor glanced around the room and palmed the bills. Sam pretended to be absorbed in his reading.

An hour passed and the doctor who had told Sam to wait outside the operating room came down the hall. He said the woman's wound was repaired, that no vital organs had been damaged.

"She'll probably sleep the rest of the night and can leave in a couple of days."

The doctor left, and Sam went back to the office where he found Carling signing some documents.

"Looks like she's going to be okay," Carling said.

"Yeah, the doctor told me. I'm going home. How about leaving word to have someone call me when she comes around."

"She your girlfriend or something?"

"No, we just met."

Carling smiled and pulled a bottle of brandy and two glasses from a shelf. "I'm calling it a day, myself. How about a drink?"

Sam looked at the bottle and shook his head. "I don't think so."

She poured one glass half full and held the bottle above the lip of the other glass.

"You sure? This is pretty good stuff."

Sam looked at Carling, and all he could see was lipstick and white teeth. Before he knew it, he said, "Okay, why not."

By the end of brandy number three, Sam and Carling were great friends and had migrated to the sofa to get more comfortable. Within a few minutes, they were close, talking softly, and sipping the good brandy. Carling's skirt rode high on her crossed legs, and her right hand caressed the back of Sam's neck. Carling did most of the talking, mainly about her eccentric clientele. Sam mentioned that the friend of the man in the lounge hadn't been too lucky.

"Yeah, he was DOA." Carling pulled Sam's face close to hers, looked from his lips to his eyes and back.

"What did he die from?" Sam said.

"What?" Her voice was almost a whisper, her eyes dreamy. She put her left hand inside his shirt and caressed his chest.

"What was it that killed him?"

"Oh, four twenty-two caliber slugs in the heart." She pressed her lips to Sam's in a long, hungry kiss. He put his hand around her waist and pulled her to him, but all the while he was trying to remember how many rounds had been missing from the injured woman's gun.

TWO

THE PHONE RANG and Sam woke with a jerk. He had
dreamed the injured woman shot him in the chest with
the .22. Putting the phone to his ear, he mumbled a
Hello.

"Sorry to wake you." It was Carling, her tone anything but sorry.

The sun pushed its way through the porthole like an
unwelcome guest, flooding the room with white light.
Sam looked at the clock: ten-past-ten. He had finally
gotten to sleep about four-thirty, and would have slept
another hour or two without the call.

He rubbed his eyes with his free hand.

"That's okay. What's up?"

"Your friend is gone."

Sam remembered about the dream.

"Gone?"

"Yeah, she got up this morning at six and left a few
minutes later."

"She had a bullet hole in her side."

"Yeah, but she's gone just the same. I thought I'd
let you know."

Sam ran his fingers through his hair, felt his face
flush.

"I wanted you to keep her there."

"Sorry, we don't do that. Oh, yeah, about your ten
grand?"

"Yeah?"

"I'll be keeping all of it."

Her voice had an edge to it, and Sam thought he knew why.

"You're still angry, aren't you?" Sam said.

"Why would I be angry?"

"Well, you know...the way I got up and left."

He still wasn't sure what had happened. They had kissed, and she was a world-class kisser, but the little voice in the back of his head said, Get out of here. He had ignored the voice before, but he usually regretted it. So he pulled himself away and told her he had to leave. It was one of the most difficult things he had ever done.

"Yeah, well, that might tend to anger a person," Carling said, "but I'm okay, forget about it."

Sam started to say something and she interrupted.

"Just don't get yourself shot again."

She hung up the phone and the dial tone droned in Sam's ear. He dropped the handset to the cradle, got out of bed and stretched in the warm rays of the sun. Carling didn't say that to wish him good luck. What she meant was, Don't come back, because you won't get in.

Sam made coffee in the galley and walked out on the deck. The newspaper lay on the gangway, encased in a plastic bag. He picked it up and carried it to one of the deck chairs under the awning.

Sipping his coffee, he scanned the paper for any mention of the woman, or of the man who died with four bullets in his heart. There were lots of crimes in Miami, but none seemed to fit. She said someone was trying to kill her. Maybe she knew something she shouldn't, or had stepped on somebody's toes. She was a great-looking woman, and that might have something to do with it. But what kept coming back to him was the gun and the probability that she had used it very efficiently to kill a man.

Sam walked to the railing, leaned on his elbows, and looked toward the inlet. The mirror of water threw the sun's glare back in his eyes. A mullet jumped near the boat, and Sam thought he and the mullet were alone until he spied a lazy pelican perched on a dock timber. The bird cast longing eyes toward the fish, probably waiting for the last meal to stop wiggling in its stomach. Its eyes blinked sleepily, and it pecked at something under its wing until the mullet jumped again. The pelican jerked its head around, flapped its wings, and dived into the water. It bobbed up a moment later, empty.

This mullet had savvy, and so did the mystery woman. Who would expect her to go up against Miami thugs and come out alive. She had taken a bullet, but had killed a man and gotten away. Like the pelican, though, they would be back, and Sam was pretty sure he would see her again.

SAM HAD BEEN running on the beach for about thirty minutes when he spotted Jack Craft about fifty yards away, tending a fishing rod. Almost a week had passed since Sam had seen the wounded woman, though he'd thought about her every day, hoping she wasn't dead. She'd said Tommy Shoes sent her to him, and Sam remembered that Jack had mentioned Tommy a couple of years before.

He slowed to a walk and angled over Jack's way. Jack turned, saw him approaching, and set the rod in a holder stuck in the sand. Sam mopped perspiration from his forehead with the bottom of his tee shirt and nodded toward a plastic bucket at Jack's feet.

"Catch anything?"

Jack Craft grinned and reached down.

"Got a bluefish." He pulled what looked like a three-pounder out of the bucket. "Thought I had something really big the way this baby pulled."

"Yeah, that's a nice one," Sam said. "Invite me over when you cook it. I'll bring the beer."

Jack nodded and dropped the fish back into the bucket.

"You got it. By the way, the tackle store had a sale on that rod you liked and I got it for you. It's on my boat if you want to come by."

Sam smiled. Jack had gotten the fishing bug after watching an old geezer drag a large Pompano in from the surf. He had been working on Sam to go fishing with him. Sam kept putting him off.

"As a matter of fact, why don't I give you a ride back. I need to get this blue in the reefer."

"That sounds good. It's too hot out here to run, anyway."

Jack gathered his tackle, Sam grabbed the bucket and they walked about two hundred yards to Jack's Mercedes.

Sam had met Jackson Craft about ten years before when they both were hired by a Government agency in Miami to bring down a notorious financier who had stolen a large fortune from retirement accounts. Sam happened to be good with a gun and Jack could run a good confidence game. The financier didn't have a chance, and Jack cruised away with his million-dollar floating home, *The Clipper*. Sam got his regular contract fee, along with a few bumps and bruises. Since that time they had been involved in a number of co-operative ventures, some of which Sam tried to forget.

Jack did most of the talking on the way back to the marina, telling Sam about his latest activity.

"I buy boats from the DEA and sell them to rich people."

"You have a boat business?"

"Actually," Jack said, "I never see the boats, I simply broker the sales."

On this particular operation, Jack said he had made an average of about thirty percent on the dozen or so boats he had brokered. He didn't mention dollars, but Sam knew that Cigarettes and Donzis, which were favored by drug smugglers because of the enormous engine power, would sell for a small fortune on the second-hand market.

Jack sounded like a legitimate businessman, but Sam knew he was actually Grand Master of the high-level con. This latest venture was just busywork until the right mark came along.

They arrived at the marina and walked down the dock to *The Clipper*. Jack led him into the galley, which was much larger than the one on Sam's boat, and pulled two beers from the full-size refrigerator. Handing one to Sam, he twisted the top off his own and took a long swallow, then reached into the bucket for the bluefish and plopped it onto a cutting board. He pulled a fillet-ing knife from the wall, sliced into the fish, separat-ing a four-inch-wide slab of meat from the backbone.

Sam sat in a chair next to the table, watching the op-eration. Jack skinned the two filets, zipped them inside plastic bags, and tossed them into the refrigerator. He rinsed his hands and said, "Be right back."

Jack left the galley for about thirty seconds and returned with a seven-foot surf rod. "It's a beauty," he said, scanning the rod from handle to tip, running his fingers over the ceramic eyelets.

Sam took it by the handle and looked it over. "You don't see many like this anymore."

"Better believe it. Why don't we try it tomorrow morning on the changing tide? We'll kill those blues."

"You've got a deal."

Sam stood the rod in the corner next to the table and turned back to sip his beer. Jack sat down at the table and rocked back in his chair.

"Funny thing happened last week," Sam said. "A woman, a real looker, came to my boat about midnight on Tuesday. She said Tommy Shoes sent her. Turns out, she'd been shot and fainted before she could tell me anything else."

Sam told the rest of the story, leaving out the part about him and Carling on the sofa.

"Oh, yeah, Carling said to tell you hello."

Jack's face softened, and his eyes drifted off to a pleasant place for a couple of seconds.

"Carling, huh, I bet she still looks great."

"She's gorgeous."

He smiled and shook his head. "I took her out a few times, but never got to first base."

"Maybe it wasn't meant to be."

"Yeah, maybe," Jack said. He took a long swallow of beer. "So, you haven't heard anything from this mystery woman since she left Carling Research?"

"No. I thought I might talk to Tommy Shoes, if I can get a meeting with him."

"You want your ten thousand back?"

"It's not that. I just thought I'd make sure she's okay."

"You said she's pretty. You wouldn't want to cash in on a debt of gratitude, would you?"

Sam looked at Jack and smiled.

"C'mon, Jack. That's something you'd do."

Jack winced.

"Hey, I was kidding. Anyway, I can set up the meeting with Tommy if you want."

"You can?"

"Sure, no problem."

Sam stood up to leave.

"How much did the rod cost?"

Jack closed his eyes, waved Sam away.

"Forget it. It's a present."

Sam knew there was no need to argue, so he thanked him and turned to leave.

"What about Tommy?" Jack said, "you want to see him this afternoon?"

"Sure, if you can arrange it."

"Why don't we get some lunch first and drop in on him."

Jack must know Tommy pretty well. He nodded, said he had to go take a shower and would be back in thirty minutes.

Sam walked off *The Clipper* and turned his eyes toward the water. Fifteen or twenty boats drifted on Biscayne Bay. Their sails, fat with the eighty-degree Miami breeze, colored the sea with green, red, and white dots. The scene made him envious for a split second, but he wasn't sure why, because he could do the same if he wanted to. Maybe he would take a cruise down to the Keys in a week or so if he could tie up a few loose ends, and see if Carling wanted to go along.

JACK WANTED TO try a new seafood restaurant and said he'd drive. Sam noticed a car following them, and it stayed behind them all the way to the restaurant. Sam and Jack went inside, ordered grouper sandwiches and beer. Two men came in a few minutes later and took a table about ten feet away.

"You see the tail?" Sam said.

Jack nodded. "Gray Dodge, picked us up right outside the marina."

"I think they just walked in," Sam said. "Maybe Feds."

"Yeah, maybe."

"You call Tommy?"

Jack shook his head. "I figured he's probably home. He usually is this time of day."

Sam chanced a glance at the table where the two men sat; a tingle ran up his neck when he recognized one of the faces. The waiter brought their beer and poured it. Sam turned up the glass, took a long drink, and set it down. For the second time in a week, he wished he'd brought his gun.

THREE

SAM KNEW THE man only as Grimes. He used to work for the Government, and their paths had crossed on a couple of jobs. Both times, he left death in his wake. He looked different from what Sam remembered, beefed up, his spiked hair lighter, almost white, but the eyes were crazy as ever.

They ate crab cake sandwiches with fries and left the restaurant. Sam checked the side mirror. Grimes and his sidekick followed.

Jack drove into Coral Gables and up to a Mediterranean mansion, built in the twenties by a man who helped kill the Everglades. Many others had owned it since then, most of them wealthy. Jack waited for traffic to pass so he could turn into the driveway.

"Used to be Mickey Jay's place," Sam said.

"You knew Mickey?"

Sam shook his head. "I just know he lived here."

"Tommy moved in when Mickey disappeared a year or so ago," Jack said.

Sam remembered the story circulating at the time: The owner of a tee-shirt shop at the beach got tired of paying protection money, hit Mickey on the head with a hot tee-shirt iron, and took him on a one-way trip to the Gulf Stream. He probably got what he deserved.

"Did Tommy take over Mickey's business?" Sam asked.

Jack shrugged. "I assume that went with the house."

The Dodge kept going down the street when Jack turned into the driveway. Grimes and the other man looked straight ahead as they passed. They didn't realize they had been made.

Jack drove up to the gate, reached out his window, and pressed a button.

"Yeah?" an anonymous voice said from a speaker.

"We need to see Tommy Shoes," Jack said.

A couple of seconds later the gate opened and they rode into the expansive turnaround in front of the house. They stopped close to the entrance, got out of the car and walked onto the portico. A short, fat man in a cheap brown suit opened the door.

"Nice to see you, Mr. Craft." The man smiled. He had perfect teeth, and he also had a black eye, the edges of it turning yellow.

"Hello, Frankie," Jack said, "Tommy in?"

"Sure. Step this way." The man turned and walked very gracefully for a person who had to weigh more than three hundred pounds and stood only a foot or so higher than the door knob.

Sam first met Tommy Shoes a dozen years before in Chicago. A guy named Roland had run up gambling debts and borrowed money from someone on the street. Roland couldn't pay the money and was getting threats. He asked Sam for help.

Sam and Roland met two guys in the back room of a restaurant where Roland told them he needed more time. One of the men was named Tommy Shoes; he wore a pair of white, patent leather wing-tips with flamingos painted on the toes.

Tommy had said to Roland, "How much more time do you think you should have?"

"A month," Roland said.

Tommy squeezed his lips together and shook his head. "You got 'til midnight."

"What if I don't make it?"

Tommy's eyes narrowed. "Believe me, you better make it, or you ain't gonna like what happens next."

Roland pulled a gun Sam didn't know he had and grinned. "That's okay, I'd rather settle the debt right now."

Sam knew Roland would kill both men, and had planned to do that all along.

Tommy and the other man were caught off guard and fumbled for their guns. Sam back-fisted Roland, grabbed the gun from his hand, and laid it on the floor. Tommy had drawn his own gun by that time, and said he would kill both of them. Sam somehow talked him out of it, promising that Roland would have his money the next day. Tommy wanted to work Roland over, but he settled down after a while and told them to beat it, saying if he didn't get the money when promised, that he would drop both of them into Lake Michigan.

Roland didn't have any way to raise the cash, so Sam called in some markers. Tommy played it pretty cool when Sam paid the debt. He counted the money, leaned back in the chair, said, "Okay."

Sam nodded, and was halfway to the door when Tommy called after him.

"Hey, Mackenzie?"

He turned around.

"I appreciate you not letting Roland shoot us. I'm

gonna remember it. I'll probably have to teach him a lesson, though."

Sam said he understood and left. He hadn't seen Tommy Shoes or Roland since. He often wondered if Tommy had dropped Roland into the lake anyway, just on principle.

Now the fat man led them into a large study where Tommy Shoes sat at a desk. Tommy stood when they entered and walked around to greet them. He hadn't changed much in the last dozen years: a little thicker around the face and the midsection, the shiny pompadour graying around the edges. He didn't seem as tall as Sam remembered. Tommy gave a nod and the fat man disappeared down the hall.

"Mr. Craft, what can I do for you?" Tommy asked.

He shook hands with Jack.

Jack smiled. "You know Sam Mackenzie?"

Tommy glanced at Sam.

"Sure, Mackenzie, I remember you." He grinned, pointed his index finger at Sam, thumb raised like the hammer of a Colt 45, and made a popping sound with his tongue.

Sam nodded, said, "Tommy."

Tommy wore a charcoal suit with a pink knit shirt unbuttoned at the neck. He turned back to Jack, grinned, and pointed at his own feet.

"Check out the shoes."

He wore dark green loafers made from alligator skin, with the heads of twin baby reptiles covering the tops. There were penny slots cut right between the little eyes. The backs of the shoes above the heels were pointed, with an inch of gator tail sticking out from each like cowboy spurs.

A smile teased at the corner of Jack's mouth.

"Those are interesting, Tommy."

"I can get you a pair, just say the word."

"Maybe later." Jack lost the smile. "Sam wants to talk to you about something."

Tommy's smile slipped away, too, and he nodded at two wing chairs.

"Sure. Have a seat."

Tommy offered them drinks and both men said they would have a beer. Tommy pressed an intercom button and told Frankie to bring in three Coronas.

Sam told Tommy what had happened and Tommy squeezed his lips together, frowned, and shook his head.

"I haven't seen her since that night," Sam said.

"That's too bad," Tommy said. "'Cause I haven't talked to her in over a week." He glanced down at one of his hands and picked at a thumbnail. Frankie entered the room and floated to the desk with a tray in his fat little hands. He poured the beer for Jack and Sam, and left Tommy's beer in the bottle. Tommy nodded and Frankie left the room.

Sam took a swallow of beer and set his glass on a table next to his chair. "Why'd you send her to me?"

"Pretty simple. I had to stay out of it. Mr. Craft speaks highly of you, and I remembered you from, you know, back in Chicago."

Tommy turned up the Corona bottle and drank about half of the beer. He set it down on the desk and wiped his mouth with the back of his hand.

Sam eyed him for a few seconds.

"Okay, who is she?"

Tommy held his hands up in front of him, palms out. "Like I said, I can't get involved in this."

"I'd consider it a personal favor, Tommy," Jack said, his tone not that of a request at all. Tommy seemed nervous. He glanced at Jack, studied his face for a split second. "Okay, but this is probably going to get me in trouble."

"We'll keep it confidential," Jack said.

Tommy glanced at the door, got up and closed it, and returned to his chair.

"Her name is Candi Moran. That name ring any bells?"

Sam stared at Tommy for a second and looked at Jack. Jack smiled.

"Moran," Sam said, "I remember Philip Moran. Disappeared with a few million dollars his clients had invested in his lending company."

Tommy made his hand into a gun again, pointed it at Sam and popped his tongue.

"He turned up in the Miami River with about a hundred bullet holes in him," Sam said. "And I heard they never found the money."

Tommy nodded and glanced at Jack, whose eyes might have narrowed slightly. Tommy looked back at Sam, stuck his thumbnail between his teeth and chewed.

"So, who's Candi Moran? His daughter?"

"Yep." Tommy pulled his thumbnail from his mouth, looked at it, spat something invisible from his lips.

"Who plugged her?" Sam asked.

"Had to be La Salle."

Tommy's voice dripped venom when he said the name, and his lip peeled back in a sneer.

"La Salle?"

"Yeah, Vince La Salle. Big guy with long hair, looks like a weight lifter or something. You know him?"

"No. What does he have to do with anything?"

"He took over Philly Moran's company."

That meant he probably put the body in the river.

"He killed Moran?"

"Sure, but the police came around here busting *my* chops about it, 'cause I used to work for Philly. I told 'em I hadn't seen the man since I started my own business a year or so ago. They said that's a good reason for us to be having problems, but we didn't have any problems. When I left, he asked me to stay away from his clients, and I respected his wishes."

Several seconds of silence passed, Tommy with a brooding look on his face. He glanced at his watch, said, "That about it?"

Sam looked at Jack, then back at Tommy. "Why would La Salle go after the girl?"

"I don't know. Maybe she threatened him for killing her old man."

Sam nodded at Tommy and glanced at Jack, who shrugged, as if to say he couldn't think of anything else.

Sam drained his Corona. "What happened to Frankie?"

"La Salle's men came by here a few days ago. Tried to get me to tell 'em where Candi's hiding. Frankie got pissed off the way they talked to me and mixed it up with one of 'em. He's kind of protective...you know what I mean. You think he looks bad, the other guy ran out of here carrying one of his own ears. Frankie clipped him with a sap."

"Why would they think you know anything about Candi?"

Tommy looked wistful and his eyes softened.

"I used watch out for Candi, made sure nobody bothered her."

Tommy looked as if he might say more, and Sam waited for several seconds until Tommy finally leaned back in his chair, crossed his arms.

"What about the Government? Where do they fit in?"

Tommy shook his head.

"They don't fit in nowhere, far as I know."

THEY FINISHED THEIR beer, said goodbye, and left. As they rode through the electronic gate and pulled into the traffic, Sam looked for the gray Dodge. He spotted it turn onto the street several cars behind them.

"You knew all along, didn't you?" Sam said.

"Knew what, Samuel?"

"About Candi Moran, her father, the money."

Jack glanced at Sam and grinned. "What?"

Sam smiled and shook his head.

After several seconds Jack sighed. "Okay, I just didn't want you to think I was in the middle of this. Tommy called me last week about Candi. He said this La Salle character had already threatened him about dealing with Philly's former clients, and he didn't want to make matters worse. I told him to send her to you."

"Thanks a lot."

Jack raised an eyebrow and looked at Sam. "Hey, I knew you'd know what to do. And you did. This could be really big, you know."

Those were the key words: *really big.* Millions of

missing dollars get a lot of attention, especially from an old con man like Jack Craft. And Sam hadn't missed the look Tommy and Jack exchanged at the mention of the money.

"Why all the games, then?"

"No games, I thought you might want to hear everything from Tommy."

Which meant he would never have said anything if Sam hadn't guessed it.

"Yeah, well, I couldn't help but notice that you and Tommy are pretty chummy. Why is that?"

"I helped him out of a situation a while back. I suppose he thinks he owes me."

The Mercedes whisked north on US1, crossed the Miami River and turned right on the MacArthur Causeway. Sam looked out over the channel at a thunderhead rolling in from the Atlantic. The cruise ships wouldn't like that. They passed the Coast Guard Station and Sam could see a curtain of rain in the distance sweeping across the tip of Miami Beach, coming fast toward the causeway. He was glad when they rolled off the bridge ahead of the storm and slowed for the turn into the marina.

"He's lying about the Government," Sam said. "He knows something."

Jack glanced at him. "Maybe he didn't pay his taxes?"

"I recognized one of the men in the Dodge. His name is Grimes, and he isn't a tax man."

"Yeah?" Jack drove into his usual parking space and turned off the engine.

Rain pounded the roof of the Mercedes, and wind assaulted it like a grizzly tossing its prey. Jack turned on the radio and tried to get a weather report. A news program played, and the reporter said pieces of what was thought to be a missing fishing boat had washed up in Grand Cayman that morning. The authorities suspected an explosion of some kind. Sam wondered what might have happened to the boat. Lots of things can go wrong on the open sea. The weather man came on and said the rain would last through the night and be gone by morning. Jack turned off the radio.

"You should remember Grimes," Sam said, "from that operation that went bad in Marseilles a couple of years ago."

Jack nodded and Sam watched his face for some reaction, but he just leaned forward and gazed out the windshield at the sky. He looked at Sam, frowned and said, "Doozy of a storm, huh!"

FOUR

SAM RAN IN the downpour to his boat, a newspaper from Jack's car over his head. In his stateroom, he stripped off the wet clothes and changed into dry khakis and a sweat shirt. Still shivering from the sudden drop in temperature, he poured a shot of brandy and carried it into the lounge.

He picked up the phone and punched in a number he had not called in a long time, but knew from memory. He took a sip of the brandy while the phone rang. The vapors felt good in the back of his throat.

"Massage parlor," the voice on the other end said. Sam heard rock music in the background. The music faded away to nothing.

"J.T.," Sam said. His full name was John Templeton Smith III, and Sam had known him since his days in the military with Naval Intelligence. Now he spent his time as a computer criminal, taking money from the rich. Sam often wondered how well J.T. might have done in honest computer work, and concluded that he would have done poorly, because larceny fueled his genius.

"Sammy! I just thought about you."

"What's that massage parlor business all about?"

"Oh, nothing, I didn't recognize your ID. I see you finally broke down and got a cell phone."

"Yep, sure did." Sam had registered the phone to a fictitious person, as J.T. surely did with his own phone.

"Well, how you doing, buddy?"

"Not bad. You?"

"Hey, you know me, man. I'm doing great." J.T. hesitated for a couple of seconds and Sam heard computer keys clicking. "If I could keep the bad guys off my ass I'd be even better. Anyway, what's going on?"

People who lost large sums of money had been after J.T. for as long as Sam could remember, but J.T. always seemed to stay a step or two ahead of them.

"I wondered if you would check out some things for me."

"Sure, what do you need?"

"You know anything about Philip Moran? I think he went by the name 'Philly.' Somebody killed him, maybe a couple of months ago."

"Oh, yeah. I remember him. I figured he did something pretty bad to end up like he did."

"The rumor mill said he stole a lot of money, and someone killed him for it."

"Hmmm. How much?"

"I don't know. A lot."

J.T. clicked the computer keys again.

"Any chance some of that money's still laying around?"

J.T. could smell money almost as well as Jack Craft, and he usually tried to cut himself a slice of the pie. Sam didn't really care. He just wanted to find out about the girl and the guys trailing him. If J.T. found some cash in the process, more power to him. Besides, he had saved Sam's life a year or so before, and used a computer better than anyone Sam had ever seen. He always came up with answers no one else had.

"I heard they never got the money back," Sam said, "which is kind of strange. Why would you kill somebody before you recovered the money?"

"Yeah, bizarre."

Sam could almost hear the gears turning in J.T.'s head.

"His daughter also might be involved in it, so see what you can find on her, too. Her name is Candi. Probably Candace."

Sam also asked him to see what he could find out about La Salle. That might be overkill, but it couldn't hurt to get the information. This La Salle sounded like someone he needed to know about, even if he never saw Candi Moran again.

"Yeah, okay, I'll see what I can do. Anything else?"

"That should take care of it…no, wait, you remember a guy named Grimes?"

"Yeah, I think so. Crazy dude and real skinny."

"That's him. He's here tailing me. He looks a little different, but I'm pretty sure it's him."

J.T. said he would call Sam as soon as he had something, and hung up. Sam set the phone on the table, looked at the empty brandy glass, and got up for a refill.

The rain quit almost as quickly as it had started. Sam walked on deck and leaned on the rail, looking toward the parking area. The gray Dodge sat there, empty, but he knew they lurked close by with their eyes on his boat. He had been trying to figure how they had gotten on to him, and decided that they probably were listening in on Candi's phone when Tommy Shoes said Sam would help her.

Sam glanced up the dock and saw Grimes and the other man walk from the direction of the marina restaurant carrying cups of something, gazing out over the channel like they were tourists.

J.T. DIDN'T CALL back until a few minutes past seven. Sam sat in the Marina Bar and Grill, finishing a bowl of conch chowder when the phone chirped. He couldn't hear well because of the bar noise, so he went outside to a walkway overlooking the water. The beer sign came on and popped a couple of times. He pressed the button on the phone and said, "Hello."

The Dodge was still in the parking lot. The man with Grimes had come inside about fifteen minutes earlier and picked up an order of food.

"There weren't any newspaper stories worth anything," J.T. said. "This guy Philly Moran was just another citizen who met up with foul play, as far as they were concerned. My source had some stuff, though. He said the word is he stole millions from a bunch of investors and tried to disappear. Apparently, the other man you mentioned, La Salle, is the one who had him killed, but nobody could prove it."

"What about the daughter, Candi?"

"I found out she's missing, and might have something to do with the money."

"Huh," Sam said.

"La Salle's story proved a little harder to find, though. Looks like he didn't exist until Moran got killed. That tells me he changed his name from something else."

"What about Grimes?" Sam said.

J.T. chuckled. "My source says he died about five years ago."

LA SALLE KICKED the air near the Sensei's head. The Sensei jumped back and returned with a kick to the midsection. La Salle stepped back and blocked the kick, then spun and threw another kick toward the face. The Sensei's eyes narrowed in the millisecond La Salle's foot came toward his nose, and he dropped to the floor, swept his leg behind La Salle's knee and La Salle hit the floor on his back. The thin mat did little to cushion the blow, and the boom of flesh striking the wood floor reverberated throughout the magnificent old beach house.

The Sensei stood and pulled La Salle to his feet, an awkward move since La Salle towered over him by at least a foot and a half and outweighed him by more than a hundred pounds. La Salle winced as he got to his feet.

Little dude better be glad I'm paying him to do this, La Salle thought, otherwise he'd be dead. The Sensei bowed and smiled. He enjoyed this. The little man possessed a tenth degree black belt and had trained students of the martial arts for more than twenty years.

"You very good, quick," Sensei said. "Need work on defense, less on attack. All for today."

La Salle drew deep breaths from the effort, and his shoulder-length hair dripped with perspiration. He bowed and mumbled his thanks, and the Sensei walked out of the room. La Salle watched him open the door and leave and saw Marcus outside the door grinning. Marcus came into the room, uninvited.

"You kick his ass again, boss?"

"Sure," La Salle said. He never let the help watch his training. They might lose respect seeing a five-foot guy knocking him around the room. They wouldn't appreciate his remarkable ability to just hold his own with the Sensei.

La Salle walked to the refrigerator at the far end of the dojo and found a bottle of spring water. He opened it and gulped it down, then tossed the empty to Marcus.

"I'm going for a shower. Let me know if Danilov calls."

"Okay, Sally, will do."

La Salle turned and walked toward the wall where a Japanese fighting sword hung on two brass brackets. He reached up, took the sword from the brackets and looked at it, admiring the nineteenth-century crafts-manship.

"You ever look at this sword, Marcus?"

"Sure, I seen it. One day when nobody was around I snuck a peek at it. It's a beauty."

"Yes, it is," La Salle said, still looking at the pol-ished metal. "Would you do something for me, Mar-cus? Would you hand me the cloth there on the table?"

"Sure."

Marcus reached for the cloth and turned back, and La Salle slammed his hand over Marcus' wrist, pin-ning it to the table, and swung the sword down as if chopping a pork loin. The blade cleaved the tips from Marcus' four fingers.

Marcus screamed and jerked his hand away.

La Salle wiped the blood from the sword on the polishing cloth. He could tell that Marcus didn't know what had happened until he saw the tips lying there, splattered with blood. His eyes went wide and he gasped when he looked at his hand.

"Why'd you do *that*?"

La Salle looked at Marcus and smiled.

"Don't ever address me as Sally again," La Salle said, his voice calm and soothing. "It's either Mr. La Salle or boss. Okay?"

Tears flowed down Marcus' cheeks. He glanced at his injured hand and nodded. "Splendid. Now, don't forget about Danilov."

La Salle re-hung the sword and walked out of the room. He untied his black belt with his free hand and looked down at the blood spattered on his white uniform. He made a mental note to send Marcus to the store for a fresh one.

SAM STEPPED ONTO *Slipstream* as his phone chirped again.

"Some help you were."

It took a second for Sam to recognize the voice as that of Candi Moran.

"What do you mean? I saved your life."

"Yeah, you took me to that quack house, where I was a sitting duck for those guys."

"Well, sounds like you're okay, now. How's the bullet hole healing?"

"It's all right," Candi said.

He opened the hatch and went inside. "I went to see Tommy. He said he didn't know where you were, but I guess he lied, huh?"

"Yeah, he knew. He told me to call you because you're a stand-up guy."

At the refrigerator, Sam pulled out a beer. He twisted off the cap and took a swallow.

"Are you?" she asked, "a stand-up guy?"

He turned off all the lights and parted the lounge curtain so he could see the lighted parking lot. The Dodge guys were back from dinner. "Sure," he said. "If Tommy says so, why would you have any doubts?"

"Yeah, well, he doesn't lie to me, if that's what you're getting at."

"So what do you want?"

"You going to help me or not?"

Sam drew a deep breath and sighed. "It depends on what you want me to do."

"Meet me and we'll talk about it." She gave Sam the name of a coffee house in Little Havana.

Sam looked outside again, and said, "Okay, but make it in a couple of hours. I've got to take care of something first."

He hung up the phone and went to his stateroom where he found an overnight bag and packed some clothes and travel items. Thinking he might not be back for a while, he stuffed a couple stacks of cash in the zippered compartment, then put on a light jacket and dropped his Glock 9mm into the pocket.

Sam locked the hatch on his way out, walked to his car and got inside. The Dodge came alive, headlights flashing in his rearview mirror, and it followed a hundred feet or so behind him driving out of the marina.

He drove across the MacArthur Causeway and headed west toward the Everglades, the traffic light for that time of day. After about thirty minutes the city's neon lights disappeared and thickets of mangrove and palmetto sprang up in the headlamps. Black water glistened just inches below on either side of the road, broken only by the occasional thrashing of creatures clinging by a thread to the ecological chain. Pieces of dead reptiles and raccoons dotted the side of the road, casualties of high speed assault by the humans.

An alligator waddled across the road not a hundred yards ahead and Sam slowed the car to let it pass. The gator never turned toward the car's lights and displayed no urgency in escaping their inspection. It reached the other side and slid into blackness.

The old Indian store was near, so Sam kept his speed about forty and clicked on his brights. He spotted the sign within another mile and then the weathered wood building that had squatted there for at least a hundred years and now seemed to be sinking into the earth. An image of the place had stuck in his mind from a few months before when he drove to Naples. It had closed for the night, and no light escaped the ghostly structure. No one would find the guys tailing him until morning.

Slowing to turn into the shell-and-sand driveway, he glanced at his rearview mirror. The Dodge trailed a couple hundred yards back. Sam took his time so they wouldn't lose him, and turned in, watching the Dodge's lights go off as it neared.

He drove to the right side of the building, stopped, and turned off the engine, leaving the lights on. The car's beams illuminated the side of the store and an abandoned old stilt house about seventy feet beyond, down a narrow, overgrown path. He stepped out of the car, walked down the path, and reached the house in a couple of minutes, about the time the automatic feature turned off the headlights. Perspiration trickled down his neck inside the warm jacket.

Just before the lights turned off, Sam noticed a wooden stair leading up to the old house. He felt his way along, walked around the corner to where he thought he would be hidden and took his gun from his pocket. After a few minutes, his vision improved and he saw two men inching down the path.

They walked to the stairway, and one of them stumbled and cursed. A second later the man turned on a flashlight and held it low as they started up the stair. Sam stepped around the corner and swung the butt of his gun at the head of the one with the light. The man grunted and crumpled on the stairway. The light dropped onto one of the steps and rocked back and forth on the warped wood, illuminating the other man's legs. The man turned and fired. The shot went skyward as Sam pulled the man's feet from under him and dragged him down.

Sam picked up the light and shone it on the man with the gun. Grimes. He grinned as if he had just found twenty dollars.

"Hey, man, we aren't after you."

"I know," Sam said.

"Then why all the violence? We're the good guys."

"Get up."

Grimes seemed to be struggling to his feet when he jerked his gun toward the beam. Sam hit the gun with the flashlight, knocking it away, and smashed his own gun against the side of Grimes' head. Grimes fell back to the ground and lay still. Sam pulled the gun from Grimes hand and stuck his own in his pocket.

The light still worked and Sam shone it on the other man, who continued to nap on the stairs.

Something large rustled in the water only a few

feet away, and Sam shone the light into the wet under-growth. Two large red spots bounced back. An alliga-tor, maybe even more dangerous than the two reptiles from the Dodge.

Sam reached his car, drove out the driveway and found the Dodge parked on the highway about where he expected. He shot all four tires with Grimes' gun, threw the gun into the black water next to the man-groves, and drove away to meet Candi Moran.

FIVE

THE DOORS OF the coffee shop stood open, and the sounds of low-riders floated through the entranceway on a balmy breeze. A silent ceiling fan turned lazily overhead. Candi was the only customer in the place at this late hour, and she glanced up when Sam walked to her table. She looked different from the last time he'd seen her, her hair in a pony tail and her face tan, as if she might have spent the last week in the sun. Although in pretty bad shape a week ago, she seemed to be okay now. She wore jeans with a low cut blouse, and glasses too large for her face. Her lips seemed fuller than Sam remembered, and he wished they were meeting for a romantic dinner, rather than to discuss someone trying to kill her.

"You sure you're Mackenzie?" she asked and raised an eyebrow.

"I'm sure."

"Sorry. I never got a good look at you." She glanced toward the door and then back at Sam. "Sit down. You're attracting attention." She nodded toward a short old woman next to the cash register who looked as if she might have her fingers wrapped around a weapon underneath the counter.

Sam took the seat across from Candi, which gave him a view of the door she watched so carefully.

An awkward silence lay between them until a waitress arrived at the table and took their order for *cafe con leche*. He watched her retreat toward the counter before speaking.

"So, what is it you want me to do?" Sam said.

"I don't know. I mean, Tommy said to go see you and you'd know what to do."

Sam nodded and wondered about the wisdom of getting involved in this mess. He didn't owe Tommy Shoes or this girl anything.

"Did you plug La Salle's guy with that little gun of yours?" Sam said.

Candi Moran's eyes widened behind the glasses. "Well…yeah. But he shot me first. I just happened to be better with a gun. I heard he died, and that's too bad. Too bad, he didn't linger awhile, that is."

"I still have your gun, but I didn't bring it with me."

She smiled for the first time. "Don't worry, I got another one."

A car drove by with the radio playing a song Sam didn't recognize.

"Why don't you tell me what happened to your dad?" Sam said as the music faded away.

"Tommy told you about him, huh?"

"A little."

"Philly got a raw deal."

Yeah, I bet. The sound of a jet approaching Miami International droned in the distance. Sam, feeling warm inside the jacket, removed it and laid it on the chair to his right. The gun in the jacket pocket made a clacking sound when it touched the wood bottom of the chair. The waitress returned with a tray in her hand. She narrowed her eyes when she heard the gun, as if she had heard that sound before, then set cups of coffee in front of them. Sam waited until she left before speaking again.

"I heard he stole a few million dollars and got caught."

Sam studied Candi's face. She pursed her lips, glanced at the doorway and blinked her eyes. She took her time, trying to be cool, but Sam could see the blood rising in her face.

"Maybe you should just hit the road if you believe that."

Sam took a sip of the coffee and kept his eyes on Candi. He held the cup in front of his lips and had another sip.

Sam shrugged. "I never met your dad."

"Well, it didn't happen like that." She took a sip of her coffee.

"Okay, then tell me," Sam said.

"These guys are after me. That's the only thing that's important."

"Yeah, but I need to know why, and I assume it has something to do with the money."

"Well, I know what happened to it. That's why they want me dead."

Sam sat back in his chair and sipped his coffee. She looked at him, took a deep breath and sighed.

"Okay. Philly called me about three months ago and told me something funny was going on. La Salle had bought the business and Philly stayed on for a while to help him get on his feet. Philly said La Salle started moving a lot of money into dummy corporations. Most of the money belonged to clients."

"Clients?"

"Yeah, they handled…investments."

"What kind of investments?"

Candi raised an eyebrow.

"High risk."

Candi took a sip of coffee and then jerked her head as a car with loud pipes passed outside. She took another deep breath and set the coffee down.

"Philly said La Salle had tampered with the books. He made the entries look like Philly stole the money. That's when he started worrying about taking a fall. About a week later he went on the lam."

Candi's eyes became shiny and looked as if they might tear up.

"Did he take any money with him when he left?" Sam said.

"He took what belonged to him, about two million. He called me and told me all about it. Then, the next thing I know, they're fishing him out of the Miami River."

She took off the glasses, laid them on the table and turned away, tears running down her cheeks. Sam handed her a napkin and she dabbed her face with it. After a few seconds, she rubbed the corner of her eye with her knuckle and gave Sam a pained smile. She looked like a little girl who had just fallen and scraped her knee on the sidewalk.

"He tell you what he did with his money?"

"Yes, he said he put it in a bank in the Caymans. He gave me the account number and PIN, said if anything happened to him that he had my name on the account. I checked it out on the Internet and found it there, a little over two million. But I checked it again after he died and the balance was zero. The account transaction log showed that I took it out."

Candi looked at the door and her eyes widened. He glanced outside and saw the end of a black limousine sliding silently by the doorway, the windows so dark that he couldn't see inside.

"What did you do?" Sam said.

"What?" Candi seemed distracted.

"About the money."

"Oh. I didn't do anything at first. Then, after the funeral, I got steamed just thinking about it and called La Salle." Candi shook her head and sighed.

"Did you talk to him?"

She looked as if she might be thinking about something far away, and several seconds passed before she answered.

"Yes. He asked if we could meet and talk. He said he regretted what had happened and he wanted to do what he could to make things right. He said he didn't know anything about the money. I knew he was lying, but I set up a meeting with him anyway. Then, right after that they started trying to kill me."

"You didn't know La Salle before that?"

Candi blinked her eyes a couple of times and shook her head.

Sam nodded, wondering why she would lie about that. Her relationship with Tommy Shoes also confused him. Tommy could have more in mind than met the eye. He wanted La Salle out of the way, and might have a master plan for him to die at the hands of an outsider like Sam Mackenzie. If so, did Candi Moran work with him in this setup, or did he just use her situation as a convenient catalyst to solve his own problem?

Sam glanced back at Candi and saw her studying his face.

"Did Philly have any other problems before this started?"

"No. He seemed to think everything was going great until the money started getting siphoned off."

Sam leaned back and stared at her. His hand rested on the gun inside his jacket. "So, what do you want to happen now?"

She replied quickly, as if she had thought about it a lot, or rehearsed it for Tommy Shoes.

"I want the person who killed Philly, but I also want the money they stole from him."

"Sounds like La Salle is the one responsible," Sam said, "whether he pulled the trigger or not."

"No kidding. I know he did it. But he has men protecting him and isn't exactly the easiest target."

Sam nodded and frowned. "So, you want me to kill him tonight, or find the money first?"

A slow smile spread across Candi's face. "All right, we'll decide who can be the biggest wise ass later. Are you going to help me or not?"

"I'll give it a try and see what develops," Sam said. "Do you know where La Salle lives?"

"Sure, in a house on Miami Beach. Philly lived there before La Salle moved in."

Sam gave her a questioning look.

"I checked the deed records at the courthouse and it shows that La Salle bought it from Philly. That's a lie, but I don't have any way to prove it."

She gave Sam the address and he wrote it on a napkin and put it in his pocket.

"What's your fee?"

Sam shrugged. "We'll talk about it later." If he could get the money back for her, he'd just take some for himself. If that didn't happen, a fee probably wouldn't matter much anyway.

Candi watched his face and looked as if she might know his thoughts. She finally nodded and drained her coffee.

"One other thing," she said.

"What?"

Candi smiled. "I want to go with you."

Sam felt a flutter inside his chest. A bad sign. No, it wouldn't work to have her along. He could think of all kinds of reasons, but mainly it would be way too dangerous for both of them. Sam only wanted to find a place to sleep for the night.

Candi glanced at the doorway and said, "Stay here."

The limousine Sam saw earlier had stopped outside the coffee shop, its back window halfway down. Candi stood, walked out the door to the car and talked through the opening in the tinted glass. Sam caught a glimpse of shiny black hair that rose about three inches above a forehead. Tommy Shoes. Candi stopped talking and looked to her left over the roof of the car, as if she saw something, and then dismissed it.

Sam felt a tingle at the nape of his neck, which he had come to know as an alert from somewhere down on the plasma level. Within a couple of seconds he'd run halfway to the door with his gun in his hand.

"Down!" he yelled.

Candi turned and gazed at him, confusion on her face. The tinted glass went up before Sam reached the car. He grabbed her and pulled her to the sidewalk as a half-dozen holes punched through the plate glass door of the coffee shop. Sam dragged Candi through the doorway, the limo shielding them a couple of feet above the walk. The old woman hunkered behind the counter, eyes wide, and the waitress lay on the floor with a red spot the size of a quarter on her temple. More rounds burst through the plate glass and slammed into the back wall of the shop.

"Get out of here!" Sam yelled as he and Candi sprang to their feet.

Tires screeched outside, the limo tearing away from the curb. The old woman ran through double doors that led to the kitchen and Sam and Candi followed. A split second later an explosion ripped the doors from their hinges and deposited them atop Sam, Candi and the woman.

Sam's ears rang from the blast. A couple of minutes passed before he pushed up from under the rubble and slid the doors aside. Candi looked stunned, but otherwise seemed unharmed. She and the old woman struggled to their feet and peered into the coffee shop. Sam glanced past the hunks of glass, torn metal and smoke to see the destroyed limo, its rear two-thirds blown away. Smoking parts of it now lay scattered inside the coffee shop.

Sam pulled Candi toward a door in the rear of the kitchen and they stepped into an alley. He thought about Tommy Shoes, and how he might have drummed up a thimbleful of sadness for the man's death, but that had been used up on the waitress, far too young and innocent to die. Tommy's death only simplified the equation by one tiny variable.

SIX

SAM AND CANDI rambled through alleys for three blocks before venturing toward the main drag to reach Sam's car. They stopped at the corner and Sam peered around the edge of an old limestone building. He saw only the burning frame of the Cadillac limo. The attackers probably had gone. A siren blared in the distance on its way to the scene.

Sam stuffed the gun in his waistband and pulled his shirt over it. "How did you get to the coffee shop?"

"Tommy dropped me off." Her voice trembled. "Do you think he's dead?"

Sam looked at her face in the glow of a street lamp on the corner of the street. Tears welled in her eyes. She shook, as if chilled from the night air, and the tears broke loose and ran down her cheeks. She had seen the same thing he had seen, but didn't want to face the truth. He wished he knew how to make it better.

"Maybe he got out before the blast."

She nodded and rubbed the moisture from her face.

He thought about his jacket, which still lay in the coffee shop, probably buried under a few pounds of glass. Too bad, he really liked that old jacket.

He took Candi's hand and nodded toward the sidewalk. They hurried another block to the car, got in, and drove away, turning right to avoid the coffee shop disaster. Two police cars sped up the avenue from the opposite direction, sirens wailing and lights flashing, and made a quick U-turn in front of the smoldering heap of metal. More sirens whined in the distance as Sam's car disappeared down the side street.

The clock on the dash displayed 10:50. He'd arrived at the coffee shop around ten. It seemed like hours ago.

"We need to find a place to stay tonight," Sam said.

"We can go to my hotel."

Sam glanced at Candi in the glow of the dash lights. "They probably saw Tommy pick you up."

"Oh, yeah, right." Candi lay her hands in her lap and looked out the window.

"We have to ditch this car, too. They know it by now."

Sam drove toward Miami International and spotted a taxi waiting by a hotel. He pulled into the hotel lot and parked where his car couldn't be seen from the street. They got out and Sam retrieved some things from the trunk that he couldn't afford to lose if the car got hauled away, primarily burglar tools, fake passports and IDs, and a noise suppressor for the 9mm. He put the items, along with a flashlight and a pair of field glasses, into a bag, and they walked over to the taxi.

The driver had his eyes closed and his head against the headrest. Sam opened the back door and he and Candi got inside. The driver, a young black man with dreadlocks, jerked awake when Sam slammed the door.

"We need to go to Avis," Sam said.

The man nodded, rubbed sleep from his eyes, and started the engine.

It took only a few minutes to reach Avis, and Sam had the driver drop them out front. He used a driver's permit from his bag that he knew would be difficult to track, and rented a black Chevrolet Impala. It looked as if it would blend in as well as any of Avis' cars, and it had decent engine power. There were few customers that late at night, and Sam and Candi were on their way in ten minutes.

Sam drove to South Beach and left the car at the front door of the Palma Hotel. Only three vacant rooms remained, each on a different floor. The clerk, a tall young man about as wide as a pencil, showed Sam the choices.

"You sure you don't have anything closer together?"

The clerk shook his head and smiled, as if wondering why they needed two rooms. "Sorry, we got lots of vacationers. These rooms have two queen beds, if that helps."

Sam sighed and turned to Candi. "You mind sharing a room?"

Candi raised an eyebrow and pressed her lips together. "Looks like we don't have much choice. I don't want to be on a different floor."

Sam tried to read something into her look, but then let it go and told himself that they were here only because of the threat on her life; this wasn't a date.

They went to the room and Sam dropped his bag onto one of the beds. A smell of stale cigarette smoke lingered in the air, surprising for a three-star hotel.

Candi glanced around the room and smiled. "Not bad. I'm going to take a hot shower." She unbuttoned the top button of her blouse and flipped on the bathroom light.

His pulse quickened at her smile. *Don't read too much into this.*

"Okay, I'll be back in a few minutes. I need to move the car."

He went downstairs to the rented Chevy and parked in the lot, keeping his eye out in case anyone might be following. A young couple ambled down the street. They seemed interested only in each other.

Returning to the lobby, Sam wished he had something to drink, but the bar had closed. He walked to the counter and looked at the kid who had rented them the room, probably a college student with a chronic need for cash.

Sam slid a folded fifty across the counter and asked if the kid might know where he could get some gin and tonic. The kid leaned against the counter with his hands spread wide and stared at the bill. He glanced at Sam and then to either side. Seeing the lobby empty, he scooped up the fifty and walked around the counter past Sam toward the bar. Gone less than five minutes, he returned carrying a paper bag with two bottles, the hint of a smile on his face when he handed the bag to Sam.

Back in the room Sam found Candi in a short hotel robe, standing next to one of the beds, pulling back the spread. Her legs were tanned and beautiful. The pony tail gone, her damp hair hung loosely around her face. Her skin glowed from the heat of the shower. The bathroom door stood open. Shower steam and the smell of expensive soap floated on the air, making Sam's head feel light as a helium balloon.

He set the bottle on the table and glanced at Candi. "How about a drink?"

She looked at the bottle and smiled. "Okay."

Sam picked up the plastic bucket and started for the door. "I need to get some ice."

When he returned, Candi had glasses on the table and the bottles open. He filled the glasses with shaved ice and made the drinks. Handing her one, they sat down opposite each other, the little round table separating them by only a couple of feet. Sam hoisted his glass in a toast.

"Here's to being alive."

The image of the dead waitress flashed into his head and he felt a twinge of guilt. Candi must have read his mind; she gave him a smile and held up her own glass.

"Alive in Miami Beach."

Candi drank half of her drink, then set the glass on the table. She looked at Sam and swept her hair from across her eye with her fingers.

Sam managed a slow smile and took a drink of the gin and tonic. She had natural beauty, even with wet hair and no makeup, but it made him feel like an amateur flutist, charming a cobra from a basket.

"So," Candi said, "Tommy didn't say much about you. How did he know you, anyway?"

Sam told her the story about his friend who owed Tommy the money, and about how they had come to an understanding.

"Yeah, that sounds like Tommy, actually a pretty nice guy. You know, all those years he hung around, he never made a pass at me. There were a few guys who did, and they didn't stay around long if he found out about it. I'm going to miss him. I really am."

Candi looked as if she might be in another place, but then took another gulp from the glass and drained it. Mixing herself another drink, she looked at him and raised an eyebrow. He tossed his drink back and set the glass down for her to fill it up.

Tommy Shoes had done some bad things in his life, but Candi didn't seem to know about that. She probably liked the funny shoes, the slick hair and the cool dialogue.

"You been in Miami a long time?" Sam said.

"Yep. All my life, except when I went off to college."

"Where did you go to college?"

"Berkeley. I majored in accounting."

Sam smiled. "Accounting?"

Candi tilted her head and narrowed her eyes.

"Yeah, my dad worked as an accountant. What's wrong with that?"

"Were you planning to follow in his footsteps?"

"Is that supposed to be some kind of wisecrack?"

Sam shook his head, realizing he treaded in dangerous territory.

"No… I just can't quite picture you poring over ledgers and stuff like that."

"Yeah, well, I'm actually pretty good at accounting. The only problem is, I hate it."

Sam gave her a questioning look.

"Philly always said everybody needs something solid to fall back on."

Sam nodded. Pretty funny, advice like that coming from a guy who probably had worked unsavory angles most of his life.

"So," Candi said, "what are we going to do?"

"Too early to say. Lots of things to consider."

"But you do have a plan, though, right?"

"Oh, yeah, of course," Sam lied.

Candi gave him a "Don't kid me" look and drank the remainder of her second drink.

They talked for another thirty minutes and had two more drinks. Then Candi stood up.

"I'm going to bed." She went into the bathroom and stayed for a couple of minutes, came out and padded over to Sam. Leaning over, she gave him a quick kiss on the lips. She tasted like mint.

She walked to the bed, stopped and looked at the floor for a few seconds, as if contemplating something.

"I guess Tommy knew you pretty well."

"What do you mean?"

She turned and looked at him.

"You saved my life."

How do you respond to a remark like that? Besides, he still had the kiss and those smooth, long legs on his mind.

Candi opened the robe and dropped it to the floor.

"Look if you want to," she said over her shoulder. "I'm just too tired right now to care." She slid under the sheet with the grace of a cat.

Sam did look, only because he couldn't tear his eyes away. She looked very sexy settling under the thin sheet. He wondered if her remark might be a cue for him, but he had his answer a few seconds later when she fell asleep.

He sat at the table for another hour, drinking gin with very little tonic, thinking about his plan for La Salle, and he got slightly toasted by the time he finally got up and went into the bathroom. He took a long, cold shower and tried to wash away the searing image of Candi Moran lying naked just a few feet away.

THE SHAFT OF morning sun sliced its way through the east window, illuminating the tiniest of airborne particles, and covering the table with a pleasant brilliance. La Salle sipped espresso from a tiny cup and read the front page of the *Miami Herald*. The limousine explosion and death of the coffee shop waitress garnered only four square inches of news space.

La Salle looked up from the paper at Marcus who stood on the other side of the table with his hands hanging crossed in front of him, his right hand bandaged with gauze and tape and appearing twice its normal size. Poor Marcus. Maybe he had learned his lesson. Marcus glanced away from his boss and rolled his shoulders, then glanced back, probably to see if he still stared at him. La Salle ate a bite of toast and marmalade and had another sip of coffee.

"Tell me again how it happened," La Salle said.

"Gino waited up the street until he had her in the cross hairs, but by the time he fired, she dropped out of sight."

"He missed?"

"That's correct, Mr. La Salle."

"So he thought he would salvage the operation by blowing up Tommy's car."

"Them was his words, exactly."

"He knew Tommy was in the back?"

Marcus' eyes slid away for a split second, and then came back.

"Yes, sir. That's how he found Candi, by following Tommy."

"How did he blast the car?"

"I believe he said he used a rocket launcher."

La Salle sipped espresso and nodded.

"Is Gino outside right now?"

"Yes, sir, I believe he is."

"Ask him to come in. I want to speak with him."

Marcus turned and walked out. He returned a few seconds later with Gino in tow.

"That will be all, Marcus."

Marcus glanced at Gino and then nodded to La Salle and made a fast exit. Gino sidled up to the table, his face flush and hands trembling.

La Salle leaned back in his chair, crossed his arms in front of him and stared at Gino. Gino, about forty, carried a little extra weight and had thin black hair with a business cut. Though he seemed nervous, his eyes stayed steady and gave away nothing. La Salle liked that.

"Marcus told me how you blew up Tommy's limo. Do you realize the kind of damage you caused on that street?"

"Yes, sir. I didn't realize the rocket thing could do that."

"You put me in a bad position, Gino. The authorities are already after me about Philip Moran, and they know Tommy and I are competitors."

"I'm really sorry, boss. I didn't mean to..."

La Salle waved his hand in the air and closed his eyes. Gino stopped talking.

"No explaining, Gino. You screwed up, big time. But your biggest problem is that you missed your target. I want you to get out of here and find her, and this time you'd better not miss. Is that understood?"

La Salle leaned forward and his eyes connected with Gino's.

Gino nodded. "Don't worry, boss, I won't miss."

"Okay, see that you don't." He gave Gino the look again. "I'd hate for you to miss out on our little project."

Gino had to know what that really meant. He would be dead if unsuccessful again. Gino took a breath, let it out and nodded.

"That will be all."

Gino thanked him and walked out of the room.

La Salle leaned back in his chair and thought about Tommy Shoes. Without a doubt, he *now* would keep his nose out of things that didn't concern him. The law probably wouldn't be a problem.

He picked up the telephone and punched in a cell phone number. The phone rang several times before Grimes answered, and then a clacking sound followed, as if the phone might have been dropped. Then Grimes answered again.

"Hello." He sounded as if in a hole, and something made a swishing noise in the background.

"What's your status?" La Salle said.

"We're in the hospital. Olsen has a machine hooked up to his insides, pumping stuff, and my leg is gone."

"What do you mean your leg is gone?"

"I think an alligator ate it."

They had botched it. This fellow Sam Mackenzie led them down the garden path. Mackenzie would have to be eliminated, of course.

Grimes said he'd be back on the trail when he could get a pair of crutches and a supply of heavy duty pain-killers. He also said Olsen would be out of commis-sion for a while, so he'd be flying solo. La Salle shook his head and sighed; these guys might be too stupid to live. He would have to think about that.

He punched the intercom button and told Marcus he

wanted to go see Danilov in one hour. Then he poured another cup of espresso, picked up the *Miami Herald* and went back to his toast and marmalade.

SEVEN

Sam woke at ten-thirty and found Candi gone. He got out of bed, put on a fresh pair of pants and went into the bathroom to shave. A few minutes later he heard Candi come in the door and set a rustling paper bag on the table.

She leaned into the bathroom and said, "I got breakfast from the restaurant."

Sam rinsed off the shaving cream, dried his face and walked out.

"You know, La Salle's place is close by, and his men could have been in the restaurant."

Candi shrugged. "Yeah, but they weren't; I was careful. I happen to know something about these guys, remember?"

Sam nodded, reached for the bag and pulled out the coffee and sandwiches. "I've been thinking. If I could get inside La Salle's house, I might find some information about the money he took from you."

Candi picked up her sandwich and said, "Maybe, but it'll be dangerous."

"I'm sure of that," Sam said. He took a sip of coffee. "What would be the easiest way to get in there?"

Candi reached into her pocket and came out with two discolored keys on a wire ring. "There's a back door that not many people know about. Philly showed it to me a long time ago. He said I should use it if anybody ever came to kill us."

Sam took a bite of his sandwich and looked at her. "It must have been tough growing up like that, always afraid."

Candi smiled and said, "I wasn't afraid. I had an escape hatch."

She laid the two keys on the table in front of Sam and he picked them up. "How long have you had these?"

"Ten or fifteen years." She shrugged.

Sam nodded and put them into his pocket. The locks might have changed since then, but he could try the keys.

THEY LEFT THE hotel at eleven. Sam drove them to La Salle's house, slowly passed the front grounds, and turned up a side street that bordered the property. The street was narrow, cars parked on either side with little room for traffic to pass. An eight-foot wrought iron fence surrounded La Salle's place. It looked like a thousand pitch forks lined up side-by-side, not something Sam would want to climb.

"You can go through a gate behind that thicket of palmetto," Candi said, pointing toward the back corner of the fence. "One of the keys should open the padlock."

Sam turned the car around and parked where he could see the entrance to La Salle's driveway from the street. He pulled the field glasses from his bag and focused.

"Two guys are always in the house when La Salle's at home," Candi said.

"You know them?"

"Sure. Marcus and Gino. I don't remember their last names, but they've been there for years. They have bedrooms on the back side of the house."

"Do you know if they have a safe for keeping valuables or important papers?"

Candi frowned. "I don't know."

"What about an alarm?"

"Philly didn't have one. He never thought he needed it."

They sat for an hour before an old Ford came into view and drove down the driveway toward the street. A middle-aged woman with skin the color of cinnamon sat behind the wheel. Sam gave the glasses to Candi. "Who's that in the Ford?"

Candi put the glasses to her eyes. "Miranda, the maid. She comes in for a few hours each morning and usually leaves about noon."

An entrance gate opened and Miranda drove out. They waited thirty more minutes before a white Jaguar sedan came down the driveway.

"That's La Salle's car," Candi said.

Sam dropped the glasses and glanced at Candi.

Candi shrugged and said, "So, I know what kind of car he has."

A Cadillac Seville followed the Jaguar. Two men rode inside and Sam assumed they were Marcus and Gino. The entrance gate opened, and both cars drove out and turned toward South Beach.

"Okay," Sam said, "I'll go inside while they're gone. Why don't you follow La Salle and keep an eye on him?"

Candi agreed and Sam got out of the car and took his

bag from the back seat. Scooting over to the driver's side, Candi sped off to catch up with the Jaguar and the Caddy.

Sam ambled to the palmetto thicket and looked around to see if anyone watched. A couple of cars passed, and an old man walked by on the other side of the street with a poodle on a leash. He glanced at Sam, then at Sam's bag. The dog jerked on the leash and pulled the man into the grass along the street. The man lost interest in Sam, talking baby talk as the poodle bowed up with an urgent expression on its wooly jaws. Within a few seconds the dog scratched the earth and they walked on.

Sliding behind the thick foliage, Sam found the gate with the padlock Candi had mentioned. The lock appeared to be new and neither of the keys fit. He unzipped a pocket inside his bag, pulled out a noise suppressor and screwed in onto the business end of the 9mm. Stepping a couple feet away, he held the tip of the suppressor to the lock, turned his head and fired. The mechanism burst open with a noise that sounded like a cow bell clanking. He put the gun in his waistband and removed the remains of the lock. The gate groaned as he pushed it open and slid inside the yard.

Mangrove, banana trees and palmetto grew in thickets. Although well manicured, the grounds had been designed primarily to limit visibility. He made his way through the well-tended jungle to the side of the house and found the escape hatch Candi had described. It was a full-size door, close to the rear corner of the house, encased in the limestone base.

Satisfied that no one could view him from the street, he tried one of the keys in the lock. The lock snapped and he felt the door release. Pushing it open, he looked inside. It was dark, and he pulled his flashlight from his bag. He stepped through the doorway, closing the door behind him. The light illuminated a basement straight ahead and to Sam's right. The air felt damp. An odor of mildew reminded him of the smell in his grandfather's cellar a lifetime ago.

Sam shone the light to the right. A stair led up to a door. He climbed the steps, turned the doorknob and heard the lock click. The door swung inward to a room dimly lit and cool. Stepping through the doorway, he found himself in a pantry. He turned to push the door closed and saw that it actually served as a swinging pantry case containing several shelves of canned soups, vegetables and meats. A key hung from a hook underneath one of the shelves. Probably for the gate, and now they would need a new one. He turned off the flashlight, dropped it into his bag and walked through the pantry to the kitchen.

Soft music played somewhere in the house, and fractured notes of a by-gone era floated in the air. Sam wondered if someone might have been left to watch the place. He pulled the 9mm from his waistband and eased through the kitchen and down a wide hall. He passed a huge living room with paintings on the wall, wool rugs partially covering hardwood floors, and lots of blond, antique furniture. Next door was an office with a desk in the center. The music came from a radio on the desk corner. A computer sat on a table beside the desk. Sam eased inside and turned off the radio. The silence made him feel vulnerable. The drawers of the desk were unlocked and he opened each one and looked inside. A few loose papers dotted the center drawer: old utility bills and charge card receipts be-

longing to Philip Moran. None of them held any interest for Sam. The other drawers contained only pens,
pencils and paper clips.

Sam figured there had to be a safe. He searched a
credenza next to the wall and behind two paintings.
Then he looked at the desk and saw a black chair pad
underneath. He slid the chair back, lifted the pad, and
found a loose piece of wood about the length and width
of a phone book. Underneath the wood, someone had
put a safe with a combination lock.

Sam removed his equipment from his bag and stuck
the rubber cups next to the lock. He turned the dial and
watched the digital screen flash numbers as the tum-
blers fell into place. It took about five minutes to get
the door open.

The safe, about a foot deep and half full of cash in
bound stacks, also contained a note with a telephone
number. Sam put the note into his pocket and looked
at the cash. The bills were hundreds, and he counted
thirty stacks of about a hundred each. Probably walk-
ing-around money for this guy. He put all the cash and
his equipment into his bag and shone the light into the
bottom of the safe. Empty. He closed the door, spun the
dial and replaced the board and the chair pad.

Sam's cell phone vibrated in his pocket, causing
him to jerk. He pulled the phone from his pocket and
pressed the answer button. "Hello," he said, his voice
a whisper.

"You have to get out of there," Candi said. "La Salle
just slammed on his brakes and made a U-turn. He's
headed back to the house."

The safe had a silent alarm.

"Where are they now?"

"MacArthur Causeway, probably less than five minutes away. Get back to the fence as soon as you can, and I'll pick you up."

"Okay," Sam said and broke the connection. He wanted to check out the computer before he left, and they were at least five minutes away, considering the traffic, so he punched the power button and waited for the machine to boot up. It required no password. Familiar icons appeared on the screen and he started the e-mail program. Finding the Inbox empty, he checked the other message folders. They were all empty, and he opened the one for deleted items. He found a single message from a person named DeliveryBoy and opened it. Dated about four months earlier, the message contained only a string of numbers. Sam thought the numbers might be for a bank account, and he wrote them on the note from the safe.

Sam searched for other documents on the computer and found nothing of interest. Someone had recently gone through the system, purging it of all information. But the person who got the e-mail message didn't realize it would hang around in the deleted files folder after being deleted. Sam turned off the computer and glanced around the office.

The paintings on the walls appeared to be works from the Renaissance period, but surely were copies. Photographs covered the remainder of the wall space. A middle-aged man appeared in several, some posing with Candi and some without, and Sam assumed he might be Candi's father, Philip Moran. In another photo, Candi posed with a younger man. He appeared to be a giant, at least a foot taller than she, with longish hair. His arm draped around her waist as she stood on tiptoe, kissing him on the side of the mouth. He looked uncomfortable, as if the photographer might have caught him off guard. Sam thought the big man must be La Salle.

He had the sudden feeling of intruding on something private, and backed away, bumping into an easel and grabbing the board cradled in its tray to keep it from falling. The board contained an artist's rendering of some sort of coastal development project with structures resembling those in Vegas, each with a showy theme of some kind. Casinos. The shoreline didn't look like Miami Beach, though. He wondered where it could be, with gambling illegal on all the Florida coasts. Maybe La Salle had something working in the legislature.

The cell phone vibrated in his pocket. How long had it been?

He started out the door and answered the phone.

"What are you doing in there?" Candi, her voice frantic.

"I'm on my way out now."

"Well, forget about the side gate. Marcus dropped Gino off there and headed toward the front to meet up with La Salle."

Sam put the phone into his pocket and pulled the 9mm from the bag, which he slung over his shoulder by the strap. He raced down the hall. Gino would be coming in through the pantry, so he went through the kitchen and a utility room to a back door he thought led to the garage.

He heard the tinkle of a key in the front door, the door open, and the sound of footsteps. They would go to the office first, which would give him time to go out through the garage. Sam reached for the doorknob and it turned in his hand. He stepped back and waited. The door opened, spilling light into the room, and the man Sam had seen in the waiting room of Carling Research stepped inside. He had a gun in one hand, the other hand bandaged. Must be Marcus.

Marcus turned to close the door, and Sam grabbed him and jammed the 9mm muzzle against his neck.

"Don't make a sound or you're dead."

Marcus' face and neck were flush, and he blinked a couple of times. He opened his mouth as if to shout.

Sam gave the muzzle an extra jab.

"Last warning," Sam said, "you understand?"

Marcus hesitated for a second, then nodded. Sam glanced at the floor-to-ceiling shelves next to the door.

"Lay the gun on the shelf. Real easy."

Marcus followed orders.

Sam jerked him toward the door, which still stood open, and pushed him through it. The garage was empty, and all the doors were closed except for one, raised about five feet. The Jaguar and Cadillac sat on the driveway outside. Sam moved the gun point to Marcus' back and let go of his arm hold. He reached into his bag and pulled out a long plastic tie.

"Okay, put you hands behind your back, wrists crossed."

Sam wrapped the tie around Marcus' wrists and connected the fastener.

"Hey, man, it's too tight."

"Quiet. We're going out. If you make any noise I'm going to kill you."

"Okay," Marcus said with an edge in his voice as he turned back toward the door.

"You better believe me," Sam said, "I've got nothing to lose."

They stopped at the door and Sam leaned down and peered around the corner. The Jaguar sat just a few feet away, the Cadillac on the other side. He saw no one around the cars.

"Let's go."

They stooped under the garage door and went out. Sam saw keys dangling from the ignition of the Jaguar and opened the passenger door.

"Get in."

"Man, I don't think I'd take this car."

"Get in." Sam shoved him toward the door.

Marcus climbed inside. Sam closed the door as quietly as possible, hurried around to the driver's side, and got in.

In the rearview mirror, he saw a large man exiting the house with a gun in his hand. The man ducked through the door, as if his head might scrub the jamb, and turned to glance at the car, his long hair swinging. Sam thought he looked like a television wrestler in a suit. He also looked like the man Candi had kissed in the photograph.

Tossing his bag into the back seat, Sam started the engine, jerked the shifter into gear and pressed the accelerator to the floor as La Salle bounded down the steps to the edge of the circular drive. The tires screamed on the brick tiles for what seemed like an eternity, then shot them forward, pinning Sam's back tight against the sumptuous leather of the seat. La Salle ran after the car and pointed the gun at them. Then he stopped and dropped his arms to his side.

Sam reached above the visor and found a remote control labeled "Gate" and "Garage" with colored plastic tape. He pressed the gate button and dropped it on the seat. The gate opened before the Jaguar reached it. Sam slowed for a split second and then accelerated onto the street. He pulled directly in front of a courier van, causing its driver to slam on brakes, and missed hitting an oncoming stretched Mercedes by only a few feet. He kept his eye on the rearview mirror, and a few seconds later he saw the Cadillac tear out into the traffic and smash into a silver Lexus. The Lexus spun around in the street and banged into two other cars, boxing the Caddy in. Sam glanced in the mirror one last time before turning toward Miami. La Salle climbed out of the car, dusted something from the sleeve of his suit and stared at the rear end of his stolen Jaguar.

EIGHT

MARCUS SAID NOTHING until they started across the causeway.

"You gonna let me go?"

Sam looked at him on the edge of the bucket seat. His head almost touched the dash, his face pale, bound hands shaking behind him.

"Sure, in good time."

"You're a dead man; you know that, don't you?"

Sam glanced at him again and grinned.

"You think so?"

"La Salle's a lunatic, and he loves this car more than anything. He'll get you if it's the last thing he does." Marcus took a deep breath, let it out and turned to look out the window. "Trouble is, he's going to get me too. He'll blame me for you ambushing me like that."

"Hey, happens to the best. Person in his position should know that."

Marcus turned his head back to look at Sam.

"Yeah, but like I said, he ain't no ordinary person. He's crazy as a bat. He cut my fingertips off for not calling him Mr. La Salle."

"You're kidding?"

"No," Marcus said, shaking his head, eyes wide.

"He smashed the Caddy coming out the gate," Sam said.

"Yeah. That'll be my fault too, but this car is going to be the big problem."

Sam looked at the polished wood on the dash. A GPS screen the size of a small television shone from the console. "It is a pretty nice machine. I think I'll keep it."

"Who are you, anyway?"

"Sam Mackenzie." He didn't see why his identity should be a secret. La Salle probably already knew it, and if he didn't, he soon would.

"You're the guy I saw at the Carling place that night Eddie died. Tommy mentioned your name too. How about my hands, man; this thing is killing me."

"I'll cut you loose when I drop you off."

"I don't know how long I can take this. I think my hand's bleeding again." Marcus grimaced and shifted in his seat.

"You knew Tommy, huh?"

"Yeah, I knew him. Not exactly my best friend, but a stand-up guy. He didn't deserve to die." Marcus shook his head. "First Philly, now Tommy."

"La Salle killed them?"

"He killed Philly. Gino did Tommy, but La Salle probably gave him the order."

"Why is he after Candi?"

After a long silence, Sam glanced to see Marcus twisting his wrists, trying to break the plastic tie. Marcus finally gave up, sighed and dropped his sweating forehead to the dash.

Sam repeated the question about Candi.

"I guess she knows too much."

"About what?"

Marcus squirmed in his seat. "La Salle's operation."

"Tell me about it."

"Why should I tell you?"

"He cut off your fingers, didn't he?"

Marcus remained silent for a moment. "Just the tips."

"I guess it didn't hurt, then."

"It hurt like hell," Marcus shot back.

"Okay, get even with him. Tell me what he's up to." Marcus sighed.

"He's had this project going on somewhere in the Caribbean, but I don't know where. He hasn't let us in on it for some reason. And I don't ask no questions. Could be bad for your health."

"Does anyone else in the house know about this project?"

"I don't think so. He keeps Gino in the dark like he does me. Hey, man, you got to cut me loose or I'm going to go crazy here."

"I'll let you go a lot quicker if you answer the questions." Sam turned on the radio and found a rock station. He cut the volume low.

"Yeah, okay, let's get it over with."

"Does this have something to do with the painting that's on the easel in the studio?"

"Yeah, I guess so. He's been taking phone calls and flying down there for several months."

"Tell me something else about the project."

"I don't know nothing," Marcus said.

"Sure you do."

Marcus shot a glance at Sam, said "Aw, man," then took a deep breath and sighed.

"He's been talking a lot to this guy named Danilov. But that's all I know. We were on our way to see him when La Salle called us on his cell phone and said somebody had broken into the house."

"Do you know Danilov's first name?"

Marcus shook his head. "That's all I know."

"Sounds Russian," Sam said.

"He don't talk American like you and me. Got this heavy accent, like foreigners have."

"What else?"

"That's it, man. I don't know nothing else. Believe me or not, I really don't care."

Marcus turned his head toward his passenger window and looked out. He probably had told the truth. La Salle wouldn't trust a flunky like him with anything important. Sam would drop Marcus off on a highway outside the city, where he couldn't get to a phone for a while. He pulled the note from his pocket and held it out for Marcus to see.

"You recognize these numbers?"

Marcus looked at them and shook his head. "Don't mean nothing to me."

The traffic thinned as Sam drove out of downtown toward Hialeah. He turned into a shopping center that looked as if all the stores had packed up and left town. Windows were boarded or covered with paper. Weeds grew through cracks in the parking lot. Remnants of a sign stood out front to remind shoppers of what they had missed.

Sam pulled a knife from his bag in the back seat and cut the plastic tie. Marcus rubbed his wrists. The bandage on his hand was soaked with fresh blood. He looked at Sam as if he didn't know what to do.

"Get out," Sam said.

"I need to call somebody."

"Sure you do."

"Not La Salle. I'm not going back there. He'll kill me for sure. I need to call a girl to pick me up."

Sam looked at him for a second and handed him the phone.

Marcus started to get out of the car.

"Call right here," Sam said.

Marcus nodded, punched a number into the phone and held it to his ear.

"Hey, babe. You gotta come get me." He looked up and down the street and told her the approximate address of the shopping center. "Okay, about ten minutes, then." Marcus told her goodbye and punched the power button.

Sam took the phone. "You interested in doing some work?"

"Work for you?"

"That's right."

Marcus gave him a look that said, *I don't believe this.*

"What would I have to do?"

"It might involve doing something bad to your boss."

Marcus glanced out the window.

"Can I have an advance? Everything I got is back at that house."

Sam had anticipated that request, and would have been disappointed had he not gotten it. He reached into the bag for a stack of the cash he'd stolen from La Salle and handed it to Marcus.

"This belonged to La Salle," Sam said.

"Even better."

"Double-cross me and I'll tell him you took his money."

"Don't worry. I don't plan on seeing La Salle again if I can help it."

Marcus gave Sam his girlfriend's number and got out. He stood there looking like a beaten dog as Sam drove away. The phone vibrated and Sam answered it.

"What do you think you're doing?" Candi.

"I don't know what you mean?"

"You drove off in La Salle's Jaguar. That can only lead to trouble."

"He won't need it when we finish with him."

A silence on the line stretched into a couple of seconds.

"Where are you, anyway? I lost you in traffic going over the causeway."

Sam gave her his location and told her where to meet him in a half hour. He drove to a garage run by a struggling Cuban businessman. Sam turned into the potholed parking lot and stopped next to the office. A small man with thick, graying hair walked out and leaned down to look inside as Sam lowered the window.

"Senor. Good to see you."

"Hello, Hector," Sam said, "I need to hide my new car for a few days." He reached into the back seat, grabbed his bag and got out.

Hector looked at the Jaguar and then at Sam and grinned.

"Someone, perhaps, is looking for this car?"

"Yes," Sam said, "perhaps."

"Policia?"

Sam shook his head.

"No problem. It will be safe here."

Hector opened the car door.

"Just a minute," Sam said. He got back in the car,

found the registration in the glove box and put it into his shirt pocket. "Okay, thanks, Hector. This'll make us square." Sam had loaned him five thousand dollars a few months ago, and Hector had repaid about half the money.

Hector smiled and displayed a gold tooth.

"You are too generous, Senor. I will make sure no one knows about the beautiful Jaguar."

The older man opened a large door on the end of the garage, got into the car and drove it inside. Sam watched as he pulled a nylon cover from a shelf and threw it over the Jaguar. He closed the garage door, locked it and held the key out to Sam.

"You keep it," Sam said.

"Come into the office. I have cold beer in the ice-box."

They went inside and Hector pulled two bottles of Dos Equis from a refrigerator that looked forty years old.

"Not Cuban, but it is good," Hector said.

Sam nodded. "How's business?"

"Pretty good, especially today." Hector grinned and handed Sam his beer. They clinked their bottles together and drank.

Sam sat in a lime-green, plastic-covered chair that had seen better days, and Hector sat behind an old brown metal desk. An oscillating fan whirred on the corner of the desk, and soft Latin music emanated from a cheap CD player perched in the window behind Hector.

A toy hula girl stood in suspended animation on the desk. Hector punched a button and she did a dance for them.

"If only women were that simple, eh, Senor?" Hector shook his head and had a sad, faraway smile on his face. He punched the button and the dancing stopped.

"Trouble at home?"

Hector took a long drink from the Dos Equis and said, "Papa moved in with us, and he drives Consuela crazy."

Sam nodded as if he understood perfectly.

"He just sits in the kitchen drinking coffee, talking about the old days in the cane fields, like they were golden times or something."

"Maybe they were," Sam said.

Hector tilted his head for a second, looked at Sam and grinned.

"Yes, maybe they were. But Consuela does not think so. She says she is going to leave if Papa stays much longer."

A bell rang behind Hector's desk. Sam looked out the window and saw an old truck roll into the driveway. Hector drained his beer and went out the door to take care of business.

Sam pulled the Jaguar registration from his pocket and saw that a company named NeoWorld Corporation owned the car. He called J.T. on his cell phone. "Anything on La Salle yet?"

"No, there's no record of him, as far as I can tell. And I've just about exhausted my resources."

That didn't sound good. Sam gave him the string of numbers from La Salle's computer and asked him to check the banks, thinking it might be an account number.

"How about looking up the NeoWorld Corporation too." Sam spelled it out for him.

"Never heard of it."

"Yeah, me either, but NeoWorld owns La Salle's Jaguar, and it could be a key to what happened to all that money that went missing."

J.T. said he would call back when he had something and hung up.

Sam saw Candi drive into the parking lot a few minutes later and went outside. Hector stood leaning under the hood of the truck, talking to the driver and pointing to something on the running engine.

Sam walked by and said, "I'll call in a few days. Good luck with your dad."

Hector smiled and nodded, and Sam got into the Chevy with Candi.

"What'd you find?" Candi said as she drove back onto the thoroughfare.

Sam unzipped his bag and showed her the cash.

"How much?"

"About three hundred grand," Sam said.

"Huh." She looked annoyed. "Where do you think he has the rest of my money?"

Sam shrugged. "What did you expect; maybe he'd have a few million dollars stuffed in his mattress?"

She nodded and said, "Yeah, did you check his mattress?"

"No, I never went into the bedrooms."

"Well, maybe you should have."

"Maybe you should have gone in there yourself."

Candi took a deep breath, sighed and looked straight ahead. Sam wondered why he'd signed on for this job. He waited a few seconds, then broke the silence and told her about the list of numbers he'd found on the computer.

"Maybe a bank account?"

"Yeah, maybe. I asked a friend who's good with computers to check it out."

"You think that's wise, giving someone a bank account number where you know there's a lot of money?"

Sam knew the risks when he dealt with J.T., and it made him even more uncomfortable for her to point it out.

"I couldn't do anything without more information."

Candi pressed the accelerator and the engine revved. They shot around an SUV, narrowly missing an oncoming truck before getting back into the right lane. The truck horn blasted.

"Oh, yeah," Sam said, "I had to take Marcus with me when I took the Jaguar. I just let him out a few minutes ago."

Candi shot a glance at him, her eyes wide.

"What did he say?"

"He said you know something, and that's the reason La Salle wants you dead."

Sam watched her face for a reaction. She rolled her eyes, nothing else. The traffic thinned out and Candi jammed her foot on the accelerator.

"He said *I* know something?"

"That's right."

"I don't know what that would be other than he took Philly's money and then knocked him off. That's the reason he wants me dead."

"He said La Salle has something cooking with a Russian named Danilov. You know anything about that?"

Candi pressed her lips together and sighed. "No, I don't. I told you what I know."

The car had sped up, and Sam peered at the speed-ometer; they were going almost seventy miles per hour.

"Better slow down. We don't want to get stopped by the cops."

Candi glanced at the speedometer and took her foot off the gas.

Candi had kissed La Salle in one of the photos. She had lied about her relationship with him, and now about what she knew. Sam felt the familiar tickle at the back of his neck and wondered if this might be a good time to say goodbye to Candi Moran.

"I'll split the money with you and we'll go our separate ways."

"What?"

"And you can have the account number, if that's what it is. Maybe you can get your own money back."

Candi's face turned red and she glanced at Sam, back at the windshield, then at Sam again.

"Wait a minute. You *have* to help me, there isn't anybody else."

"Sorry, no can do," Sam said, his tone firm.

Candi stepped on the brakes and turned into the edge of a liquor store parking lot, the Chevy's tires screeching to a halt. She turned off the engine and looked at Sam, her eyes watering and her lips pouting.

"Please…" Then her lips parted as if to say something else, but remained silent. She reached her hand to Sam's face and touched his cheek.

Something fluttered inside his chest, and he wondered if having her close to him might be as fatal as putting a gun to his head. He wished he had the strength to tell her where to go.

Sam sighed and looked out his window. A pay phone

hung from the outside wall of the liquor store, and he decided to try the telephone number from La Salle's safe.

"I'll be right back."

He glanced at the note, dropped coins into the phone and punched in the number. It rang four times before a man answered and said, "About time you called."

Sam listened for a second and his head began to throb. He hung up the phone, walked back to the car and got inside.

"Who did you just call?"

Sam looked at her and wondered why things had to be so complicated.

"I don't think you know him."

"Try me."

"His name is Jackson Craft."

NINE

"WHO'S JACKSON CRAFT?" Candi asked, her face a question mark.

"He's the man whose phone number happened to be in the safe with La Salle's money."

Maybe Jack had been waiting for La Salle to dial the number. Sam didn't know the answer, but he knew Jack Craft, and that man could be up to just about anything.

"So, what does that mean?"

"I don't know, but I'm going to find out." Sam opened his cell phone and punched in the number he normally used to call Jack Craft. Jack answered immediately.

"Sam?"

"Yeah."

"Why did you hang up?" Jack sounded like nothing out of the ordinary had happened, just shooting the breeze with an old friend.

"Well, I guess I might have been a little surprised to learn that La Salle had a pipeline straight to you, especially since you never mentioned anything about knowing him."

"Yes, I can see how you might have that reaction."

"How did you know it was me calling?"

"La Salle called about an hour ago and said you had the telephone number. He also said you cleaned out his cash." Jack chuckled on the other end of the line.

"How did he know *I* did it?"

Jack didn't say anything for a couple of seconds. Probably making up his answer.

"He might've learned about you from those guys who followed you," Jack said.

Sam decided to let it go for now.

"How about telling me what's going on, Jack."

Another pause.

"Not on the phone. Meet me in the parking lot of the restaurant where we last ate. I'll be on the far side toward the back at seven o'clock."

"Why would I do that? Could be a set-up."

"When did I ever betray you, Samuel?" His voice had an edge to it.

Sam took a deep breath and sighed.

"Okay, I'll see you then." Sam closed the phone and put it into his pocket.

Candi started the car again and pulled out into the traffic. "Okay, what's the deal?"

"I'm not sure. He said he'll tell me about it if I meet him tonight."

"You trust that guy?"

Sam thought about Jack Craft, shook his head and said, "I really don't know. I need some answers."

He decided they would go back to the Palma Hotel, since no one knew they were there, and wait for his meeting with Jack. They ordered room service and were finishing the meal when J.T. called on the cell phone.

Sam held his hand over the phone and said to Candi, "It's the guy checking on the numbers for me." He went to the sitting area where a sofa and a picture window overlooked the Atlantic and spoke into the phone. "What did you find out?"

"Those numbers don't have anything to do with a bank. I checked several, especially those in the Caymans, and none of them resembled that coding structure."

"That's too bad," Sam said. "Might have been an easy answer."

"Yeah, tell me about it. I did have another idea, though. The numbers might be GPS coordinates. Reading the string of numbers like it's written points to a place up around Greenland. In another order the numbers point to somewhere in Asia. But one sequence puts the location on Grand Cayman."

Sam remembered what Marcus had said about the project in the Caribbean, and wondered if there might be a connection.

"Yeah, well, might not be anything important, but tell me the Grand Cayman sequence anyway."

J.T. called off the numbers and Sam wrote them down.

"Did you find out anything about Danilov?"

"Oh, yeah. If it's the same guy, he's been involved in a couple of shady business deals in Florida. He lived in Havana before the Russians packed their bags and checked out."

"What would he have to do with La Salle?"

"Beats me, except they're both criminals."

According to Marcus, La Salle had been talking regularly with Danilov, who, it turns out, used to be stationed in Cuba. Cuba is in the Caribbean and La Salle has some kind of project going on in the Caribbean. Did that mean the project could be in Cuba, or at the Grand Cayman location J.T. had interpolated from the string of numbers?

"Hmmm." Sam closed his eyes and kneaded his brow. "What about NeoWorld Corporation?"

"Oh, yeah, NeoWorld is a pretty big deal. It incorporated a few months ago in the Cayman Islands, and my sources show that they have assets of close to a billion dollars."

Philip Moran's two million sounded to Sam like a drop in an enormous bucket. It also sounded like it might be a lot harder to find than by just digging around in La Salle's portfolio.

"That sounds like more money than somebody like La Salle would be able to scrape up."

"Yeah, it does sound a little rich. I didn't see any mention of La Salle, though."

No surprise there, but NeoWorld owned La Salle's Jaguar, so he figured in there somewhere.

J.T. continued. "NeoWorld's business is stated in their Articles of Incorporation as 'Financial,' but that doesn't mean much. They can do just about anything they want by owning holding companies, and nobody is the wiser."

"Anything else?"

"That's about it, I guess."

Sam looked around at Candi, who appeared to be reading a hotel brochure. He turned back to the window and spoke as quietly as possible into the phone. "Okay, this information has been a big help. Just let me know your fee and I'll make a deposit to your account, if that's what you want. I'm going to slide out of this one pretty quick. It's getting too risky." He planned to stay on the job until he learned what was going on, but J.T. didn't need to know that.

A pause on the line stretched into several seconds.

"That's too bad. I wanted to come down and help you out."

He wanted to get his fingers into NeoWorld's money, and he figured Sam might uncover just enough inside information to make that happen. Just what Sam needed right now, J.T. busting up the china shop.

"Thanks, but I'll take a rain check."

"You sure? I can be there on the next flight."

"Yeah, I'm sure. I'll let you know if anything changes, though."

J.T. said okay, and Sam heard disappointment in his voice. He told Sam to forget about paying him, that he didn't have much time invested. That worried Sam, because J.T. usually got paid, one way or another, for everything he did. Sam closed the phone and turned to see Candi standing directly behind him.

"I heard what you told him," Candi said. "Can I say anything to make you change your mind?"

"Maybe. It depends on what you say."

She gave him an innocent, pouting look. "What do you want to know?"

The photograph bothered him more than anything else. There had been a romantic relationship between Candi and La Salle, and that could cause a dangerous situation at some point down the road.

"How about you and La Salle?"

"What do you mean?"

"Were you intimate?"

Candi's eyes widened and she glanced out the window, then sat on the sofa and looked up at Sam.

"What if I said we were?"

Sam nodded and said, "Keep talking."

"I didn't want to tell you about it because I was embarrassed. He killed Philly, and I felt like a traitor. I promised myself I'd get him, and I came to you." Candi's eyes turned shiny with tears and her mouth twisted out of shape as she began to cry. She wiped her eyes with the backs of her hands and composed her face. "I told Philly to watch his back, and he must have known what that meant, because he tried to get out."

Sam nodded.

"So you haven't seen or talked to him since then?"

"I had the phone conversation I mentioned to you, and then he put out the hit on me like I said."

Something had to be missing from the equation. La Salle wouldn't try to kill her because of her father.

"How about what Marcus said, that you know something important about La Salle?"

"All I know is he lined up a bunch of investors to set up some big operation in the Caribbean."

"What do you suppose it might be?"

Candi shrugged. "My first guess would be something to do with gambling."

Sam remembered the sketch of the scene that looked like Las Vegas, except on a waterfront.

"Maybe you're right. The company that owns La Salle's Jaguar also has a billion dollars in assets."

He sat on the sofa, pulled the car registration from his pocket and showed it to her.

Candi's eyes widened. "You're saying this is La Salle's company?"

"Maybe."

"If he has that much money, why would he be interested in Philly's measly two million?"

Sam shrugged. "I'm sure he didn't get rich by turning down money."

"Do you believe me?"

Sam nodded. "I still believe you might know something else, but I'll settle for what you said for now."

"And you'll stay on the job?"

Sam sighed. "I might as well. For the time being, at least. La Salle's going to be looking for me whether I do or not."

Candi smiled and her eyes got dreamy. She slid closer on the sofa and put her hand on his chest. Then she pressed her lips to his for a long, hungry kiss. Alarms sounded off in Sam's head; or it could have been the blood pulsing in his ears. He ignored the noise, reached his arm around her waist and pulled her to him. She held the kiss for another second or two, then broke away, took a deep breath and let it out.

"Whew," Candi said. "We should cut back on the voltage a little if we're going to work together."

Sam leaned back on the sofa and ran his fingers through his hair. "Sure."

She had total control of the voltage and could turn it off as fast as she turned it on. Maybe it *would* be better if they kept their distance for now.

SAM LEFT CANDI sleeping in the room and drove to meet Jack Craft. He hadn't planned on her going anyway. If things got dangerous, it would be a lot easier if he were alone.

The sun lay on the horizon over the Intracoastal Waterway by the time Sam entered the restaurant parking lot. He spied Jack's Mercedes toward the rear of the place, away from the other cars. The spot overlooked the waterway to the East, with a wall about three feet high bordering the property. Sam saw a man behind the wheel of the car, but with the tinted windows he couldn't be sure it was Jack. He pulled in next to the Mercedes, stuck his gun in the pocket of the new jacket he'd purchased in the hotel gift shop, and got out.

The air was still and smelled of fish spawn. A brown dog sat close to the wall. His ears stood up and he had large intelligent eyes. He had a stately manner, and looked as if his name should be Prince Alfred. Sam saw a stick lying next to the wheel of the car; he picked it up and threw it in the air. The dog glanced in the direction of the stick, then back at Sam, and raised an eyebrow, as if to say, "You must be kidding." Sam shrugged and walked around the rear of the Chevy toward the Mercedes.

He saw something moving in his peripheral vision and turned to see a man in a motorized wheelchair bouncing across the shell-and-sand lot. *Grimes.* His head and leg had been wrapped with bandages and he made a beeline for Sam. It looked as if part of his leg might be missing under all that gauze. Grimes lifted a silenced handgun from his lap and pointed it at Sam. Sam dived behind the Chevy as Grimes fired three times. The shots made a noise like an angry cat spitting: *pffft pffft, pffft.*

Each round punched through the trunk lid with a clank. Sam pulled the gun from his jacket pocket, pushed back the slide, and stood so he could peer over the edge of the car. Grimes had come to within a couple of feet of the car, the wheelchair moving fast, his eyes wild, and he raised the gun to fire again, but didn't seem to notice the car in his path. The wheelchair slammed into the bumper, bounced and turned over.

Grimes fell out of the chair and landed on his side. The chair's wheels continued to turn, even faster now without any weight on them, and threw sand and pieces of shell into Grimes' face. He cursed and retrieved his gun from the sand where he'd dropped it. Shielding his eyes with his hand, he fired two rounds at the chair. The chair's motor hissed and smoked, and then the wheels jerked to a stop. Grimes crawled on his hands and one knee around the bumper to the space between the two cars. Sam backed up until his legs touched the wall behind him. *No way out.*

"This is all your fault," Grimes said. His speech slurred, as if he had been drinking or taking drugs.

"Put down the gun," Sam said.

Grimes kept crawling toward Sam, now only a couple of feet away.

"Final warning," Sam said.

Grimes pointed the gun at Sam's midsection and Sam kicked it. The toe of his shoe made contact with the barrel and the gun spun in Grimes' hand and fired. He dropped it and grabbed the side of his head. Blood seeped through his fingers, and when he looked at his hand, his eyes rolled up like slipped window shades and he fell to the ground. Sam saw something fall from the sky several feet away. Prince Alfred trotted over, picked it up in his teeth, walked past Grimes, and dropped it at Sam's feet.

Sam had forgotten about Jack Craft in all the excitement. Jack got out of the car and looked down at Grimes. His eyes narrowed.

"What's *he* doing here?"

"You didn't see him try to kill me?"

"No, I saw you drive up. I waited for you to come over and get in the car, but you disappeared." He stared at the thing lying at Sam's feet. "What's that?"

"It looks like what's left of Grimes' right ear."

TEN

JACK GLANCED AT Grimes' unconscious body lying between the cars. "Let's get out of here. You want to go to your hotel?"

"My hotel?"

Jack shrugged. "I knew you weren't on your boat."

Had Jack led Grimes to him intentionally? Whether he did or not, Sam didn't want to go to the Palma Hotel. He glanced at Prince Alfred sitting at his feet looking up at him, as if awaiting further orders.

"Let's go up the road a few blocks. There's a bar on the right."

Jack looked at Grimes and said, "What about him?"

"He'll live."

Jack nodded and got into his car.

Sam pushed the wheelchair away from the Chevy and opened the driver's door. Prince Alfred brushed by him and jumped into the car seat. He glanced at Sam and blinked his eyes.

"No, you can't go with me," Sam said. Just what he needed, something else to look after. Sam pointed at the ground and said, "Out."

Prince Alfred shook his head and hopped into the passenger seat. Sam looked up and saw Jack's car leaving the parking lot. He also saw the front end of a Cadillac parked behind the restaurant with two men sitting in front. It didn't look like the Cadillac La Salle wrecked while chasing Sam in the Jaguar, but he probably had others. Sam got into the car and said to the dog, "Okay, but you're getting out at the next stop."

Prince Alfred grinned at that and looked out the windshield, ready for his ride.

After backing the car out, Sam pressed the accelerator. The tires spun and propelled the Chevy down the driveway toward the street, leaving Grimes and the crippled wheelchair lying on the ground. In the mirror, he spotted the Cadillac ease around the edge of the restaurant and follow him onto the driveway.

Sam entered the street, drove about a quarter-mile, and turned into the parking lot of the Coral Corral, a country-western bar. Jack's Mercedes sat next to a wide pickup truck with dual tires on the rear. A car backed out a couple of spots before Jack's and Sam took its place. The Cadillac Sam had seen at the restaurant idled past as he turned the engine off.

Sam got out of the car and the dog followed. He stepped over to Jack's Mercedes, got inside and closed the door. The dog waited by the car.

"Who's in the Caddy?" Sam said.

"What Caddy?" Jack turned and looked.

"It's parked somewhere down the way."

"Oh, I didn't see it."

"Same one as behind the restaurant we just left. I didn't recognize the guys inside and thought they were with Grimes."

Jack nodded and said, "Maybe. We'd better talk fast, in case he decides to crash the party."

"Yeah, good idea. So, what's your deal with La Salle?"

Jack sighed and said, "Someone gave him my num-

ber and told him I could put him together with a person
to broker a big land deal."

"When was that?"

"Five or six months ago."

Sam thought about the sketch of the casinos.

"This is about gambling?"

Jack looked at Sam and smiled. "Ah, I see you've
been busy. How did you know that?"

"A painting in La Salle's house looked like a devel-
opers dream. Like Las Vegas, only on the seashore."

Two men with cowboy hats got into the pickup next
to Sam's side of the car, backed out and drove away.
A couple of seconds later a large man with thinning,
slick black hair appeared at Sam's window and tapped
on the glass.

Sam looked at Jack and Jack nodded.

"Better open it," Jack said.

Sam lowered the window.

"You need to step outside, Mackenzie."

"Who are you?"

"La Salle wants his stuff back."

The other man, who had spiked hair, stood with his
hand inside his sport coat. They wouldn't kill him until
they had the money and the car back. Maybe Jack could
just drive away. Except they would be sitting ducks if
one of the guys panicked and started shooting.

"See you later," Sam said to Jack.

With his hand inside the pocket of his jacket, Sam
wrapped his fingers around the stock of the 9mm and
got out of the car. Slick and Spike stepped backward
into the vacant parking spot, keeping their eyes on
Sam.

"Take your hand out so I can see it," Slick said.

"All right."

Sam pulled the 9mm from his pocket and pointed it at Slick's chest. Slick drew his own gun and Spike flashed a broad grin and leveled another gun at Sam.

"Looks like you're outnumbered," Spike said.

Sam shrugged. "You kill me and La Salle will drop you in the Miami River like he did Philly Moran. I don't have anything to lose, so I'm going to walk away from here. If either of you move, I'm going to kill you. Do you understand?"

The men looked at each other and frowned as if they hadn't thought about that.

"You're crazy, man," Spike said, "you're going with us."

Sam shook his head. "No way."

Slick lunged, swinging his gun at Sam's gun hand, but Sam jerked out of range. Slick stumbled and cursed. Prince Alfred sprang between them, his lips curled back in a snarl, and sank his teeth into Slick's groin. The man dropped his gun, screamed and fell back against Spike. Both tumbled to the ground. Prince Alfred growled and tore at the man's pants as if fighting another animal over a fresh kill.

"Get him off me, get him off!"

Spike struggled to his knees and pointed his gun at the dog. "Hold still and I'll shoot him."

"Shoot the dog and I'll shoot *you*," Sam said.

The dog let go of Slick and leapt at Spike, locking his jaws on the hand holding the gun, while Slick moaned and rolled around on the asphalt. Spike's gun dropped to the ground with a clack, and he screamed out a string of obscenities while trying to free his hand from the dog's teeth.

Curses replaced the moans from Slicks gaping jaws as his blood-covered hands grabbed for the gun he had dropped. Sam took a long stride and kicked him in the face. The man fell over and the gun fired in the air, the round exploding like a small bomb. Sam grabbed the gun from his hand and stuck it into his pocket.

"Get him to stop, man," Spike screamed, eyes bulging like tiny balloons. "He's chewing my hand off! Please!"

"Easy, boy," Sam said.

Prince Alfred stopped growling, let go of the hand and backed away. Sam looked at the dog, wondering if it might be his guardian angel. He reached down, picked up the gun and eased around the rear of the Mercedes toward the Chevy. His guardian angel followed.

Jack backed the Mercedes out of the space, lowered his window and said, "If I were you, I'd go with Candi somewhere for a long vacation until this blows over."

Before Sam could answer, the Mercedes engine roared and the big car shot out the driveway.

"Hey," Slick said, "you got my gun." He pressed his hands against his crotch, as if something important might fall out if he didn't.

Sam turned back and said, "This dog might have rabies, so both of you should get checked out."

They glanced at each other, scrambled to their feet and headed toward their car, dripping splotches of blood on the white parking space stripes on the asphalt.

A throng of cowboys and cowgirls stood on the porch of the Coral Corral, most of them with beer mugs in their hands. One of the men with a belly like a watermelon, slurred, "Hey, man, what happened over there?"

Sam nodded in the direction of the two bleeding men and said, "Dude tried to shoot my dog."

The man looked at Prince Alfred and then at the two men and took a sip from his beer mug. "I hope he chewed them up good."

Sam didn't answer, already inside the Chevy, the dog in the passenger seat. The Cadillac drove from the parking lot, tires screeching as it sped south. Sam drove out a couple of seconds later and turned in the opposite direction.

Jack Craft hadn't told him everything he wanted to know, but that would have to wait. He called information and got the number for Cayman Airways. When he reached the airline, he learned that the last flight of the day left Miami International in forty minutes.

He spotted an electronics store in a shopping center, turned in and parked. Prince Alfred sat next to the car while he went inside. A chubby young man with gelled hair and pimples ambled over and asked if he could help.

"Do you have any GPS units?" Sam said.

The pimpled man showed Sam a mouthful of crooked teeth and said, "Global Positioning System." His look said, "Finally, someone to appreciate my knowledge in fine electronics," but he only said, "Sure, follow me."

They had several different varieties and the pimpled man began his spiel about the virtues of each.

"I don't have much time," Sam said, interrupting, "I have some coordinates for a place I want to go, and I just need something that will help me get there."

The pimpled man nodded and reached for a unit slightly larger than a cell phone. He spent a few seconds demonstrating the unit until Sam said, "Okay, that's enough."

He purchased it for cash and hurried out, leaving the register still printing the receipt and the pimpled man talking about the warranty.

The dog wagged its tail when he returned, and Sam wondered what he could do with him. He hated to leave him at the airport, but he didn't have time for anything else. A Burger King stood at the entrance to the shopping center and he used the drive-through to buy two Whoppers. Prince Alfred looked at him and at the bag of burgers, and whimpered as they rode out onto the street. Sam dropped the bag onto the floor, pressed the accelerator, and drove the few miles to the airport in less than five minutes.

He parked in the short-term lot, the closest to the terminal, and got out of the car. Prince Alfred jumped out after him and stood next to the back tire as Sam unwrapped the burgers. He placed them in front of the dog and turned to leave. The dog started to follow and Sam pointed at the food and said, "Stay."

Prince Alfred looked almost as if he nodded, went back to the burgers and wolfed them down. Sam thought about the guns in his pocket, went back and opened the car trunk. He put in his own gun and the ones liberated from the mob men. Then he got the bag with La Salle's money and took enough cash to last a couple of days. He also took one of his passports and a Florida driver's license. Prince Alfred polished off the second of the burgers as Sam went inside to purchase a ticket for Grand Cayman. The agent looked at her watch and squeezed her lips together.

"I don't know if you'll make it. You still have to go through security."

"Yeah, I'll make it," Sam said.

He did make it. A pretty flight attendant, about to close the door, smiled and took his boarding pass.

The flight was about half full, which surprised Sam, thinking most people would travel earlier in the day to Grand Cayman. He took his window seat, opened his cell phone and called Candi at the Palma Hotel. Candi sounded as if she had just awakened.

"I have to make a trip," Sam said, "and won't be back tonight."

Candi paused and said, "What do you want me to do until you get back?"

"Hey, the room's paid for, so order room service and watch some movies. It won't hurt you to rest awhile. You seemed to be pretty tired earlier."

"You're just mad because I wouldn't...you know."

"No, not a problem, believe me. I just have to do something." After a long silence, Sam said, "The plane is taking off, so I have to hang up. I'll see you tomorrow." He punched the off button and put the phone in his pocket.

A smiling young man sat in the seat next to Sam's, his eyes jittery and wide. He introduced himself as Harold Shakes.

"I'm scared to death of flying, especially over the water."

"There's nothing to worry about," Sam said.

"Yeah, I know, but it still scares me. I wouldn't be here except I have to return to Grand Cayman. I found this job in a hotel on the island and went back home to get rid of all my stuff. I start work tomorrow. I hope I don't throw up."

Harold's plans didn't interest Sam, but he didn't want him to be sick, at least not sitting next to him, so he decided to keep him talking.

"Did this have anything to do with a woman?" Sam said.

Harold's eyes got wide and his mouth stretched back in a quick smile. "How did you know?"

Sam looked out the window and said, "Just wondered." It was a pretty safe bet. Most things men did had something to do with a woman. He thought back about the situations he'd gotten himself into over the years, and couldn't seem to think of a single case where a woman didn't play a prominent role. It might be a weakness of some kind, and a psychologist would have a fancy name for it to stick onto Sam's forehead, if Sam showed enough interest to find out.

The plane lifted off and the lights of nighttime Miami sped by below the window, getting smaller by the second. The pilot banked the plane and the sky turned dark.

Candi Moran, the catalyst in this latest quagmire, remained a mystery. Something about her bothered Sam. The involvement with La Salle aside, Sam still needed to determine her true motivation and knowledge about La Salle's operation before he would be satisfied.

Sam turned and noticed Harold talking again.

"...she works at the hotel, too. It was love at first sight. You know what I mean?"

"Oh, yeah, man. I know what you mean." Did he ever.

Harold seemed to settle down after they reached airspace, and Sam opened a magazine in hopes that Harold might take a nap. He didn't. They both ordered a couple of drinks from the flight attendant, who seemed too young to serve alcohol, and Harold's monologue seemed to relax a little. Even so, Sam learned more than he wanted to know about Harold's jitters over the new job, his worry that his new girlfriend didn't like him as much as he liked her, and his fear that she might have flown the coop while he went home for the past three weeks. Harold seemed to be afraid of a lot more than flying.

The flight attendant announced the plane was approaching Grand Cayman. It had been a while since Sam had been there, and he couldn't remember the flight taking so long, being only a few hundred miles from Miami. He guessed that flying around Cuba might be one reason. The lights of beach hotels rose under the plane, pale in comparison to those of Miami. This happened to be the home for much of the money in the world that people wanted to hide, probably many billions. But for all outward appearances, the island was just a laid-back tropical paradise with nothing on its mind but sun and drinks and slow, warm afternoons. Sam might come back again when he could stay a few weeks, and lie in the sun and drink rum until his head buzzed. Right now, though, he had to find the place identified by the coordinates written on a note in his pocket.

A few minutes later the plane descended to the runway and Harold grabbed onto Sam's arm. Once on the ground, Harold wiped perspiration from his forehead and thanked Sam for his patience.

"Glad I could help. Good luck with the new life."

They deplaned and Sam pointed him toward baggage claim. Sam got in line, showed the passport and license to an airport official, and headed for the taxi stand outside.

He had to wait in line a few minutes before a taxi became available.

"Where to, Mac?" The driver appeared to be American, probably retired from a factory job in the northeast.

"I don't know, give me a minute."

The old driver looked at him with one eyebrow raised and just nodded. Had he been in Miami, the driver probably would have told Sam to get out of the cab and gone on to the next customer. Sam fired up the gadget, compared the coordinates on the screen with the ones J.T. had given him, and found he needed to go north. He vaguely remembered a main highway running north and south on the west end of the island.

"I want to take the road that heads northwest."

The driver hesitated and said, "Not much going on up there this time of night, and it's pretty dark out. You sure you know where you're going?"

"Yeah, I know exactly where it is," Sam said with as much confidence as he could muster.

The driver shrugged and started the engine. They rode for about twenty minutes, passing a turtle farm that lit up the dark, but not much else. The latitude coordinate on the GPS unit increased in numbers and got closer to the coordinate on the note, then the road turned slightly east and the longitude coordinate, which had stayed right on the money since their journey began, started moving away from the target. Sam hadn't seen a building or anything else that might be his destination, but he asked the driver to stop and turn around.

"I think the place I'm going is close to here, so go slow."

The driver mumbled something Sam didn't understand, but he did as asked. They approached a path on the side of the road, a swath about ten feet wide cut in the scrub, and Sam said, "Turn here, I think this is it."

The driver put on the brakes. "Sorry, I can't go down there. The sand might be soft and we'd get stuck."

Sam looked at the GPS screen. The place couldn't be more than a hundred yards away.

"Okay, how about waiting for me, then? I won't be there more than a few minutes."

The driver shook his head. "I don't think so, I—"

Sam handed him a hundred dollar bill and said, "Here, I'll give you another one if you wait twenty minutes and take me back to the airport."

The driver took the bill and nodded. "All right. But after twenty minutes, I'm gone." He looked at his watch and back at Sam with a warning stare.

Sam nodded, got out of the car and strode down the dark path.

ELEVEN

THE TAXI'S LIGHTS grew dim as Sam entered the woods. He heard something sliding in the grass a few feet away, and wondered what kind of snakes might be indigenous to Grand Cayman. The sound stopped a moment later, and he continued through the woods. About two hundred yards from the road the swishing of surf reached his ears and a metal building appeared through the trees. A flood light glowed from a pole on its corner, a steel fence surrounded it, and a business van sat outside the fence. He stepped closer and saw that the land inside the fence had recently been scraped clean of all vegetation, and the musty smell of raw earth hung in the air.

The fence had a gate with a padlock, and Sam didn't have any tools with him that would open it. Beyond the gate, a strip of light glowed underneath a door entering the building.

He went to the passenger side of the van and pulled the door handle. It popped open, almost without sound, and the interior dome light flashed in his eyes. He reached into the door jam, ran his fingers along the surface until he felt a button, and pressed it. The light went off, and he stood for about thirty seconds, listening to his heart pound in his ears, wondering if anyone had seen him. A bead of perspiration rolled down his cheek.

With his free hand, he reached in, snapped open the

glove box, and felt around inside. An envelope aroused his interest. Taking it, he closed the glove box and pushed the van door shut.

He went past the building along the outside of the fence. The property ran right up to the sand dunes where the surf lapped just a few feet away. The back yard, if it could be called that, was illuminated by the glow of a dim, yellow light mounted on the rear eave of the building, and two large dish antennas stood in the dirt like twin sentries. Between the roar and hiss of the surf, Sam heard a whirring noise as one of the big antennas moved.

A plastic chair sat next to the wall of the building, and cigarette butts lay in a pile underneath. Sam wondered what could be going on inside. It obviously was some kind of communications facility, but it could be a perfectly legitimate business enterprise. He thought about the envelope from the van and stepped behind the trunk of a large pine. He opened the envelope, unfolded the piece of paper inside and turned on the GPS unit. Faint markings of a government form were visible in the glow of the screen. It looked different from a Florida vehicle registration, but it had to be the same kind of document. He searched in the dim light for several seconds before finding the name of the vehicle's owner: NeoWorld Corporation, the same as with La Salle's Jaguar. So much for the idea of the legitimate enterprise. NeoWorld, the new company with almost a billion dollars in assets. Sam turned off the GPS unit and returned it and the papers to his pocket.

J.T. had hit the nail on the head by interpreting the numbers in the e-mail as transposed GPS coordinates. The e-mail confirmed delivery of the dish antennas and whatever else was inside the building. But what did it have to do with La Salle's project?

An air conditioning unit kicked on a few feet away and screamed like a wounded animal. Sam jerked at the sudden noise, and then felt foolish when he realized what the sound was. He also felt angry at himself for flying all the way to Grand Cayman on a hunch, and not learning anything of real value. There might be lots of places like this owned by NeoWorld that had absolutely nothing to do with Candi Moran's misfortunes.

Sam thought about the taxi and pressed the illumination button on his watch. It had been more than half an hour. He wished he had paid more attention to the time, because the driver probably had gone.

Stepping into the trees, Sam found a dead limb, threw it onto the roof of the building, and hurried back to the side of the van. The limb made a loud thump when it hit, and probably reverberated inside. A few seconds later, the door opened and two men came out arguing.

"It's probably just an animal. Something came out here last night and ate the chicken bones I threw out."

"I don't care. We must check it out. And I will not remind you again to close the door when you go out to smoke. If you cannot handle the job I will tell your boss to send someone else." The second voice had an accent that sounded Russian, and Sam wondered if it belonged to Comrade Danilov.

"I can handle the job. All you do is flip a few switches and stand watch."

"Yes, but I will be gone tomorrow and you will be alone. This is more important than you can imagine. If it is compromised we might have nothing."

"Compromised? What's the big deal? Why would anybody be interested in all that computer junk? You act like we're sitting on a gold mine or something."

The Russian paused, as if trying to decide what to do. After several seconds, he sighed and said, "Just do as I say, Mr. Cicero. I will speak to La Salle in the morning." His voice had an edge, and Cicero opened his mouth as if to speak, but no words came out. He turned and stomped toward the rear of the building. The Russian shook his head and went back inside. Cicero came back in a couple of minutes, mumbling something under his breath. He went inside and slammed the door, and Sam heard the snap of a lock.

The Russian sounded worried about someone breaking into the building. But he would be gone tomorrow, leaving only the wise ass to stand guard. If Sam wanted to get inside, he would be better off to wait until then. It still wouldn't be easy. He'd have to figure out how to get over the fence without setting off any alarms, he would have to deal with the man and he'd need some tools. But at least it gave him some time to figure out his next step.

Sam took one last look at the building and turned to leave. Something moved in the path leading from the highway, and he dived for cover behind a bush where he could still see the path. A silhouette of a tall man made a sudden stop and scrambled into the trees. The sound of crunched leaves reached Sam's ears a few seconds later, and seemed to be advancing in his direction. Running his hand through the leaves, Sam found a tree limb and picked it up. The man kept coming, now just a few feet away. He had to see Sam if he passed, especially if he turned on a flashlight. Sam stood and raised the limb for a home run swing.

The leaf crunching stopped and a voice whispered, "Sam, is that you?"

It was too dark to see the man's face, but Sam recognized his voice: J.T.

"You almost got yourself a concussion," Sam said. "What are you doing here?"

"Probably the same thing you are."

Sam had hoped J.T. would stay out of this, but right now he just wanted a ride away from here. "You have a car?"

"Yeah, parked back there in the woods. I got here right before you pulled up in the taxi and didn't want to come down and screw things up, but after the taxi left I wondered if something might have happened to you. You find out anything about this place?"

"Yeah, I think so. Let's get out of here and I'll tell you about it."

They went to the rental car and J.T. backed into the highway and headed south. Sam told him about the vehicle registration and the conversation he had overheard.

"I planned to go back there tomorrow. Now that you're here, we can both go, if you're game."

"Sure, you know me, man," J.T. said and smiled in the glow of the dash lights.

J.T. hadn't changed much in the year or so since Sam had seen him, his hair a little more gray and slightly shorter, but still long enough for a pony tail. He had put on a few pounds, more like muscle than fat, and he still looked pretty dangerous, especially when he smiled.

They checked in at the Marriot, which Sam had

passed in the taxi from the airport. J.T. had an over-night bag and a portable computer with him. Sam had only the clothes he wore. They got their room keys and started toward the elevator.

"How about a drink before we go up?" J.T. said.

Sam looked across at the bar and nodded.

"Yeah, that sounds good."

They sat at a table in the corner. A waiter came and took their beer orders.

Sam knew why J.T had come to Grand Cayman; there was the possibility that the facility would lead to some of the billion or so in assets of the NeoWorld Corporation. If anyone could liberate some of that from NeoWorld's offshore deposits, John Templeton Smith III would find a way. Sam only worried that if there happened to be a fork in the road, one road leading to the money, the other to keeping Sam alive, Sam couldn't be sure which road J.T. would take. He'd decided long ago, that as long as he knew the man's motivation and planned for it, he would be okay. No doubt, Sam could use his help. He'd had the nagging feeling that if he did get a peek inside that facility, he might not know what to look for. J.T. would know. So…what was he worried about?

Not long ago, J.T. had killed a man about to shoot holes in Sam. J.T. had ended up with something worth a lot of money, but he had come through when Sam needed him. The beer came and Sam took a long pull on the bottle. He set it down and looked across the table.

"What?"

"Nothing," Sam said. "I'm glad you're here."

"Sure, buddy, anytime."

They talked a few more minutes and Sam ordered a bottle of gin to take with him. Back in his room, he called Candi Moran at the Palma Hotel, but got no answer. That bothered him, so he called back and asked for the young desk clerk, who said Candi had left no messages. Sam told him he had another fifty for him if he would give him some information. The clerk said she left the hotel a couple of hours before, about 9:30, with two men.

"I remember because she was hot, even more than when you brought her in last night. I watched her pass the desk and she said, 'Where are we going?' The man next to her glanced at me, like I might be trying to eavesdrop or something, and told me to mind my own business. He grabbed her by the arm and they left. I didn't think too much about it, because we get a lot of characters in here."

Sam thanked him, hung up the phone, and thought about leaving for Miami, but remembered the time and guessed there wouldn't be any flights out after midnight. He also thought about the men, probably La Salle's employees, and wondered how they'd learned Candi's location. Candi had been angry when Sam told her about going to Grand Cayman, but he didn't think she would call La Salle. On the other hand, she and La Salle did share some history that she failed to mention. He decided he couldn't do much about it in the middle of the night.

DR. FIXX, OF the Fixx-It Animal Hospital, took off his white jacket and hung it on the coat rack. He glanced in the mirror and smoothed his mustache. Amy, his pretty assistant, should be just about ready by now, after the triple dose of animal tranquilizers he'd slipped into her pop can. She'd said she was sleepy and Dr. Fixx told her to take a nap in the back room while he finished cleaning up.

A noise came from the outer office. Fixx glanced at his watch: 7:40. *Another customer at this hour?* A man with spiked blond hair stumbled through the double doors, hopping on one leg, and pointed a long handgun at Dr. Fixx's chest. Fixx thought his pounding heart might burst. He'd never seen a gun that big, especially one pointed at him.

"You gotta sew this on for me," the man said, pulling something from his shirt pocket. It resembled a piece of bloody calamari.

"What *is* that?"

"It's my ear, you dope." The man sat on the examination table, his gauze-wrapped stub of a leg sticking straight out.

Dr. Fixx wished he had left at closing time, rather than stay around and try to get Amy into bed. He glanced at the door to the back room. The drugs should keep her sedated for a while. He could sew the piece of ear onto the man's head and be done in ten minutes.

Fixx stretched on a pair of surgical gloves. "How did this happen?"

"That's none of your business, just start sewing."

Dr. Fixx gave him a couple of shots of local anesthetic, retrieved a needle and suture material from his cabinet, and started reattaching the piece of ear.

"That hurts, man, give me another shot."

"All right, all right, just hold on."

Dr. Fixx looked at the blood on his gloved hands and sighed. He filled another syringe, stuck the needle an

inch or so below where he had administered the last
shot, and pressed the plunger. It would have been better if he had just given the man a knock-out shot and
called the police, except for his drugged assistant. He
had wanted only to make her carefree, but had given
her too much. Anyway, he couldn't call the police, so
he would just hurry up and sew the ear back on and
maybe the guy would leave. Who cared if it fell off
tomorrow?

Dr. Fixx did the work quickly, and inserted the last
suture a couple of minutes later. He tied it off and
snipped the excess thread. He stepped back and as-
sessed his handiwork. It did look something like an
ear if he squinted his eyes a little.

GRIMES LOOKED SIDEWAYS into the mirror the doctor
handed him and grinned at the bloody reflection.

"That ain't half bad."

"I'm glad you like it. Now, will you please leave so
I can tidy up here?"

Grimes looked through the glass door of the medicine cabinet. Hundreds of little pill boxes sat inside.

"Yeah, I'll leave, just as soon as you sack up everything in that cabinet."

"You can't take my medicines. They're prepared
for animals and could harm you, maybe render you
unconscious."

Grimes pointed the gun at him.

"Alright, alright, the medicine is yours. Hold on."

The doctor found a cardboard box and began stack-
ing the little boxes inside.

"Stand back," Grimes said. He hopped off the examination table and bumped the doctor out of the way.

Reaching his arm into the cabinet, he raked everything off the shelf into the box. He did the same with the other shelves and sat back on the table to look inside the box.

"What's this stuff good for?"

The doctor told him that the blue boxes contained painkillers and the others mostly antibiotics, but something in his smile made Grimes wonder if vets have to take the Hippocratic oath, like human doctors. He quickly forgot the thought when the back door to the room opened and a young woman wearing only a tank top and bikini underwear pushed through. She looked at Grimes, then at the doctor and her eyes narrowed.

"You drugged me, you slime bag."

Her words came out slurred.

The doctor glanced at Grimes and then at the girl and grinned.

"Now, Amy, I did no such thing," he said, shaking his finger in her direction.

The doctor did it all right, but Amy *was* pretty fine to look at, standing there in her skivies. As a matter of fact, he might just have to rescue her from this pervert.

"I'll take you home if you get in my van outside," Grimes said.

Amy looked at him, trying to focus her eyes, and a slow smile grew across her sleepy face.

"Are you that rock singer? I can't think of the name." She sounded like a teenager.

Grimes smiled and said, "Yeah, baby, that's me. Get in the van and I'll sing you a song when I come out."

"Cool," Amy said, her voice dreamy. She didn't seem to notice that he had only one leg and had a gun with a two-inch noise suppressor attached to the barrel.

She turned and staggered toward the door, but glanced back at the doctor and said, "You won't get away with this, you know. Just wait."

"Here, take this with you."

Grimes handed her the box of drugs. She took it and went out the door. Grimes grabbed a towel and wiped down the things he remembered touching.

"What are you doing?" the doctor said. But then he seemed to realize his situation and his face contorted. "No, you can't—"

Grimes pointed the gun and pulled the trigger. It made a sound not unlike that of an air-powered pellet gun, and a red spot the size of a nickel splattered on the veterinarian's forehead. Amy was right, the doctor wasn't going to get away with it. His body pitched backward and dropped to the floor, and the man who looked like a rock singer with one leg turned and hopped out of the room.

TWELVE

SAM AND J.T. ate breakfast in the hotel restaurant at seven the next morning and checked out a half hour later. They got in the car and J.T. drove up the highway to the place they had been the night before. He went beyond the driveway and pulled the car into a brushy spot hidden from the road, but with a clear view of the entrance. They sat and waited.

"I thought about this last night after I got to the room," J.T. said. "If I can get inside for a couple of minutes, I can install a program on their computer that'll automatically send a copy of everything they do to my Internet site."

"Won't they know it's doing that?"

"Not unless they're looking for it. It'll do the work in the background. But, like I said, I have to get inside and get access to their computer for a few minutes."

Sam looked out the windshield and watched a car pass the entrance on the highway, going east.

"I think I know a way in," Sam said. "The guy's been getting takeout for his meals. After Danilov is gone, he'll probably have food delivered. If that's the case, we'll intercept the delivery and I'll take it down to the fence and get him to come outside. While he's out, you can slip in and do your thing."

"It's worth a try."

At a few minutes past nine, a taxi turned into the

entrance and went down the driveway to the facility. The taxi returned five minutes later with Danilov in the back seat, probably headed for the airport. Sam expected a food delivery about noon, but that didn't happen. The car heated up, even though shrouded in shade from the trees, and Sam's shirt stuck to his chest from the perspiration. Hunger struck about one-thirty and they rode to a store down the road for a sandwich and a drink, and a chance to run the air conditioner. They returned to their place in the trees within ten minutes and sat there for another hour before a car with a pizza sign on top passed the entrance. The driver, an old man, stopped, backed up and turned in. Sam and J.T. got out of the car, hurried to the edge of the driveway and waited for the car to reach them.

Sam held up his hand and the car eased to a stop. He stepped to the window and said, "Thanks, I'll take it from here."

The man looked at the bill stuck to the pizza box and said, "Are you Mr. Cicero?" He spoke with an English accent, like someone of nobility.

"Yeah, I'm Cicero. I thought I'd take a walk. How much do I owe you?"

Nobility looked at the box again and read off the price of the pizza. "And it's a long way up here, don't you know."

Despite the smooth voice, he looked a little threadbare, and Sam speculated that he might be a nightclub performer down on his luck.

"It sure is, and this is for your trouble." Sam handed the man a big bill.

The man smiled and pushed the pizza through the window.

"That's a pretty nifty sign you have on top," Sam said. "I wouldn't mind having one of those for my den. What would you charge me for that?"

Nobility raised an eyebrow. "Oh, I don't think the sign is for sale."

Sam pulled a larger bill from his pocket and held it out.

"How about this? You could always tell your boss it blew away."

The man seemed to consider that for a half-second and then the money disappeared into his wrinkled hand.

"Take the bloody thing."

Sam handed the pizza box to J.T., unscrewed the mechanism holding the sign in place, and pulled it from the roof of the car. Nobility tossed an electrical wire out the window and backed his car out of the driveway. They went back to the rental car and Sam fastened the sign on top. He stood back and looked at it. "What do you think?"

"Not bad. You don't see many new cars like this delivering pizza, but the guy probably won't notice."

"Okay, let's go." Sam got into the driver's seat, put on his sunglasses and started the engine. J.T. lay down in the back seat. They eased through the scrub and trees and turned into the driveway toward the facility. Daylight made the path look different, and it seemed much shorter than when Sam had walked it the night before. The van sat in the same place, and Sam pulled the car past the far side until he could see the door of the building, leaving most of the car hidden behind the van. He lowered the windows, turned off the engine and blew the car horn.

"Stay where you are until he comes out the door,"

Sam said, "in case there's a camera that isn't visible from here."

Nothing happened for a minute or so and Sam blew the horn again, this time standing on it for several seconds. He waited and listened to the whisper of the surf in the distance, the breeze from the Caribbean cooling his sweaty face. The door of the building finally popped open and the man Danilov had called Cicero came out. He saw the car, glanced up the driveway and the woods beyond, and looked back at Sam.

"Bring it to the gate."

"Can't. I hurt my leg yesterday. You'll have to come to the car."

Cicero rolled his eyes. "Why didn't they send somebody that can do the job?"

Sam glanced in his side mirror and saw the back door of the car open. J.T. got out, squatted next to the car and closed the door with barely a sound. He duck-walked to the rear of the van.

"I told 'em I needed to be off for a few days," Sam said, "but two guys quit and they didn't have nobody else."

"Okay, hold on." Cicero sauntered to the gate and unlocked it with a key from his pocket. "Tell them I'm not gonna do this again, okay? Next guy delivers pizza here'll have to bring it to the gate."

"Yeah, okay, I'll tell 'em. We should have another person in a day or two."

Cicero went through the gate to the car window. Sam looked beyond him and saw J.T. pass and enter the building.

"Okay, gimme the pizza."

"Ten-ninety-five," Sam said.

The man dug into his pocket and pulled out a ten and a one and handed the bills to Sam.

"It's a long way up here, you know."

"Yeah, I know, but I ain't giving you a tip. You didn't even bring it to the gate like I asked."

"I told you, I'm crippled."

Cicero sighed and shook his head. "Crippled? I thought you said you hurt your leg yesterday."

"Yeah, I did."

"You just said you're crippled."

"Yeah, as of yesterday."

Cicero snapped his fingers and held out his hand. "Well gimme the pizza. I ain't giving you no tip."

"You're not?"

"No, I'm not."

Sam glanced at the door of the building. It had been only a minute or so.

"Did I say, ten-ninety-five? I meant thirteen-ninety-five."

Cicero's face twisted and his upper lip peeled back in a sneer.

"Hey, fella, I ain't giving you no fourteen dollars for a pizza."

"You sure about that? 'Cause that's the price."

"Yeah, I'm sure. And I'm gonna call the store and tell them what you tried to do to me."

"Won't matter," Sam said, "the owner's my uncle."

"I don't care, I'm still calling."

"Well, looks like there's nothing I can do about that," Sam said.

Cicero balled his fists and narrowed his eyes.

"Listen, you gonna give me the pizza or not? If you

ain't, you better give me my money back or I'm gonna drag you out of that car and—"

"I told you I got a busted leg."

"I don't care, just give me my money."

"Yeah, you'd like that, wouldn't you? That would mean I came out here for nothing."

Cicero reached for the door handle and then looked as if he thought better of it. He stepped back and took a deep breath.

"On second thought, just get out of here."

He started to turn and the door of the building cracked open.

"Hey, wait," Sam said.

Cicero turned back and said, "What?" His voice dripped with venom.

"I didn't mean to make you mad. Here, take the pizza. I'll make the tip on somebody else."

Cicero had a confused look on his face, but he glanced at the pizza box, licked his lips and stepped back to the car window. He reached for the pizza, and when he did, J.T. sneaked through the gate and ducked down behind the van. He waited until Cicero started through the gate before he got into the back seat.

Cicero glanced at the car before going into the building. "Get outta here."

Sam put the car in reverse, turned it around and drove away.

"What did you find?"

"About what you'd expect," J.T. said, his voice shaky. "A high-powered computer and some fancy communications equipment in the end of the room nearest the door. On the other end was what looked like a couple of bedrooms and a little kitchen."

"Did you install your program?"

"Sure, piece of cake."

"Are you okay?"

"Yeah, why?"

"I don't know, you just sound a little strange."

SAM AND J.T. went straight to the airport and bought tickets for the next flight to Miami, which didn't leave until 6:20 PM. That gave them a couple of hours to kill. They found a table in the corner of the ice-cold airport lounge and ordered beer.

Sam leaned back in his chair and glanced at J.T., who had been unusually quiet after leaving the facility.

"How does this program of yours work?"

J.T. sighed. "Every time the computer issues a command, the program copies it to my web site. If they access a file, it copies that too. All I have to do is access my site and see what's there, for what it's worth."

The waiter brought the beer and poured it in tall glasses. Sam didn't speak again until he left the table. "What do you mean, 'for what it's worth'?"

"Well, I just don't think they're doing anything with offshore bank accounts in that building."

"Why do you say that? You weren't in there long enough to do much on that computer."

"Yeah, but it wasn't the computer that tipped me off."

"What, then?"

J.T. took a long swallow of beer, draining half the glass. He leaned his elbows on the table, rubbed his eyes with his fists, and looked up at Sam.

"There was no ceiling in the building. I could see all the way to the roof, and a panel on the seaward side looked like it could be slid back like a skylight in a car. Only it wasn't a skylight."

"So, what's the big deal about an opening in the roof."

J.T. shook his head and sighed. "That wouldn't be a big deal, but the stuff underneath might be."

"Yeah, go on."

"It looked a lot like a missile launcher."

THIRTEEN

WIND AND RAIN pelted the plane on the flight home, and Sam and J.T. didn't arrive in Miami until after eight o'clock. They got through Customs without fanfare and went to Sam's rental car in the covered parking area. Prince Alfred sat next to the driver's door like a stone sentry.

"Hey, you have a new friend," J.T. said.

"Yeah, he jumped in the car last night before I left and wouldn't get out. I left him here eating hamburgers."

Sam mentioned how the dog had chewed up La Salle's goons.

"Man, this is a special dog. Look how his ears stand up and how steady his eyes are. He might have been a show dog or something. He have a name?"

"I've been calling him Prince Alfred, but I don't know his real name."

"Prince Alfred, huh? That fits pretty well."

J.T. squatted next to the car and reached out his hand. Prince Alfred glanced at Sam and then went to J.T. as if they were old friends. J.T. opened the passenger door and the dog jumped in and over to the back seat, as if he had done it a hundred times before. Sam started the car and weaved his way out of the airport's network of loops and access roads. He got onto Highway 836 and pointed the Chevy toward Miami Beach.

"I bet Prince Alfred is hungry."

Sam glanced and saw J.T. rubbing the dog's ears.

"Hey, you trying to steal my dog?"

"Your dog? You just said he's a stray."

Sam grinned. "Yeah, he is, and he probably is hungry."

After crossing the MacArthur Causeway, they turned north on Miami Beach and rode to a Burger King drive-through. They ordered three of the largest burgers on the menu and ate them on the way to the Palma Hotel. Prince Alfred jumped out when they arrived and stood by the car.

"They might have someone waiting here for me," Sam said, "but it's been an entire day, so I'm hoping they've given up."

J.T. shrugged. "I'm not worried about it if you're not."

Sam thought he must be over his scare at the facility on Grand Cayman.

"Okay, let's go."

He retrieved two handguns from the trunk and gave one to J.T. They took the side entrance, avoiding the lobby, and went up the stairs to the fourth floor. No one waited in the hall, so they went to the room and inserted the card key. It still worked; that meant she hadn't checked out. Sam nudged the door open with his foot and peered around the corner. The room appeared to be empty. He stepped inside with the 9mm extended and J.T. followed, easing the door closed behind him.

Sam went into the bathroom and found it empty as well. He put his gun in his pocket, ran his fingers through his hair, and looked around the room.

"There's nothing here that belonged to her, but there wouldn't be, because she didn't have a bag."

The room seemed undisturbed, the bed not slept-in, or re-made since Candi left.

"Who knew she was here?" J.T. said.

"No one but me, unless she told someone."

Sam went to the phone by the bed and pressed the re-dial button. An internal number popped up on the display and the phone rang twice before a man answered.

"Concierge, how may I help you?"

"My wife called you from our room last night and asked for assistance," Sam said. "I just got back from a trip and seem to have missed her. Do you have a record of the call?"

"Room 417?"

"That's right."

"Umm, yes, sir, we should have a record. Please hold." He came back after a few seconds and said, "She called at 9:18 and asked if we would buy her some clothes from the hotel store and send them up."

"Did you get the things for her?"

There was a pause on the line. "Why, yes, of course, is there a problem?"

"No, not at all."

"You can preview the charges if you call up your room bill on the TV."

"Oh, yeah, I'll do that, thanks."

Sam hung up the phone and told J.T. what had happened. He turned on the TV and punched up his bill using the remote control. It indicated purchases of a dress and articles of underwear. The charges would cover three or four outfits in a downtown men's store.

"She didn't make any other calls, according to this," Sam said. "Probably used her cell phone to call the guys who picked her up."

Sam used the system for express checkout, then put a fifty in an envelope from the desk and sealed it. On the outside he wrote, "For the young man on the night counter," and left it on the desk. Maybe the kid would get the money. He deserved it for the information he'd given Sam.

"Let's get out of here. I paid cash for a week in advance, and the excess will more than pay for the clothes."

They went back down the stairs and slipped out the door they had entered.

THE VAN SAT four parking spots beyond the Chevy. Grimes and Amy, the former Veterinarian's Assistant, had been waiting twenty minutes for the two men to exit the hotel.

"There he is," Grimes said.

"Who?"

Grimes didn't want to say much, knowing she wouldn't appreciate the fine points of the assassination business. After leaving the vet's office, they'd driven to a motel where he crashed and lost almost a day in a delirium of painkillers. She played the perfect nurse, so grateful for getting rescued from that pervert vet.

"His name is Mackenzie, and he owes me something. Start the van and follow their car, but don't get too close."

Amy did as he said, waiting for the Chevy to leave the parking lot before pulling out.

"I still think I should call the cops about what Dr. Fixx did to me."

"We've been over that. Like I told you, he'll make it sound like it was your fault." If someone hadn't found the body yet, they soon would and it would be in the news. He hoped that didn't happen for a while; she was pretty nice to have around, even if she wouldn't get into the sack with him.

"What are you going to do?"

Grimes grinned in the dash lights.

"Nothing much, just rough him up a little."

He actually planned to kill him, but she didn't need to know that right now. The phone chirped in Grimes' pocket and he pulled it out and punched the talk button.

"Yeah."

"What is your position?" La Salle.

"I'm leaving the Palma now, following Mackenzie's car."

"Excellent. Which way is he going? I'll have a couple of my men head him off."

"No way, Jose."

"Pardon me?" La Salle's voice had an edge in it that Grimes didn't like.

"I can handle Mackenzie."

"Negative. I want him alive. He still has my money, and if anything happens to him I'm going to hold you responsible. Do you understand?"

"Sorry, we're breaking up," Grimes said and terminated the call. Money, schmoney, who did he think he was? Mackenzie had caused Grimes to lose a leg and almost lose an ear. He touched the re-attached ear and shock waves rippled through his head. *Not good*, he would need to double the antibiotics. Mackenzie would have to die, no doubt about it. If he had the money with him, that would be fine, otherwise, La Salle would have to get his money on his own.

DRIVING AWAY FROM the Palma, Sam punched in the telephone number for Jack Craft's boat and got no answer. Then he tried the cell number he had found in La Salle's safe. Same result.

"Who're you trying to call?" J.T. asked.

"Jack Craft."

J.T. grinned. "Good old Jack. What's he up to these days?"

Sam brought him up-to-date on Jack's involvement, at least what Sam knew of it.

"Sounds just like something he would do. You think he knows what happened to Candi Moran?"

"Maybe. I'll try him again later."

Sam drove onto the causeway and headed toward Little Havana where Hector lived.

He turned into the driveway of the old Spanish cabana. The house was dark. They got out and Sam knocked on the door. After a couple of minutes, a light came on inside and Sam knew Hector peered at them through the peep hole in the door.

Hector opened the door wearing a pair of dark pants and no shirt. He looked as if he had been sleeping, but not very well, his hair mussed.

"Sorry to wake you, Hector," Sam said.

"No, no. Not a problem. I tried to call you today but you did not answer."

Sam nodded. "Yeah, I've been away. What's wrong?"

Hector stood back and asked them to come inside.

They went through a small entry hall to a living room and sat down.

"Someone broke into my garage and took the Jag." Hector grimaced and shook his head. "I don't know what to do when I can't reach you, and I am really sick about it."

Sam shrugged. "Forget it. It didn't belong to me anyway."

Candi probably had told La Salle how to find it. Or someone else had stolen it. Happened many times a day in Dade County.

Hector took a deep breath and let it out. "You mean you are not angry?"

"Not at all. I just need to talk with you."

"Then, by all means, let me get you a drink." He hurried out of the room, returned a couple of minutes later with three bottles of beer, and eyed Sam. "So, what is wrong?"

"Have you ever heard of a man named Danilov?"

Hector's eyes widened for a split second. "I might have heard that name. Why do you ask?"

Sam told Hector about Candi Moran and La Salle. "This guy, Danilov, plays into the situation too. My information says he was stationed in Cuba at the Russian embassy, but after the Russians left, he showed up in South Florida. He and La Salle are working together."

"But if this Candi Moran called Senor La Salle, why are you worried about her?"

Sam didn't know the answer to that question himself.

"I'm not certain she called him. She might have told someone else who sold her out."

Hector looked at Sam and smiled for the first time

since they had arrived. "Yes, that might have happened." He frowned and looked as if deep in thought for a couple of moments. "I have heard of this man; he is a criminal, but I know nothing else about him. My papa might know more. As I told you, he worked in the cane fields as a young man, but he knows many people. His cafe friends know much about what goes on in the old country. Papa listens to the radio in bed until after midnight, sometimes two in the morning, so he will be awake."

Hector stood and ambled out of the room.

"You think his dad would know anything about this business?" J.T. said. "He must be pretty old, and probably has been here for years."

"Worth a try, I suppose."

When Hector returned, he handed a piece of notepaper to Sam. "He wouldn't tell me anything, but he said if you talk to this man you will learn about Senor Danilov."

The piece of paper contained the name, Ricardo Miro, and an address Sam didn't recognize.

"Do you know this place?" Sam asked.

"No, but the street is not far from here. Papa said he has a nice house."

Sam nodded. "Okay. I'll see what he has to say. Thanks, and please thank your father for me."

Hector shook his head and waved his hand. "We are happy to help."

Sam and J.T. finished their beer and left.

J.T. accessed a map program on his computer and found Miro's address within minutes. It took them a while longer to get there through the maze of streets and lanes.

The house sat deep in the lot, obscured by a thicket of palm and banana trees. Sam turned into the driveway and eased the car around the dense growth until the headlights splashed on a Spanish villa with wood beams protruding from the eaves. A nice house, as Hector's father had said, but it looked as if it had been neglected for the last ten years. Paint peeled from the beams, windows and the front door. The grass had gone to seed long ago, and weeds sprouted through hundreds of cracks in the driveway. No lights glowed inside, and Sam wondered if the house might be abandoned.

"What do you think?" Sam said.

"Let's go in. The old man must have thought this guy is important or he wouldn't have put you on to him."

Sam nodded and turned off the car. They got out and headed toward the front door. Prince Alfred went to the thicket of trees, his nose to the ground.

Sam shone his light on the entrance and knocked. He also pressed a cracked plastic doorbell switch that looked as if it hadn't worked in a decade. No one came to the door. He knocked again and waited a couple of minutes, then retrieved his pick and inserted it into the lock. An airplane whined overhead from Miami International and then the noise disappeared, off to the Caribbean or other points south. Sam took a couple minutes to open the loose old door lock. For the time of night it seemed very hot, and Sam wiped perspiration from his forehead with his sleeve. He pulled the 9mm from his pocket and pushed the door open.

A wave of hot air and stench hit Sam in the face. His heart raced, the odor unmistakable.

J.T. shook his head and said, "We should get out of here."

"Yeah, we should, but I want to take a quick look inside."

They stepped into a foyer, and Sam shone the light into a large living room to the left. Threadbare furniture sat on a worn and dusty wood floor. It looked as if no one had been there in a long time. Sam peered down the hallway and saw an open door mid-way down and another closed at the end. They eased toward the open door. Boards squeaked underneath a stained carpet runner. They stopped at the door and Sam shone the light inside a bedroom, the bed unmade. A large roach, the kind locals called a palmetto bug, ran across a dingy pillow.

They went on to the closed door, listened for any sounds inside, and heard nothing. Sam twisted the doorknob. It snapped and the door sprang open an inch or so. J.T. gagged at the odor that escaped and turned away. Sam pulled a handkerchief from his pocket and put it over his nose and mouth. Light flashed from somewhere inside and Sam nudged the door all the way open with his foot. The light came from a muted large-screen television against the opposite wall, an old rerun of the Andy Griffith show playing. A reclining chair sat in front of the TV, and in it slumped a large man. Sam put the light on him. He had a grin on his face, as if having a good chuckle about the TV. The right side of his head had a dark spot on it. A mass of clotted blood covered the other side, and a spatter the size of a suitcase decorated the wall to the man's left.

"Must be our man," J.T. said in a muffled voice.

He had pulled the neck of his shirt up over his mouth and nose.

"Yeah, I'd say."

Empty boxes and old shoes lay spilled on the floor from a closet to the right of the chair.

"Someone searched the place," Sam said.

"I can't stand it; I've got to get some air." J.T. turned and hurried out of the room.

Sam shone the light inside the closet. A hat lay on the top shelf. Tangled wire hangers clung to the clothes rod like old bat skeletons. He went back to the bedroom they had passed. A similar closet contained the man's clothes on hangers, most of which were new. The shelf above the hangers had been cleared. A string hung from a ceiling light fixture, so he pulled it and heard the snap of a switch, but nothing happened. *Bad bulb.*

He glanced at the things on the floor: only shoes, men's jewelry, and old photographs. Squatting on the floor, he shone the light on one of the snapshots, a family pose that looked at least forty years old. A boy in it might have been a teen-aged Ricardo Miro, though he bore no resemblance to the corpse watching TV in the next room.

Sam searched the top and bottom of the closet and found nothing out of the ordinary, except a light scattering of plaster dust on the edge of the closet shelf directly under the light fixture. He dragged a chair from the corner of the room, stood on it, and loosened thumbscrews on the four corners of the fixture. It came loose in his hands and he laid it on the shelf. The bulb and sockets had been removed, and only a square hole in the ceiling remained. He reached inside, touched what felt like a small metal box, and pulled it out. The top snapped open with the press of a button, and inside he found a stack of papers that looked like Miro's financial records. He replaced the fixture, wiped down everything he remembered touching, and went out the front door with the metal box.

J.T. stood next to the car, looking toward the street, Prince Alfred next to him, growling from deep in his throat.

"What's wrong?" Sam said.

"We've got company."

FOURTEEN

GRIMES SAT IN the passenger seat with the rifle tip extended out the window, the night scope trained on Mackenzie, cross hairs centered on his chest in fluorescent blue. This would be easy. He would hit him and then the other guy for good measure. Grimes remembered the other guy from somewhere, but he couldn't quite place him.

"What are you doing?"

Grimes glanced at Amy behind the wheel, her eyes large, her voice urgent.

"Don't worry. I'm just going to nick him a little so he's easy to deal with. I need all the help I can get; I only have one leg, you know." He tried to sound pitiful, and thought it worked because Amy nodded and looked away.

Grimes went back to the scope and zeroed in on Mackenzie again. Amy reached for the bottle of rum Grimes had sent her into the liquor store to buy. *She's just getting a drink to settle her nerves.* He applied pressure to the trigger. In a half-second, Mackenzie would take the round and it would be over for him. Grimes felt the trigger snap under his finger, and at the same time he heard a loud thump and the shatter of glass. The back of his head felt numb and on fire at the same time, and his nostrils filled with the bite of alcohol. His head went into a spin, he thought he might throw up, and before he could comprehend exactly what had happened, the lights went out.

SAM HEARD A familiar high-pitched whistle as the round went under his left arm. It jerked him sideways and he dropped to the ground.

J.T. fired the 9mm in the direction of the van parked down the street. It sounded like dynamite exploding in the night and the van sped away, screeching its tires. "Are you hit?"

"I think so," Sam said, "it feels like a red-hot knife stuck under my arm." He pushed up to a sitting position, wincing, leaned against the side of the car, and put his hand under his arm. Blood seeped through his shirt and wet his fingers. He stripped off the shirt and held his arm up, away from his body. J.T. shone the light on him and surveyed the damage. Prince Alfred nudged the back of Sam's hand with his nose and whimpered.

"You have a little groove on your side right under your armpit. Not bad, I don't think. Must have been small caliber with a suppressor. I never heard it."

"Yeah, neither did I," Sam said. "I think he's gone now, so let's get out of here. I don't want to be in the yard of a dead man when the cops arrive."

"Got that right, buddy. You need help?"

"No, I'm okay." He stood up and put on his shirt, then walked back to the driver's side to look for the metal box he had dropped. It lay on its side but remained closed. He picked it up and got into the car.

"Who do you think it was?"

Sam started the car and pressed the accelerator, speeding out the U-shaped driveway and onto the street. "Probably Grimes. The only thing is, I wouldn't think he could miss at this range, especially if he had a night scope."

"Why's he trying to kill you?"

"You know Grimes; he's nuts. Besides, he might hold me responsible for him losing his leg." Sam told the story about leaving Grimes in the Everglades.

J.T. chuckled. "Man, I'm impressed. That sounds like something I would do. You still bleeding?"

"I don't think so, but it hurts like crazy."

"What's that you brought out of the house with you?"

Sam picked up the box from the floor and handed it to him.

"Looks like Miro's financial records." Sam told him where he had found the box. "I think the killer might have been searching for them."

J.T. opened it and shone the light inside. He pulled out the document on top and looked it over.

"This is a statement on a numbered account in the Caymans. Miro had almost three hundred thousand dollars stashed away down there."

Sam turned into a small motel with a liquor store next door and parked the car in a spot where it couldn't be seen from the street.

"How about deposits?"

"There's just one for the full amount of the balance, deposited a few months ago."

"What else is in there?"

"That seems to be all there is. Hold on, here's something else in the bottom of the box."

He pulled out a laminated card and turned it over.

"It's an identification card of some kind, with Miro's picture on it." He handed the card to Sam.

"My Spanish isn't very good," J.T. said, "but it looks like he worked for a museum in Cuba, and had something to do with antiquities."

Sam looked at the card, dated several years before. He handed it back to J.T.

"Put it back in the box."

Sam put on his jacket and zipped it up to cover the blood stains before going in to register. They got connecting rooms, and Sam went into the bathroom to look at his injury: just a flesh wound. He cleaned it up with warm water and applied some antibiotic ointment and Band-Aids from his shaving kit. After changing into his last pullover shirt, he went to the liquor store for bottles of gin and tonic. Back in the room, he got a bucket of ice and made two drinks. J.T. opened the connecting door and came in. Sam glanced up and saw Prince Alfred lying on the floor in the next room.

J.T. dropped several sheets of paper on the table. "I checked out the Internet site."

"What did you find?"

"Not much. And it's like I said before, it doesn't look like anything to do with banking." He picked up the piece of paper on top and scanned it. "It looks like they're monitoring things at different locations. There's a coordinate associated with each process shown there." He handed the printout to Sam.

Sam looked at the piece of paper.

"Did you check these coordinates?"

J.T. sighed. "Yeah, I did. All of them are in the sea between Grand Cayman and Cuba."

"Wonder what that has to do with the missiles you saw?"

"I don't know, unless the coordinates are potential targets."

Sam thought about that for a minute and felt a tingle run down his back. He mentioned the news report he had heard in Jack's car the day of the storm, about the pieces of a missing fishing boat washing up on the shore of Grand Cayman.

"Yeah, it might have wandered too close to the place these guys are watching and they zapped it with one of those missiles."

Sam dropped the printout on the table, sat down in one of the chairs and took a drink of his gin and tonic.

"Why don't you keep an eye on the Internet site and see if it changes."

J.T. shrugged. "Sure. What I'd like to do, though, is get another look at Miro's records."

Sam nodded at the box on the edge of the table. "Help yourself."

J.T. opened it and pulled out the papers. His eyes grew wide.

"What is it?" Sam said.

"I didn't see this handwriting before. It might be a personal identification number; you know, a PIN." He showed the number to Sam. "There's a chunk of cash here that nobody's going to use. Might not be too difficult to get it transferred into another account, especially if that really is a PIN."

Sam raised an eyebrow. "What if he had a family?"

"He lived alone. And if he had a family, they would have found his body by now, even if they didn't live with him."

Sam thought about Ricardo Miro lying in the chair with that comic look in his eyes. Hard to tell how long the man had been dead, but from the looks of the body, it had been at least a couple of weeks. He ran his fingers through his hair and took another drink. The pain in his side had diminished to a warm glow. Couple more drinks and it might be gone altogether.

"He might still have someone in Cuba."

J.T. sighed. "You going to look them up so we can give them this money?"

"I might," Sam said.

"Wonder what Miro could have done to accumulate that kind of cash."

"Danilov probably had something to do with it."

They drank about half the bottle of gin and, about 1:00 AM, finally called it a night. Sometime in the early morning Sam heard the dog whimpering and J.T. let him out. He awoke again when the maid knocked on the door. The clock next to the bed displayed 9:00 AM, and he went to the door and told her to come back later.

Sam went into the bathroom, took a shower and changed the dressing on his wound. When he came out, J.T. sat at the table with breakfast sandwiches and coffee from a nearby fast-food restaurant.

As Sam joined him, J.T. asked, "So, what do we do now?"

Sam took a bite of the sandwich and sipped the coffee. He added sugar to the coffee and took another sip before answering. "I thought I might try Jack again, and Marcus, the guy who worked for La Salle."

"You think you can trust him?"

"Probably not. But I might not have much choice."

"You think Grimes killed Miro?"

"Maybe, but I'd guess another of La Salle's men did

it. I'm sure he has several in Miami who would make a close-up hit like that."

Sam called Jack Craft on his cell phone, but he didn't answer. *Probably avoiding me.* He cut the connection and punched in the number Marcus had given him the day he stole the Jaguar. A woman answered, her voice dreamy and slurred, as if she might have been asleep. Sam asked for Marcus and she told him to hold on.

"Yeah, who is this?"

"Mackenzie."

Marcus paused for a couple of seconds, as if he might not remember.

"Oh, yeah. What's up?"

"Have you been in touch with La Salle since we talked?"

"Uh, no. I told you, man, I ain't going near that guy. I'm on his list for sure."

"How about Candi? Have you heard from her?"

"Candi? Yeah, she called me a coupla' nights ago. Wanted to know how to get in touch with La Salle. Said he didn't answer his phone at the house."

"Why did she want to talk with him?"

"Well, now, she didn't say why. I just gave her a number I knew and she hung up. Is she okay?"

"I don't know," Sam said. "She's gone."

"Well, she was pretty thick with the big guy, if you know what I mean."

Sam knew.

"Did La Salle leave town?"

Another pause.

"Yeah, uh, I heard yesterday from a buddy that he flew out on the private plane."

"Where to?"

"I don't know. He never told any of us."

"Who's this buddy you mentioned?"

"He could get in a lot of trouble if it got back to La Salle."

"Don't worry, it won't."

"Okay, Frankie's the one called."

"Frankie?" Sam said. "The guy who worked for Tommy Shoes?"

Sam remembered the short fat man who'd been in a fight because one of La Salle's men said something about Tommy Shoes that he didn't like.

"Yeah, that's him. La Salle took over Tommy's clients and asked Frankie to look after them."

"Okay. I need to know where they went. Can you find that out?"

"Yeah, I might be able to do that. Will we be square after that? 'Cause I been thinking, it ain't exactly smart of me to be talking to you."

"That's not much for the stack of cash I gave you," Sam said.

"Yeah, but it didn't belong to you anyway."

Sighing, Sam said, "Okay, get me La Salle's location and I'll let you off the hook."

Sam told him he would call again in an hour and hung up. They put their bags in the car and Prince Alfred skipped over from the shade of a palm and got in with them. After checking out of the motel a few minutes later, they rode toward Coral Gables and the house where Tommy Shoes had lived. Sam turned into the ornate driveway, stopped at the electronic gate, and pressed the button on the speaker box.

"Yeah?" It sounded like the same voice as when he

had visited with Jack, the one word punctuated with an electronic screech from the box.

"This is Mackenzie. I need to talk to Frankie."

"Frankie ain't here right now."

"I'll wait for him."

"He won't be back for a while."

"Where is he?"

The voice paused for a couple of heartbeats.

"Hey, that ain't none of your business. Get outta here."

Sam glanced up and saw J.T. grinning.

"They were a lot friendlier when Jack did the talking," Sam said.

"Yeah, I bet."

Sam drove away and tried Jack Craft again. Still no answer. They went across the MacArthur Causeway to Miami Beach and headed toward La Salle's place. Sam slowed the car, cruised by the house and saw the garage door open, no cars inside, as if La Salle might have left in a hurry. The maid's Ford sat out front. Sam circled the block and came back, stopping before he reached the entrance, and parked where he could watch the Ford.

He called Marcus again and got an answer on the first ring. "What did you find out?"

"I didn't find out where he is, but you could talk to one of his pilots at the airstrip where he keeps the planes. He might tell you. That's the best I can do."

"Why would the pilot tell me anything?"

"Randy and the boss ain't the best of friends. La Salle smacked him against the head once when he made a wisecrack about Candi. The boss kept him on, but he gets the other pilot to do all his plane driving now."

"How about a phone number?"

"Sorry, I don't have one. You'll have to go see him."

Sam took down directions to the private airstrip and hung up the phone.

"Could be a set-up," J.T. said.

"Yeah, I know. That's why I think I should go alone."

"No way. I don't have anything better to do. Might as well go with you."

"Okay, but if it's an ambush we'd both be better off if you'd stay outside watching."

J.T. considered that and nodded. "We can work it that way. I'm not afraid of these dudes."

Sam grinned. "Yeah, I know."

A woman came out the front door of the house and walked to her car. Sam thought he remembered Candi saying her name was Miranda. The Ford started down the drive toward the gate and Sam eased out into the traffic. He turned into the entrance and braked as she stopped at the street, waiting for traffic to pass, their cars only a few feet apart.

"Miranda." It came out louder than intended.

She turned and stared through the open window at him and J.T., her eyes wide.

"Candi Moran said you can be trusted." She hadn't actually said that, but she probably meant to.

Miranda hesitated, and she had the look on her face that people get when they're trying to decide whether or not to do something they really don't want to do. "Is something wrong with Miss Candi?" She spoke with a Spanish accent.

"I think she's in danger, and the man who lives here is responsible. Do you know where he is?"

Miranda shook her head. "No, Senor. I know nothing of what he does or where he goes."

"If I don't find her, something bad might happen. Anything you can tell me—"

"I am sorry, I do not know." She faced forward and pressed the accelerator. The Ford's front tires spun on the driveway, made a screeching noise, and it sped out into the traffic.

"We could follow her," J.T. said.

"I don't think it would do any good. She probably told the truth."

SAM DROVE TO a bank and rented a safety deposit box large enough for the money and Miro's documents. He kept out a couple thousand dollars for expenses and told J.T. what he had done when he got back to the car.

"If something happens to me, go back and clean out the box." Sam showed him the bank key and stuck it under the edge of the Chevy's carpet below the dash.

THE AIRSTRIP LAY on the fringes of the Everglades. They passed a lot of farm country, but much of it looked as if it hadn't been cultivated in a while, still parched from the previous year's drought. The hangar appeared a few hundred feet ahead and Sam pulled over to the side of the road for J.T. to climb into the back seat. Prince Alfred raised an eyebrow when J.T. folded his long legs and squeezed into the space on the floor.

Sam pulled his cell phone from his pocket and punched in J.T.'s number. The phone chirped in the back seat and J.T. answered. Sam turned on the speaker, put the phone in his shirt pocket, leaving the connection open, and drove down the highway toward the dilapidated metal hangar. He turned in and followed a shell-and-gravel driveway to a tall steel fence where a gate stood open. A sign painted on the hangar advertised "CROP DUSTING" in big, peeling, blue letters, and a black Corvette sat inside the fence at the far corner of the hangar closest to the flight line. There didn't seem to be any other vehicles in sight.

Sam lowered the windows and turned off the engine. He put his 9mm into his pants pocket, pulled his shirt over the butt of the stock, and got out into the heat. Just a few feet away from the gate, an old air conditioner groaned and rattled the sheet metal wall of the hangar. The sun bore down overhead and Sam felt perspiration beading under his shirt and stinging his wound. Prince Alfred jumped out behind him, walked to a shady spot next to a bush and lay down. Sam put his hand on the gun in his pocket and walked through the gate.

He strode past a closed side door to the front of the hangar. It stood wide open and a late model twin-engine airplane sat inside. No one worked around the plane, but Sam saw an office with a large window at the rear of the building. A slim man wearing a white tee shirt and khaki pants sat at a desk inside the office reading a paperback book. The man saw Sam and laid the book on the desk with the pages down. He stood, opened a door and sauntered out toward Sam.

"Can I help you?" His eyes shone red and his hands shook like someone who drank too much.

"You Randy?"

The man looked beyond Sam and then around the hangar. He glanced at Sam's hand on the gun.

"Depends. Who's asking?"

"A friend of Candi Moran. I think she's with La

Salle, and Marcus said you might know where they went."

"Why are you looking for her?"

"He tried to kill her and he might do it again."

Randy nodded. "You alone?"

"Yes."

He studied Sam's face for several seconds and then turned and nodded toward the rear of the hangar.

"Let's go back to the office. It's air conditioned."

Sam followed him into the small room and closed the door behind him. Randy motioned for Sam to sit in front of the desk, an area so small Sam had to turn the chair sideways to sit down. The old air conditioner leaked cool air, but the smell of day-old rum hung there like the last drunk at the party.

"So, what's this business about Candi?"

"You know her?"

"Sure, she's quite a dish."

"Do you know where she is?"

Randy looked out the picture window behind Sam and shrugged.

"Maybe I do."

Sam heard a dog barking, and it took him a full second to realize the sound came from his shirt pocket.

Randy squinted his eyes and cocked his head to the side. "What's that noise?"

Sam removed the phone from his pocket and turned off the speaker.

"Just my cell phone. That's the way it rings."

"Your phone barks?"

"Yeah. Pretty catchy, huh?"

Sam feigned pressing the answer button and put the phone to his ear.

"Hello," Sam said.

J.T.'s voice came on the line, whispering.

"Two guys just drove up in a Cadillac and are getting out. The dog's going crazy."

"Okay, do your thing."

Sam put the phone in his pocket and looked at Randy.

"You expecting anyone?" Sam said.

"No, why?"

"Two guys are outside, so I can only assume they're here to see me. You have a back door out of here?"

Randy shook his head.

Sam pulled the gun from his pocket and pointed it at him. "Too bad."

Randy's eyes bulged and the left side of his face twitched. "Don't kill me, man. I didn't have anything to do with this." He pushed his chair back and it banged against the wall, as if that extra distance might get him out of range of a bullet.

Sam motioned with the gun.

"Get out there and meet them at the door on the side. I'll be right behind you, so don't try to tip them off."

Randy nodded and walked out of the office toward the door.

"Open it." Sam stood against the wall next to the door.

Randy's hand shook when he twisted the knob. The door sprang open and two men pushed through, the same men who had tried to take Sam from Jack Craft's car at the nightclub: Slick and Spike.

"Where is he, Randy?" Slick said.

"Right here," Sam said, clicking the hammer on his gun. "Lay your guns on the floor."

Slick turned, pointed his gun at Sam and grinned. "I think you're outnumbered, pal," Slick said.

J.T. stepped through the door and put his 9mm to the back of Spike's head. "You heard him. Put your weapons down."

They stood frozen for several seconds, obviously calculating the odds of walking out alive if they refused. Then the man with the gun to his head spoke. "Okay, I'm laying it down. You too, Gino."

Sam heard something move behind him and turned. The big end of a wooden crutch came around like the blade of a ceiling fan and struck him on the side of the head. J.T. yelled something he didn't understand, and Prince Alfred growled and leapt in slow motion toward the crutch wielder. Sam's head buzzed like a hornet's nest and everything in the hangar turned sideways as he descended to the concrete floor. He saw his reflection in the sheen of Slick's expensive Italian shoes, and then the buzzing stopped.

FIFTEEN

SAM AWOKE TO a throbbing headache and the drone of airplane engines in flight. He turned to see J.T. in the seat beside him looking at the clouds through the airplane window. The sun found a hole in the white fluff and cut into his eyes like a knife.

"So, Sleeping Beauty awakes." The voice came from across the aisle. Grimes. Blood and bite marks covered his face, and he held a gun pointed at Sam.

"What happened to you?" Sam said.

"A wild animal attacked me. You know a lot about wild animals, don't you, Mackenzie?"

Sam remembered the scene in the hangar right before losing consciousness. Prince Alfred must have chewed him up pretty well. Sam rubbed his eyes. "You didn't hurt the dog, did you?"

Grimes snorted a laugh and looked away.

"He's okay," J.T. said. "Grimes smacked him pretty hard, but a woman with Grimes said she works for a vet. She took him with her and said she would fix him up."

Sam looked behind him. Spike and Slick sat slumped in their seats, taking a snooze. There probably wouldn't be a better time than the present to take these guys, but Grimes had a gun, and Sam's head felt like it might fall off if he stood up.

"Where are we going?"

"You'll know soon enough," Grimes said.

J.T. touched Sam on the arm and Sam turned and looked at him.

"It looks like we're flying southeast," J.T. said, his voice a whisper.

"How long have we been gone?"

"Going on three hours. We dusted the treetops before leaving Florida, evading the FAA. Hard to tell where we are now, but I'm guessing somewhere over the Virgin Islands. I think we just passed St. Thomas."

They weren't headed for Grand Cayman unless Randy had a creative way of getting there. Sam closed his eyes and drifted off to sleep again, waking when the plane's flaps dropped. He unbuckled his seat belt, leaned over to the window, and saw land about a mile away.

"Hey, back in your seat." Grimes waved the gun and Sam sat down, closed his eyes, and wished the pounding in his head would stop.

The plane landed on a rough runway and taxied for several minutes before stopping. Randy shut down the engines and Slick and Spike got out of their seats.

"Okay, we'll take it from here," Slick said.

Grimes nodded and stuck his gun into a shoulder holster. The hatch opened and someone rolled a ladder up to it for them to deplane. Spike went down the aisle and out, and Slick stayed behind.

"Let's go," Slick said over Sam's shoulder.

Sam and J.T. got out of their seats and eased over to the hatch and down the ladder. The runway, paved with sand and gravel, stretched long and wide, as if built for large planes, possibly jets. A construction trailer stood on blocks about a hundred feet away, and about a dozen men worked on the metal skeleton of what might be a future air terminal. Palms, palmetto and pines surrounded the entire area.

A car, with a man in the driver's seat, sat about twenty feet from the plane.

"Get in the back," Spike said. They did as they were told and Spike got in with them. Slick took the front seat. The driver headed down a shiny new road cut through the foliage. Recently paved and smelling of tar, it seemed a callous invasion of the ancient jungle. Sam glanced back and saw Grimes hopping down the ladder one step at a time while supporting himself with the handrails. A man wearing a short sleeved jumpsuit stood at the bottom holding his crutches. Sam touched the spot where the crutch had struck his head and winced.

Despite the air conditioner blowing cool air, the car felt warm, and no one spoke for the next five minutes as the road curved toward the east. The landscape opened to a wide expanse of lawn and gardens, and the road surface changed into fine brown pebbles, inlaid down the center with tan circles, each containing a diamond, club, spade or heart. They passed an entranceway sculpted from coral and surrounded by royal palms and blooming shrubs. An elegant sign the color of mahogany contained the words WELCOME TO NEW MIAMI. A structure rose in the distance. It looked like a hotel, and the sea beyond was cool and inviting, glints of brilliance bouncing off its caps from the sun. A sailboat floated offshore, seemingly still and perfect, lending the appearance of a movie set. Sam wished he could board that perfect boat and sail somewhere other than this place.

The hotel, the color of oxidized copper, had been built in the shape of a treasure chest, about twenty stories high. A giant sculpture of a muscle-bound man stood out front, at least half as tall as the building. He looked a lot like Hercules, except he had one large eye in the center of his forehead. A Cyclops. Rich in detail, the sculpture might have been a work of art in another era.

They rode between the Cyclops' feet, which seemed as large as compact cars, to the hotel entrance. The car stopped and Spike got out and pointed his gun at Sam. "Okay, out."

They exited and strode through the door. The lobby, tiled with marble the color of coral, contained no furniture. A mosaic of multi-colored tiles in the shape of a large eye had been laid at its center.

Spike told them to follow him.

"And stay off the eye," Slick said, "the cement ain't cured yet."

Slick stuck a card key into a slot on the wall next to the elevator. A green light flashed and the doors opened. They stepped inside, ascended to the penthouse, and the elevator opened to a large apartment with glass on the back side overlooking the sea. The furniture looked a lot like that from La Salle's house on Miami Beach, and Sam recognized a couple of paintings he had seen there.

"Stay with these guys and I'll go talk to the boss," Slick said. Spike nodded and told Sam and J.T. to sit on the sofa.

Slick returned in a couple of minutes.

"He wants to see you, Mackenzie," Slick said and

turned to Spike. "Take this other clown downstairs and lock him in the money room."

J.T. raised an eyebrow and smiled.

They might regret putting him there.

Slick took Sam down a hall and opened the door to a dojo, a large, rectangular room with a pad on the floor. He told Sam to remove his shoes before going in. La Salle and a small Asian man stood facing each other, barefoot and wearing white uniforms with black belts. The small man had to be the teacher, the Sensei.

La Salle jumped back into a fighting position and yelled. The Sensei, fast as lightning, punched his fist toward La Salle's face. La Salle jerked his head back out of range and then blocked a front kick to his abdomen and a spinning roundhouse kick to the face, stepping back with each. He returned with a side kick to the face and the Sensei ducked below it and dropped to the pad. With La Salle's massive right leg still airborne, the Sensei kicked behind his left knee and the big man's leg buckled, dropping him to a crouch. The Sensei sprang to his feet and La Salle spun and drove his fist into the Sensei's lower back. Sam had never seen anyone that large move so fast. A grimace of pain and confusion pinched at the Sensei's face as he stumbled sideways.

La Salle glanced at Sam and Slick and narrowed his eyes. Dirty fighting, and the small man probably wouldn't forget it. La Salle climbed to his feet and spoke in a low voice. The Sensei nodded, then smiled wanly and padded toward the door. He bowed his head, almost imperceptibly, as he passed Sam and said, "You are the one," his voice a whisper.

Slick waited until he got out of earshot and said, "What did he say?"

Sam shrugged and said, "I don't know." He had heard the words, but he really *didn't* know what the man meant.

La Salle, his long hair dripping with sweat, walked over and told Slick to wait outside. "So, the thief is brought to justice." La Salle scanned the floor as he spoke, as if looking for something. Finally, he reached down, picked up a rubber band and gathered his hair into a pony tail.

Sam said nothing.

"Do you still have my money?"

"Some of it."

La Salle smiled and shook his head.

"Not very smart, you know. And I can't let you get away with it."

La Salle towered over Sam by at least six inches.

"Yeah, I figured as much."

La Salle wiped his forehead with his uniform sleeve.

"Where is the money now?"

"Sorry, you won't get it back unless you let Candi go."

"Candi?" La Salle said. "I don't think you understand."

"How's that?"

La Salle turned and motioned for Sam to follow him.

They went to the far wall and La Salle drew back a heavy drape to reveal a wall of glass similar to that in the living room. A patio outside seemed to stand at the edge of the Caribbean.

"Have a look for yourself."

Candi Moran lay on the patio in a lounge chair, face down, wearing a white bikini, the wound in her back almost healed.

"Come close. I want her to see you."

Sam sidled up to the window. She certainly didn't look like someone in distress. La Salle tapped on the glass a couple of times and Candi turned on her side and rose to an elbow. Her eyes looked sleepy. Looking straight at Sam, she made a face and waved her hand as if to say, *Leave me alone*. She turned and lay back down on the lounge chair.

Candi seemed to be there of her own free will. At least La Salle wanted Sam to believe that and had painted a pretty convincing picture. But the glass might be one-way, which Candi couldn't see through.

La Salle had tried to kill her, and she had a bullet wound to show for it. She wouldn't just let bygones be bygones and move in with him. But then, Sam wondered if he could be objective about a woman so attractive to him. And something in his head flashed red at the possibility that she might be harmed again.

Sam ran his fingers through his hair and turned to La Salle.

"I want to talk to her."

La Salle smiled and seemed about to speak, but Sam noticed a narrowing of his eyes, a warning, and lunged away at the same instant La Salle threw his fist at Sam's face. The fist still connected with his cheek. Sam shook his head, turned inside La Salle's next punch and slammed his fist into La Salle's nose. La Salle's head rocked back, and a string of blood splattered the glass. He wiped his nose and grinned. Sam hit him in the stomach and it was like punching a sack of cement. The big man only flinched, apparently feeling little pain, so Sam kicked at La Salle's midsection. La Salle blocked the kick, returning one of his own that doubled Sam over, then spun in the air, seeming as light as a feather, and delivered a roundhouse kick to Sam's head. Sam felt a buzz behind his eyes and the room started to spin. He staggered back and shook his head. La Salle back-fisted him to the temple. Sam fell to the pad and lay still for what seemed like a long time, his head in a spin. He opened his eyes and saw La Salle prancing back and forth, flexing his fists, a wild look on his face.

He wondered if the next blow might finish him. Then the Sensei's face flashed in his mind's eye and he heard the words again. *You are the one*. It all became clear: the Sensei had meant that La Salle feared Sam. La Salle had kidney-punched the Sensei to demonstrate his cold blood, and he would kill Sam now, if he could. He would want Sam looking at him when he did it.

The spinning in his head finally subsided, and Sam struggled to his feet. La Salle padded toward Sam, grinning, making a big show of rolling his fingers into fists, and launched another kick to Sam's face. Sam jerked out of range, rushed in, and slammed his fist into La Salle's ribs. He felt something give, and La Salle staggered and gave him a sidelong glance. The look told him that he would have to do better than that, but Sam also read something else in it and knew this might be his only opportunity. La Salle blinked his eyes a fraction too long and Sam drove the heel of his right foot into the side of his opponent's knee joint. The knee made a snapping sound similar to that of a fresh cob of corn being broken in half. La Salle's eyes went wide, and he opened his mouth as if to scream, but nothing came out. He fell to the pad and Sam knew he wouldn't be kicking anybody else for a long time. Dirty fighting, no doubt about it.

SIXTEEN

La Salle lay on the floor, holding his damaged leg in both hands, grunting with pain. Sam seized his wrist and twisted until La Salle turned onto his side, then untied the black uniform belt with his free hand. Designed to encircle the waist twice, the belt unwound to more than six feet. He bound La Salle's hands behind him with one end and gagged his mouth with the other.

Sam padded to the patio door and went out. Glancing back at the glass wall, he saw only his own reflection, confirming his suspicion that Candi had not seen him inside. Candi rolled onto her side and stared at him, her mouth open, eyes wide.

She stood up from the lounge chair and put her arms around him. "Sam! How did you find me?"

"Let's go, I'll tell you later. La Salle's men might be on their way."

"Where's La Salle?"

"Don't worry. He won't be causing any trouble."

Candi donned a terry robe and followed Sam back into the dojo. La Salle twisted his neck to look as they entered the room, his eyes narrow slits, sweat streaming down his face. He tried to speak, but the words were unintelligible inside the gag. They left him lying like a trussed animal at a rodeo. Sam put on his shoes and they stepped into the hallway.

Candi grabbed his arm. "You did that to him?" She seemed surprised, but pleased.

Before Sam could reply, Spike came around the corner with a can of cola in his hand. He stopped short, eyes wide, mouth open. Sam struck Spike on the cheek with the heel of his hand and slammed his head against the wall. He dropped to the carpet, unconscious, spilling cola on himself and the floor. Sam took Spike's gun from his shoulder holster.

They stepped around him and eased down the hall toward the posh room with the elevator. As they rounded the corner, Slick stood waiting and stuck a gun to the side of Sam's head. He halted, his pulse pounding in his ears.

"Gimme the piece or I'll scatter your brains on the wall."

Sam handed it over and Slick dropped it into his pocket.

"Where do you think you're going?"

"Your boss got tied up, so we decided to leave," Sam said.

"Yeah?" He looked around them down the hall. "I see you also decided to bust a hole in the wall with Jimmy's face."

Sam moved a couple of inches toward him and he stepped back.

"Come any closer and you're a dead man," Slick said, his lips tight against his teeth, his voice pitched high.

The elevator door opened and Frankie, the short man from Tommy Shoes' house, stepped out. Frankie held a golf club about six feet long, the club head the size of a grapefruit. He didn't seem the least bit surprised to see Slick holding the gun on Sam and Candi.

"Hey, Gino, let's go drive some balls."

Slick Gino gave Frankie a smirk. "Look, Bozo, can't you see I'm a little busy here?"

Frankie glanced at Sam and Candi and said, "Yeah? How about Jimmy then?"

"Jimmy's indisposed right now."

"He's what?"

"Hey, he's passed out in the hall."

Frankie took a couple of steps so he could see down the hall.

"What happened to him?"

Sam watched the tip of Gino's gun, and wondered if he could take it away from him before he shot either of them.

"Mackenzie here just busted his head. Go check on the boss while I keep them here."

"Aw, man, I wanted to drive some balls. I go talk to him and he'll give me something to do."

"Just go, Frankie."

"Okay, let me show you something first."

Maybe this is the time, while Frankie has Gino's eye.

Frankie held his club in front of him as if addressing the ball, getting ready for a drive.

"I got this new grip I'm trying. Check this out."

Sam eased in front of Candi, ready to lunge for Gino's gun, but Frankie winked at him and he stopped.

Frankie drew the club backward, in a slow backswing, keeping his head down, as if watching the imaginary ball.

"Hey, man." Gino rolled his eyes and turned to look at the short man. "This is serious—"

Frankie swung the club as if going for the green on the par five. The club head struck Gino about an inch above his eyes with a flat thumping sound. Gino stumbled backward, fell against the wall, and his eyes snapped shut, his forehead beginning to swell. Sam pulled Gino's gun from his fingers and retrieved the gun Gino had put in his pocket. He glanced at Candi and saw little reaction in her eyes.

Frankie reached down and fished something out of Gino's pocket, then pressed the button on the elevator.

"C'mon, let's go," Frankie said.

The elevator door opened and the three of them went inside.

"What's the deal, Frankie?" Sam said.

Frankie pressed the down button, grinned, and winked at Candi.

"You saw the way he talked to me. No respect at all."

"Gino'll be pretty mad when he wakes up."

"Yeah, well, he burned Tommy and he's lucky I didn't whack him. Besides, he's the one gave me the black eye." He paused for a second. "There's a hidden camera in the dojo. After you wiped up the floor with La Salle, I knew Gino would head up there to help his boss. I thought it would be a good time to settle the score."

"What about the guy who came here with me?"

"He's in the money room. I got the key from Gino." He held up a card for them to see.

The elevator door opened and they took a left down the hall past a room the size of a football field.

"That's supposed to be the casino," Frankie said with a snort, as if choking back a laugh.

"You sound doubtful."

"Yeah, well, La Salle's a high roller, and I think he'll run out of money before he's finished with this place."

"He must have already spent a fortune. Where is the money coming from?"

"Beats me. He's real close-mouthed about it. He thinks I'm going to pitch in with him, but I know a sinking ship when I see it, and I'm getting off."

They strode through a metal door at the end of the hall. The room inside looked like a long jail cell with bars from floor to ceiling. A walk-in vault filled the wall behind the bars and J.T. sat next to it on the floor. He stood up when they came into the room and looked from Sam to Frankie and back.

"This is Frankie," Sam said. "He's going to get us out of here."

"Yeah, that's cool. I knew you'd work something out. Is this Candi?"

J.T. had a funny smile on his face and looked as if he might drool onto his shirt. Candi hugged herself and mumbled something about the air conditioning. Sam saw goose bumps on her legs below the terry robe.

"Yeah, I'm Candi," she said, answering for Sam. "You're the computer geek, right?"

J.T. winced and glanced at Sam.

"I suppose some people might call me that."

"Hey, not me, pal," Sam said.

Frankie stuck the card key into the lock and opened the cell door.

J.T. nodded toward the vault and said, "You know how to open this thing?"

Frankie shook his head. "They don't trust me that much yet."

J.T. made a face. "Too bad. They had a wooden crate

on the floor when that big dude brought me in here. He called two other guys and they put it in the vault and locked it up. It looked heavy."

"So, what's the big deal?" Sam asked.

"They almost dropped it and the lid fell off. I saw gold inside."

"Gold? You mean, like, gold coins."

"No, it looked like art pieces. Masks and figurines, things like that."

J.T.'s eyes had that glow, and Sam knew it would be a problem. He looked at Frankie and Candi. "Either of you know anything about any gold?"

They shook their heads, but Sam saw something in Candi's eyes. He held her gaze for a couple of seconds and she looked away.

Frankie looked at his watch and said, "Okay, let's get out of here. Randy said he'd have the plane ready for takeoff in fifteen minutes, and it's already been that long. I want to be back in Miami by the time Gino wakes up."

Frankie opened the door and stood there. J.T. looked at Sam and Sam knew he wouldn't leave.

"Who knows how to open this vault?" J.T. said.

Frankie rolled his eyes. "There's no way you're going to get into that vault. You better forget that."

J.T. raised his eyebrows and smiled, as if to say, *Oh, yeah? Just watch.*

Frankie sighed. "Okay, you going or not?"

J.T. shook his head. Sam looked at Candi.

"I think I'll hang around, too," Candi said.

Sam ran his fingers through his hair.

"Okay, thanks for your help, Frankie. We're stay-

ing here. If the subject comes up, tell them we left on the plane with you."

Frankie grinned and shook his head. "You guys are crazy. You'll never get that gold, and they'll kill every one of you." He shook his head again, rested the golf club on his shoulder like a sentry, and went out the door.

Sam told J.T. what had happened in the dojo, handed him one of the guns, and glanced at Candi. "Do you know your way around this place?"

Candi shrugged and said, "A little, I guess. La Salle gave me a tour."

"You have a key to the penthouse?"

She shook her head.

Sam could have asked Frankie for the card key he'd taken from Gino, but didn't think about it at the time. Too bad; one of the men up there might have the combination for the safe. He remembered what Frankie had said about the hidden camera in the dojo.

"Are there any cameras in here?"

"I believe the only place they've put them so far is around La Salle's suite for his protection. They're not too worried about anyone stealing anything yet. Nobody's on the island except us."

"How about locals?"

Candi shook her head. "A few people lived here in primitive homes but La Salle had them relocated to the next island. He gave them some money and they were happy."

"Okay, they'll be coming down soon, so we need to get out of here."

"We could go to one of the bedrooms."

Candi opened the door and they went out. They

made their way down the hall to the stairwell and up one flight of stairs. Sam opened the door on the second floor and peered around it to make sure no one waited there.

"The locks haven't been activated yet, so they're all open," Candi said.

They went to the last door down the hall and entered an unfurnished room with a view of the sea.

Sam closed the door behind them. "How many men are in the building?"

"Only a couple more besides Gino and Jimmy. Also, the construction men and some maintenance guys who are working on the electrical system. I heard La Salle talking to them this morning about how the people who put in the generator messed it up."

The karate guy might still be around, and Grimes, too, unless they left with Frankie. Sam glanced at Candi and held her stare for a couple of seconds.

"What are you looking at?" Candi said.

"I think you know something about that gold you're not saying."

Candi sidled to the window, crossed her arms in front of her, and looked out at the water. A gull landed on the balcony, peered inside and flew away.

"I know they brought it in last night."

"Who brought it?"

J.T. stood with his hands in his back pockets, listening.

"One of La Salle's men, I don't know his name, and a guy named Danilov. He spoke with an accent. I think maybe he's Russian. He flew the airplane, and he told La Salle the weather was rough coming in."

Sam nodded. "What else?"

"That's about all, except he said he's going back tonight for another load."

J.T. looked at Sam and smiled.

"What kind of plane does he fly?" Sam asked.

"I don't know anything about airplanes."

"You've seen it, though?"

"Well, yeah, I've seen it."

"How big is it and what does it look like?"

"It's pretty big, probably with enough room for eight or ten people, and it makes a lot of noise. Oh, yeah, and it floats in the water."

"A seaplane?"

"Yeah, I guess."

Sam raised an eyebrow and he and J.T. exchanged glances. The computer system in the facility on Grand Cayman monitored something in the sea between Grand Cayman and Cuba. Sunken treasure.

"Anything else?"

"No."

"There's something you're not telling."

Candi looked at Sam and smiled. "Danilov said the most valuable items are still out there."

SEVENTEEN

SAM FOUND CANDI a pair of coveralls in a maintenance room down the hall. She dressed in the bathroom and came out and modeled the too-large coveralls for them. She had rolled up the sleeves and cuffed the pant legs.

"Not bad," Sam said.

"Well, it'll have to do, at least until I get off this island."

Sam nodded and raised an eyebrow. "Since we're on the subject, how did you happen to end up here? You were safe and sound when I left you at the Palma Hotel."

Candi's face turned red. "I knew you would bring that up."

"Well, it is the reason the gang is all here."

"Yeah, I know. You made me pretty mad the other night when you said you wouldn't be back for a while. I called Marcus, thinking he wouldn't tell La Salle after what La Salle did to him. He said he would come get me."

"Did Marcus pick you up?"

Her face dropped. "No. I went to the lobby an hour or so later to meet him, but I saw Gino and Jimmy instead. I guess Marcus sold me out. Probably trying to ingratiate himself with the boss after letting you get away with the car and money."

She said it in such a way as to toss the blame for

calling Marcus back into Sam's lap. He glanced out the window. The sun had scalded its way under the horizon, turning the blue of the sea into black marble with veins of pewter. A ribbon of gold rimmed the edge of the world at that faraway place where it bends and disappears. Sam wondered how many ancient people had chased the golden ribbon looking for treasure, only to end up lost in the darkness.

"I felt like a fool," Candi said. A tear broke loose from her eye and ran down her cheek. She dried it with her rolled-up sleeve.

She probably told La Salle where to find the Jaguar, too, but Sam thought it might not be the best time to bring that up.

J.T. ambled over and put his arm around her shoulders. "Hey, don't worry about it. Happens to the best of us. Right, Sam?" He gave Sam a look that said, *If you don't tell her, I will*.

Sam sighed and said, "Yeah, okay, I called Marcus too, looking for you."

"You did?"

Sam nodded. "He told me to go to the airstrip and talk to the pilot, but Gino and Jimmy showed up after I arrived, and then Grimes ambushed me. I guess I feel a little foolish myself."

Candi sniffed. "You do? Really?"

"Afraid so."

Candi kissed J.T. on the cheek, pulled out of the embrace and wiped another tear with the back of her hand.

J.T. said, "Hey, you two need to lighten up. This place looks like it's going to be pretty wild."

"Oh, yeah, New Miami." Candi rolled her eyes. "That's the plan, if the money lasts. I got the big spiel about how this is going to be the next Monte Carlo. Over two thousand rooms in a couple of years and he expects to draw a million visitors by the end of the third year. He plans to have flights coming here from all over by next month, and a Hovercraft out of Miami." Candi glanced at Sam and grinned, tears still damp on her face. "Can you believe that?"

"Yeah. Sounds pretty ambitious."

"So, where's Danilov's seaplane?" J.T. asked Candi.

"It's on the other side of the airport in the lagoon. A dirt road goes out there."

"I wonder what time they'll leave?"

Candi shrugged. "He said they would go at nightfall."

J.T. looked out the window. "It's getting dark now. We probably missed them."

"Doesn't matter as long as we're there when they get back," Sam said.

J.T. nodded. "Yeah, I guess. I just wish we knew where they're going."

Sam had to admit that he wanted to know their destination, too. He wondered how La Salle might be using the facility on Grand Cayman in his scheme.

"I wish we'd had more time to check on that web site."

"Yeah, me too," J.T. said.

Sam turned to Candi. "Do you know where we can get access to a computer?"

"They have them in Security. But somebody might be in the office."

"That's okay, let's go take a look. After that, we'll head over to the lagoon."

They went back down the stairwell, exited, and

sneaked to the security office, which lay a few doors past the money room. The door stood open. Sam leaned against the wall and peeked inside. A bank of video monitors occupied one side of the room, and a man sat in the corner, his head against the wall, eyes closed. He looked like the same man who had driven them to the hotel. There didn't seem to be much going on yet in the security department of the Cyclops.

Sam stepped inside, his gun leading the way, and the sleeping man opened his eyes. He pitched forward in the chair and fumbled with his shoulder holster. Sam pointed the gun at his face and thumbed the hammer.

"Don't do it."

The man froze and glanced at Candi and J.T., then at the monitors. One screen showed La Salle still on the floor with his hands tied. Another displayed the foyer where Gino lay unconscious.

"What happened to them?"

"Just a little misunderstanding," Sam said. "Be good and you won't get hurt. At least not by us."

J.T. went to work on the computer while Sam took the gun from the security man's fingers and made him get on the floor.

Sam said to Candi, "Unplug that phone cord and hand it to me."

After tying the man's hands behind him with the cord, Sam found a roll of packaging tape in the desk and taped his mouth and ankles. He pulled a set of car keys from the man's pocket. Hopefully the car still sat out front. Opening a closet next to the desk, Sam dragged the man inside, leaving the door ajar so he could wiggle his way out in an hour or so.

J.T. punched the computer keys, while Candi watched the monitors.

Sam peered over J.T.'s shoulder. "You find what you need?"

"Yeah, I think so. I'm on the Internet now. There were several transmissions since I looked at my web site, but the information looks about the same each time. I just need to download this one last file."

Sam joined Candi at the monitors. Most of the screens displayed views of empty rooms. He went to the one where La Salle lay on the floor and watched as the dojo door opened. Jimmy the Spike stepped into the room rubbing the side of his head. He spotted La Salle on the floor and hurried over to him. Sam turned up the volume on the speaker until he could hear their voices and zoomed in with the camera.

La Salle gurgled and jerked at his bindings. His eyes bulged. Jimmy knelt to his side and untied the belt around his gagged mouth.

La Salle gasped and said, "Where's Gino?"

"Out cold." Jimmy untied the knot that bound La Salle's hands. "Somebody hit him pretty hard. His head is all swollen up, like twice as big as it's supposed to be."

"Help me up. I think Mackenzie fractured my leg."

Jimmy got to his feet and looked down at him.

"He what?" Jimmy stood gazing at his great leader, as if paralyzed by this revelation that he might not be invincible after all.

La Salle glanced up and narrowed his eyes. The look said he would kill Jimmy if he could.

"Just pull me up."

Jimmy hesitated another second and then reached

for his arm. La Salle got his good leg under him, stood and reached for the rail against the wall. He started to hop toward the back door, but stopped and turned around.

"I heard an airplane take off a few minutes ago. Who left on it?"

Jimmy shrugged and rubbed the side of his head. "I don't know, somebody hit me, too."

"Well, find out." He started hopping again and said over his shoulder, "And tell the pilot to get the other plane ready. I need to go to Miami and get this leg fixed."

Jimmy left the dojo while La Salle still worked his way toward the back door, one hop at a time, moaning, his face contorted with pain.

"WE BETTER GET GOING," Candi said.

Sam stepped over to J.T. and said, "Let's go. La Salle's leaving for the airport in a few minutes, and I want to be long gone by then."

"I almost got it...okay, take a look at this." He turned the monitor so Sam could see. A red dot blinked in the center of the screen with several blinking white dots scattered around it. "I found this program on the computer. It uses the data file I received on the web site. The dots are the coordinates I mentioned in the Caribbean. That red dot in the center is what they're watching, maybe where the gold is located. I'm guessing the other dots are boats. These guys are watching to make sure no one gets too close." J.T. gave Sam a nervous grin. "That's what the missiles are for."

Sam remembered the rocket launcher they had used on Tommy Shoes' limo, and the destruction it had caused. According to J.T.'s description, the missiles were larger than a rocket launcher, and probably would turn a fifty-foot boat into small pieces. He remembered the radio report of the fishing boat that had washed up in pieces on Grand Cayman. Poor guys never knew what hit them.

"Did you write down the coordinates of the red dot?"

J.T. gave Sam a sidelong glance, grinned and said, "Yeah, first thing I did."

"Okay, let's get out of here."

They made it almost to the lobby when the elevator beeped. Sam led them into an alcove and peered around the corner. Jimmy came out of the elevator and sprinted toward the security room. When he went in the door, they hurried through the lobby and crossed the big eye in the floor, not bothering to step around the uncured cement.

The car still sat in the covered limousine area not far from the door. They got inside, Sam and Candi in front, J.T. in back, and Sam started the engine. They rode away from the hotel, quiet until they passed between the giant feet. Sam glanced at Candi in the glow of the dash lights. Her face reminded him of a movie star he had seen on the cover of a recent magazine. She had the looks to be an actress or model herself, instead of tying up with a bunch of criminals.

J.T. broke the silence. "How do you think Danilov figures into this?"

"Maybe he found a shipwreck back in his Cuba days," Sam said.

"And he got Miro to appraise something he found and sell it for him?"

"Yeah, that would explain Miro's bank account. But what doesn't add up is the link with La Salle. The only information you found about him was in the last few months, like he didn't exist prior to that time."

Sam glanced at Candi again and caught her eyes. She looked away.

"Maybe Candi knows," Sam said.

Candi waited a few seconds and said, "Back before Philly died, La Salle mentioned something about working in Central America. I asked what he did there and he got this real funny look on his face. He mumbled something about being a consultant, and never mentioned it again."

Sam drove past the New Miami sign and onto the road that led to the airport. The road was dark except for the car's headlights, but after a couple of minutes Sam could see lights from the airport in the distance.

"Do we have to go through the airport to get to the lagoon?"

"No," Candi said. "You can take a left at the edge of the airport onto an access road and it goes all the way around one side."

Sam turned off the headlights before reaching the airport and turned left as Candi instructed. He could see the runway lit up next to an airplane similar to the one he had flown in on. Two men stood talking inside the construction trailer. Sam couldn't recognize them at that distance. A car started up next to the trailer and raced toward the road to the hotel. Sam eased the car into a clump of trees and put on the brakes. The approaching car's headlights shone through the trees, and when it passed he saw Marcus behind the wheel. Probably going to get La Salle. A moment later the two men in the construction trailer came out and down the steps. One of them, wearing flight coveralls, hurried toward the plane. *Maybe the pilot?* The other man, dressed in a business suit, stepped to the corner of the trailer and a flood light illuminated his face. A chill ran up Sam's back. He eased the car back on the road and drove toward the lagoon, wondering what Jackson Craft might have to do with La Salle, New Miami and sunken gold.

EIGHTEEN

VISIBILITY DIMMED AS they drove away from the airport, and Sam snapped on the parking lights. Following Candi's directions, he turned onto the dirt road to the lagoon, still thinking about Jack Craft. Jack had said he put La Salle in touch with a broker to purchase some land, maybe this island. But why would he be here now, months later, unless he had more involvement in this mess than he had said? Sam wished he'd pressed Jack a little harder, and maybe he, J.T. and Candi wouldn't be in the middle of nowhere planning to rob gold from crooks.

"It can't be far from here," Candi said.

The road, paved with sand and shell and wide enough only for one vehicle, meandered like an old creek bed. Sam drove slowly and looked for a place to park where the car would be hidden. He saw a spot a couple of minutes later, turned off the road into a clearing, and eased in behind a stand of trees.

They got out and ambled along the curvy road for about fifty feet before seeing the reflection of light across water. An area half the size of a football field had been cleared, and on the far side a wooden dock jutted out into the edge of the lagoon. A yellow light cast a jaundiced glow over the boards, and an old gas pump stood next to the light like a loyal friend awaiting the return of the ship.

In a graveled area near the dock sat a business van.

"Walk in the edge of the trees," Sam said. "I'll check the van first, in case someone is asleep inside."

They eased through the brush until even with the vehicle, and Sam crept to the window and peered inside. Empty. Keys hung from the ignition, ready for a quick departure.

Sam glanced at the dock. Small bugs swarmed the light and dropped on a pile underneath when they flew too close to the globe. Maybe they wanted something they thought lay inside the brilliance, something like the gold the people on this island were chasing. Sam wondered if the bugs' demise could be a message for him.

This fiasco had started with Sam trying to protect Candi Moran. He didn't *want* the gold. There would be problems with it as long as La Salle or Danilov lived, and he certainly wouldn't kill them for it. He had gone along only because Candi wouldn't leave the island. Now he wished he had just told her to get on the plane or forget about any help from him. J.T. would have stayed with her, but Sam knew his interest, and his first priority probably wouldn't be to protect Candi. That might be just what Candi deserved. She wanted protection, but she also wanted her father's money back, and even more. There had been no question about her staying once she knew J.T. would help with the gold.

J.T. punched Sam on the shoulder. "What's the plan?"

"We take them by surprise when they come in, and nobody dies. Then we get Danilov to fly us out of here on that plane."

J.T. hesitated. "Why should we worry about keeping these guys alive? I can fly the plane."

"Yeah, I know you can."

J.T. raised an eyebrow and stared at Sam for a couple of seconds. "Okay, you're the boss."

Candi stepped in front of Sam and looked him in the eye. "Hey, don't I have anything to say about this?"

"Like what?"

"Like, I think we should take the gold from the plane and stay and get what they have in the safe. We could be missing out on millions if we don't. La Salle will be in Miami, and we'll have Danilov's full attention. Gino's probably the last of La Salle's henchmen left on the island, and I don't think he's going to be in any shape to do much of anything."

Sam considered that for a moment and said, "Okay, you can stay if you want, but Danilov is going to fly the plane to Miami and I'm going to be on it."

J.T. glanced at Candi and nodded. "Fair enough."

Candi remained silent.

An airplane flew over, heading west.

"There goes La Salle," J.T. said, watching the running lights trailing away in the sky. He turned and looked at Sam. "You leave the keys in the ignition?"

"Yeah, I did."

J.T. nodded and Sam knew he wouldn't be leaving the island until he had a look into the safe.

They got inside the van, Sam and Candi in front and J.T. in back, and waited.

"The part that's mystifying about all this," Sam said, "is how La Salle could amass so much money in such a short time."

"He told me a man came to him with a proposal to

build this place," Candi said, "and he had investors who wanted to buy in. La Salle had been planning to do it anyway, just not so soon, and out of the blue this guy shows up."

"Did he tell you the man's name?"

"No, but I know La Salle took the offer and set up the company. He said he would buy them out, at least enough to gain control of everything, when his other investments came in. I assume now he was talking about this salvage operation."

J.T. spoke up. "Did he know who the investors would be?"

"I don't think so, but he didn't care. He stood only to gain by using their money. Besides, who would try to swindle somebody like La Salle?"

"Did the guy require La Salle to buy a percentage of the stock in the company?" Sam said.

"Oh, yeah, but he had it set up so he would have three months to put in his part."

"Did he say how much?"

"Yeah, a hundred million."

J.T. whistled. "He must think there's at least that much gold out there."

"Maybe twice that," Sam said, "since Danilov is probably taking half."

They waited in the van for several hours. It got chilly in the early morning and Sam wished he had a light jacket. Sitting in the driver's seat, Sam took the first two-hour watch, then leaned his head against the headrest and dozed while J.T. took over. He didn't know how long he had been asleep when the drone of an airplane woke him.

"There they are," J.T. said.

Sam stretched and peered at the dock area.

The noise got louder as the plane neared, and running lights flickered in the distance. They got out of the van and crouched behind it. Sam pressed the light on his watch and looked at the time: 4:10 AM.

The plane landed at the edge of the lagoon and taxied on the water toward the dock. It looked like an old Grumman Mallard: no pontoons, just a big floating hull like a boat. Its engines raced a couple of times as the pilot coaxed it into place, and then coughed and went silent. The hatch popped open and a man jumped out onto the dock. Another man threw out two ropes, and the man on the dock knelt and tied them to boat cleats. Sam didn't recognize either of the men. The noise of a helicopter chattered in the distance and the man on the dock stood and looked up.

"Someone else is joining the party," Sam said.

Coming in fast, the helicopter swept the lagoon with spotlights and circled. The man on the dock pulled a gun from the pocket of his coveralls and yelled something that was garbled by the helicopter noise. The other man jumped out of the seaplane onto the dock and looked up.

"We'd better go back to the car until we see how this plays out," Sam yelled over the helicopter prop wash.

J.T. nodded. "Yeah, and we better make it quick. That chopper's coming this way again."

They hurried along the van on the side farthest from the dock and raced up the road into the trees to a spot near the car where they could still see the seaplane. The helicopter slowed, hovered above the van, and shone the light on the seaplane. One of the men on the dock shielded his eyes and aimed the gun in the air, but rounds from the helicopter hit him before he could pull the trigger, and he fell back on the dock. The other man dived into the water as bullets ripped through the boards where he had been standing. The pilot set the helicopter down in the clearing and cut the engines, but kept the spotlight on the plane. Three men with rifles got out of the copter and ran to the side of the van.

Dead silence hung in the air, as if the birds, frogs, and other wildlife stopped everything to watch the humans do battle.

One of the men yelled over the hood of the van, "Come out or we will torch the plane." He had an accent, maybe Spanish, but Sam wasn't sure.

Nothing happened for a while, and Sam wondered if Danilov might be considering his options. Had the plane not been tied down, he might have tried to take off again, but he would surely die if he tried to cut the ropes. Maybe he thought help would come from the Cyclops. Finally, he appeared in the open hatch, his hands over his head.

One of the men from the helicopter stepped around the van. "Is there anyone else?"

"No," Danilov said, "just the three of us."

The helicopter men rounded the van and stepped onto the dock. One of them kicked the man who had been shot and, satisfied he wouldn't be moving, pointed his rifle at the murky water. "The other one went in right there. Probably halfway to Florida by now." He turned toward the plane and motioned to Danilov with his hand. "Okay, out."

Danilov jumped down and one of the men from the helicopter climbed into the seaplane. He came out a few minutes later with a gold figurine in his hand and held it in the air. "This is one of the pieces. A lot more is on the plane, and the rest must be in the hotel."

These men didn't seem like run-of-the-mill pirates. They could fly a helicopter and handle weapons, and seemed more like Special Forces than thieves. But they also could be expensive hired hands.

One of the helicopter men held a rifle on Danilov while the other two went onto the seaplane. Danilov kept looking in the direction of the hotel, probably wondering when La Salle would show up. A few minutes later the two men from the helicopter stepped off the seaplane carrying a crate.

Sam heard the whine of an electric motor. He turned and saw a golf cart easing down the road toward the helicopter, the light from the dock reflecting off the driver's spiky blond hair and bloody face. *Grimes.*

The cart stopped, far enough away that no one on the dock noticed, and Grimes watched the action below. He reached for an object standing on the floorboard beside his feet, pulled something that made a snapping noise, and put the object onto his shoulder. It looked like the tube of a telescope. He pointed it and pulled the trigger. A second later the helicopter exploded, sending fifty-foot flames into the air and changing the night into day.

Sam felt the heat on his face, and the brilliance of the flames cut into his eyes like a laser.

"Man, what a blast," J.T, said.

The men from the helicopter yelled at Danilov and at each other for several seconds before all of them scrambled aboard the seaplane. They probably thought no one would blow it up because of the gold it carried.

Sam glanced at Grimes. The cart lurched forward

and made a wide arc around one side of the burning helicopter toward the dock.

Sam turned to Candi and said, "Stay here." Candi crossed her arms in front of her chest and nodded, her eyes wide.

Sam turned to J.T. "You ready?"

J.T. thumbed the hammer on his 9mm and said, "Sure, lead the way."

They ran toward the golf cart. Grimes heard their footfalls about the time they caught up with him. He stomped on the brake and grabbed an Uzi on the seat beside him. Before he could turn, Sam struck him on the temple with the butt of his handgun, and Grimes dropped the Uzi and fell over on the seat. Sam took the gun and told J.T. to make sure Grimes didn't have any more rocket launchers in the cart.

The seaplane's engines started and one of the men aboard threw the tie lines into the water and closed the hatch. The engines raced and the plane moved away from the dock.

"They're getting away," Sam said to J.T. He noticed the van still sat unharmed. "Back the van down to the water. I'll go for the plane with a rope."

Sam ran to the dock, laid down his weapons and unwound the now-slack tie lines from the cleats. The ropes seemed strong, but Sam thought they might need both of them. He dragged one end of the ropes to the graveled area next to the dock, slid into the cool water with the other end and swam to the moving seaplane. It had traveled about ten feet by the time he reached the hull. Finding the towing eyelet on the front, he grabbed onto it, ran both ropes through and knotted them.

Within seconds after J.T. tied the lines to the van's

trailer hitch, the plane pulled them taut and stopped dead in the water. J.T. gunned the van's engine and jerked the seaplane toward the dock while Sam pushed away and swam back. The engines on the seaplane roared, but the truck pulled the plane bit by bit back. Its hull scrubbed a side cleat on the dock, made a sound like sheet metal tearing, and the van kept tugging until the curvature of the hull rode up over the edge of the dirt bank and onto the gravel.

J.T. stopped the van and the plane sat still for several seconds, the propellers still turning, before the pilot finally gave up and shut down the engines. Sam climbed onto the dock, retrieved his weapons, and stepped over to the disabled craft. He grimaced when he saw the rip in the hull, knowing it would have to be repaired before it would float again. J.T. came over with his handgun, and when Sam nodded, he tapped on the hatch with his knuckle.

NINETEEN

SAM AND J.T. waited several minutes, hugging the side of the beached plane, before J.T. tapped again on the hatch, this time with the butt of his 9mm. The hatch popped open and Danilov fell out, as if pushed from behind. He stood and dusted off his hands.

"Okay, the rest of you, come out one at a time," Sam said. "Try anything funny and you'll die."

Danilov glanced at Sam and J.T. next to the plane and nodded, as if to say, *You have won this round, but it's not over.* He looked at the tear in the metal on the hull and shook his head. The plane probably belonged to him. He looked back into the open hatch, his eyes became large, and he yelled, "No! You might hit the fuel tanks."

Sam and J.T. dived away from the hatch to the ground. Bullets ripped through the skin of the aircraft, opening holes the size of dimes. Sam and J.T. lay there for a few moments after the firing stopped, then Sam got to his feet and said, "That was a stupid trick. I'm giving you five seconds to come out."

The sun's fingers pushed through the trees from the east, illuminating vapor rising above the lagoon's surface. A water bird screamed, flapped its wings and took flight. The dying flames on the helicopter snapped like breaking twigs, and the odor of cordite and burned fuel floated on the damp air.

Sam fired a burst of rounds from the Uzi into the air and yelled, "Okay, time's up."

"Wait, don't shoot. We are coming out."

Three men jumped down from the hatch. Training the Uzi on them, Sam told them to stand by the dock with Danilov.

"Get the weapons from the plane," Sam said to J.T., "and take a look at the cargo."

J.T. came back a couple minutes later with an armload of rifles and said, "There's several crates left on there. Let's push this jalopy back into the water and get out of here."

"No can do." Sam pointed to the hole in the hull.

J.T. made a face and kicked a dent in the sheet metal, then jerked back and jumped on one foot, cursing under his breath.

"You break your toe?"

"I don't think so." He tested his foot on the ground and took a few steps, then drew a deep breath and blew it out. "Okay, so what do we do now?"

"We could take this stuff to the airport in the van and wait for a plane to return. One of them has to be coming back pretty soon."

J.T. nodded, then turned and glared at the men from the helicopter. "Who do you guys work for?"

One of the men smiled and glanced at the sky, as if expecting something else to happen. Then he nodded toward Danilov and said, "Why don't you ask him."

J.T. looked at Danilov. "You know these guys?"

Danilov raised an eyebrow and shook his head. "No, I have never seen them before."

J.T. shrugged and said, "I guess it doesn't matter now."

"Move all the crates from the plane to the van," Sam said to Danilov and the others, pointing with the Uzi.

Danilov and one other man climbed into the plane and began handing crates through the hatch for the other men to carry to the vehicle. Sam wondered why Candi hadn't joined them already. He looked for the golf cart, but it had disappeared.

"Grimes got away," Sam said to J.T. "Watch them while I go check on Candi."

He handed J.T. the Uzi and pulled the handgun he'd taken from Gino out of his damp waistband. Hurrying up the road, he saw tracks where the cart had spun around in the sand, and found it in the spot where the car had been parked. No sign of Candi or Grimes. Sam wished he'd given Candi a weapon, but he hadn't expected Grimes to show up.

Sam went back to the van and said to Danilov, "Get in. You're driving." He turned to the helicopter men. "The rest of you get in the back."

"Where's Candi?" J.T. said.

"Grimes must have taken her. The car's gone too, so they could be anywhere on the island by now."

"Aw, man. Why does everything have to be so complicated?"

Danilov looked as if he might smile as he turned to get into the driver's seat. J.T. stepped over and shoved him, rapping his head on the door well. Danilov grabbed his forehead and shot him a threatening look.

"Hey, I bet that hurt," J.T. said. "Better be more careful."

The three helicopter men scrambled into the back and sat on the floor next to the crates. J.T. got into the rear seat and held the gun on them. Sam got into the

front passenger seat next to Danilov and made sure he
didn't try anything funny while they rode up the winding road to the airport.

The airport looked abandoned. Someone would have
brought La Salle to the plane the night before, but no
cars remained on the tarmac, so that meant someone
had driven away and stayed on the island. Sam told
Danilov to park the van behind the trailer where they
would be out of sight but could peer around the edge
and see the flight line.

Sam took the van keys and J.T. kept an eye on the
men while Sam got out, strode to the front of the trailer,
and looked in the windows to make sure no one hid
inside.

When he returned, J.T. said, "Watch them while I
get this guy's phone. He called somebody, but I didn't
see him until he hung up a second ago."

J.T. opened the back door and pulled the man out.
He had what looked like a satellite phone hanging from
his belt.

"Who did you call?"

The man shook his head. "No one, the, ah, recep-
tion no good."

J.T. handed Sam the phone and said to the man. "Get
back in the van."

An approaching airplane droned in the distance, and
Sam stepped to the edge of the trailer where he could
see the landing strip. The hum of the aircraft engines
grew louder by the second and a silver jet descended
onto the runway. Unlike La Salle's smaller planes, its
wings seemed to span fifty yards.

Sam hurried back to where J.T. guarded the men. "I
don't like the looks of this."

"Yeah," J.T. said, "let's go to the hotel."

They got back into the van, and Sam told Danilov to get going. He started the engine, put the van into gear and pressed the accelerator. The van darted around the trailer and headed across the tarmac, but the plane taxied ahead of them, its rear cargo door dropping open. Before the plane completely stopped, four men dressed in dark coveralls and carrying silenced automatic weapons jumped out and ran toward the approaching van. They halted less than a hundred feet from the front of the moving vehicle and trained their guns on the windshield.

"Stop," Sam said.

Danilov glanced at Sam. "No, they will kill us."

One of the men fired a burst of warning shots into the air.

Sam put the gun to Danilov's head and yelled, "I said stop. They'll kill us if we don't."

Danilov stepped on the brakes and brought the van to a standstill in front of the men. The whine from the jet's engines wound down and the man who had fired the warning shots, perhaps their leader, said, "Get out and drop the weapons." Like the men from the helicopter, he spoke with a Spanish accent.

"They knew exactly where to find us," J.T. said.

"Yeah, our friend with the telephone must have tipped them off."

J.T. looked at Sam and said, "We can take these guys."

Sam glanced at him, wondering if he might have been smoking something.

"What do you think?" J.T. said.

Getting out of the van, Sam said, "I think this is where we drop our weapons."

J.T. followed Sam and they laid their guns on the tarmac. The helicopter men burst out the back of the van, laughing and patting each other on the back.

The leader from the plane, a tall man with short, graying hair, aimed his Uzi through the windshield at Danilov and said, "Out, *bandido.*"

Danilov sighed, opened his door and climbed out. The leader spoke to them in Spanish and one of the helicopter men nodded and said, "*Gracias, Renaldo.*" The helicopter men strode to the plane and went up the loading ramp. That left only Renaldo, the leader, and the three other men from the airplane. One of the men had a scar running down the side of his face. Another had two gold teeth in front, and the third man had a tattoo of a snake on the side of his neck. They all looked deadly.

Renaldo peered into the back of the van, pointed his gun at Sam and said, "Load the gold onto the airplane."

Sam and J.T. stepped to the rear of the van and pulled out one of the crates.

"You too," Renaldo said to Danilov.

After they had loaded all the crates onto the aircraft, Renaldo pointed his Uzi toward the rear doors of the van and told Sam and J.T. to get inside. He waved the gun at Danilov and said, "You drive, *bandido.*"

Sam and J.T. got in and sat where the helicopter men had ridden a few minutes before. The man with the scar got in with them and held an Uzi muzzle just inches from their faces.

Danilov got into the driver's seat again, and Renaldo sat in the passenger seat next to him. "Go to the place where the big man with one eye stands in front."

Danilov glanced at him. "You have all the gold. If you go to the hotel you will be ambushed."

Renaldo jammed his gun into Danilov's ribs. "Just drive. You are lucky I don't shoot you where you sit."

Danilov winced and started the engine.

They arrived at the front entrance a few minutes later. Several men worked there unloading slot machines from a truck and rolling them on hand trucks through the doors. When Renaldo got out of the van, the workers saw the gun and stopped their work, got into the truck and sped away, leaving several shiny slot machines scattered around the front of the building.

Renaldo strode to the entrance where the doors stood open and looked inside. He turned back and said, "Everybody out. Let's go."

Sam wondered if Gino or others left behind might be waiting for them. If so, they might be sorry, because their handguns wouldn't stand up to the weapons these guys carried.

Inside the hotel, they went directly to the money room, Renaldo seeming to know where to go. The door to the room stood ajar, and Sam tried to remember if they had left it that way. Renaldo held up his hand and everyone stopped. He took a small canister from his belt, pulled a pin from it, tossed it inside the room, and closed the door. Sam heard muffled shouting for a few seconds and then silence.

"We are going inside and you will open the vault," Renaldo said to Danilov.

Danilov shrugged. "I don't know the combination."

Renaldo smiled and said, "You better know it, otherwise you will be of no use to us."

Renaldo put on a gas mask and Scarface handed one to Danilov. Danilov put it on, Renaldo swung the door open and they went inside. Sam peered around the doorway and saw Jimmy and the man from the security room lying on the floor near the door, their eyes closed. Guns lay next to their hands where they had dropped them. The bomb probably contained a general anesthetic that would wear off in an hour or so. Sam got a whiff of something with a chemical odor and backed up, bumping into J.T.

Renaldo shoved Danilov's shoulder and he stumbled over the men toward the door of the vault. Sam turned, thinking this might be the time to grab a weapon from one of the men, but the barrel tips of two Uzis jammed him in the side. Scarface yelled something in Spanish at Sam and Renaldo glanced at them and grinned.

Renaldo gave an order in Spanish to the man with gold teeth and Gold Teeth dragged La Salle's men away from the doorway and bound their hands with nylon ties. Danilov stared at Renaldo for a few seconds, maybe considering his chances if he just played dumb. Then he turned to the steel door and reached for the large chrome dial. Danilov worked on the dial for almost a minute and finally pressed down on the handle. The door snapped open a quarter-inch and Renaldo pushed Danilov out of the way and swung it open. Inside, a dozen or more crates similar to the ones they had taken off the seaplane sat on the floor.

J.T. stared at the crates, then glanced at Sam and shook his head. The look on his face said *That could have been ours.*

Gold Teeth and the tattoo man went outside and got three hand trucks left by the workmen while Renaldo watched the prisoners. When they returned, Renaldo took their gas masks and gave them to Sam and J.T.

"Move the gold to the back of the truck," Renaldo said.

They put on the masks and, along with Danilov, hauled the crates one-by-one to the van, then rode in back to offload them to the plane. Gold Teeth drove while Scarface guarded them from the back seats, and Renaldo and Tattoo stayed with the safe.

On the first trip to the plane, J.T. whispered to Sam, "You got any ideas about getting us out of this?"

Scarface saw him talking and said, "*Silencio*," before Sam could reply. It was just as well. With so many guns pointed at them, the only idea he had was to appeal to Renaldo and try to convince him to let them live.

It took two trips to get all the gold. La Salle's men still slept in the money room when they finished. Renaldo said something in Spanish to Tattoo as they left the money room the last time. He nodded and stayed behind with the sleeping men while everyone else loaded the last crates and got into the van. Tattoo came out a few minutes later and got in the back seat. Sam wondered if he had killed the men.

When they had rolled the last crate up the airplane ramp, Sam wiped perspiration from his face with his shirt tail and caught Renaldo's eye. "How about letting us go?"

"Sorry, we have orders."

He actually sounded sorry, probably for what he had to do next.

"We don't have anything to do with this place," Sam said.

"You tried to steal the gold," Renaldo said. He stared at Sam for a couple of seconds, as if trying to decide what to do, then pulled a satellite phone from his belt and punched in a number. Scarface, Gold Teeth, and Tattoo held their guns on their three prisoners, maybe waiting for orders from Renaldo to kill them.

A couple of moments passed and Renaldo spoke into the phone in Spanish. Pacing, he ran his fingers through his hair, and closed the phone.

Renaldo glanced at Sam, an eyebrow raised. "You are Mackenzie?"

"Yes," Sam said, wondering who he had spoken with.

"And your friend?" Renaldo glanced at J.T.

"John Templeton Smith," J.T. said.

Renaldo nodded. "Get on the plane with the *gringo bandido*." He spoke to his men in rapid Spanish and Scarface jammed a gun into Sam's back.

Sam, J.T. and Danilov sat in small seats along the starboard side of the aircraft next to the cargo. The ramp closed and the jet engines fired up. The aircraft turned and started toward a runway on the far side of the flight line from where it had landed.

Sam looked out the porthole next to his seat. A car raced down the road toward the airport. It slid to a stop at the edge of the flight line and the driver's door swung open. Grimes climbed out on his one good leg and wrestled a rocket launcher out the door. He leaned against the roof of the car, put the launcher onto his shoulder and took aim. If he pulled the trigger, there would be nothing anyone could do to stop the rocket. The plane would go up in flames as the helicopter had, and they would all die. Sam's pulse thumped in his ears, and perspiration beaded on his face. Seconds passed, the plane taxied into takeoff position and Sam wondered if Grimes might be considering that the gold would also be destroyed if he fired the rocket. Then the jet engines accelerated to maximum thrust and seconds later the plane lifted off and shot skyward. Grimes took the launcher off his shoulder and just stood there, leaning against the car, watching the fortune fly off into the sky.

Sam felt a stream of perspiration run down his face and drip off his chin, wondering who these people could be, and how they had known exactly where to find the vault with gold inside. He also wondered what had happened to Candi and sighed; there was nothing he could do about it now.

They flew east toward the midmorning sun for an hour or so, and then the plane descended. Islands were visible below, maybe the Florida Keys, connected by a long bridge. They landed on an airstrip with foot-high weeds growing on the tarmac, and taxied to an old hangar with large holes in its walls.

Renaldo unbuckled his seat belt, stood and said to Sam and J.T., "Time for you to get off." He pressed a button and the rear door dropped open.

Sam looked out at the old hangar. A piece of tin flapped in the breeze and a pelican glided in from the water and landed at the rear of the plane. It cocked its head and looked up its beak inside, maybe wondering what kind of shiny bird this might be, and how much of the food supply it would consume.

These men would leave Sam's and J.T.'s dead bodies on this desolate piece of ground where no one would discover them for a month or so. Yet, if they wanted them dead, why hadn't they killed them back at the airport after they had loaded the gold? Maybe they had to clear it with someone, and maybe that had been the purpose of the phone call before they'd taken off.

Danilov started to get up with them, but Renaldo pushed him back into his seat. "You stay."

"If you know my name," Sam said, "you know I don't have anything to do with La Salle."

"Shut up. Just do as I say."

Sam and J.T. took their time going down the ramp to the seedy flight line. Renaldo held the gun on them and told them to keep going and not turn around. *A bullet in the back?* They strode toward the old hangar, Sam's pulse firing away, and stood there for several seconds before hearing the engines on the plane accelerate. The plane circled as they turned to watch, and sped down the runway, its rear door closing as it lifted off. It ascended to about three hundred feet and then banked and headed west toward Central America.

TWENTY

A TRUCK HORN blasted in the distance. Sam and J.T. trod a couple hundred yards across crumbling tarmac and down a hill through a stand of small pines before seeing a highway and a road sign:

Key West.

48 Miles.

Cars and trucks rushed both ways on US1 in a steady stream, headed to and from the land of margaritas and sunsets.

"Looks like we're somewhere around Marathon," Sam said.

J.T. nodded. "Yeah, guess so. Who do you think those guys were?"

"I don't know, but they knew exactly where to find the gold in the hotel. I'd say someone sold La Salle out."

"Yeah, me too, and I thought they would kill us for sure."

They walked up the narrow shoulder of the highway edged with palmetto and flowering weeds until they saw a motel sign advertising three hundred feet of private beach and a cafe.

J.T. turned to Sam. "You got any money?"

"Yeah, it's probably wet from when I went in the lagoon." Sam pulled his wallet from his pocket and opened it. Several damp hundreds and twenties stuck together when he pulled them out.

"That's okay, it'll spend."

The motel, a one-level cinder block structure, looked like it had been around for seventy years or more. They ran across the highway when they had a clearing in traffic, went into the cafe and sat down at a table. A waitress barely out of her teens with purple hair and silver rings in her eyebrows came over with a pad in her hand and took their order for fish sandwiches and beer. She gave them a big smile when she left the table and Sam wondered if she might have been on her way to Key West when her money ran out. Marathon probably didn't have much to offer a twenty-year-old with purple hair and piercings.

A woman sitting with a man at a table close by looked at Sam as if he might have smallpox. Sam smiled and the woman looked away and whispered something to her companion. They got up and left.

"You scared her off," J.T. said.

"I can't imagine why."

"Could be that dried blood on the side of your face."

"Yeah, that might do it."

Sam went into the restroom. He looked into the mirror and saw dark circles under his eyes and the streak of blood where Grimes had hit him with the crutch. The streak led to a cut about an inch long below his temple. He washed his face with hand soap, careful to not open the wound, ran his fingers through his hair to smoothen it, and went back to his table.

The food arrived and they ate. When the server came with the tab, Sam handed her a hundred.

"How about calling us a taxi? We need to go to Miami."

She looked at the damp bill and smiled, showing a

shiny bead in her tongue. "Miami, wow. Can I go with you?" She seemed serious.

"Sure," Sam said, "you can ride along."

The smile leaked away as she glanced toward the kitchen. "I've been helping this old man run this place. He'll probably go under if I leave."

"Hey," J.T. chimed in, "some old guy's problems aren't your responsibility."

She paused, biting her bottom lip as if thinking about it, then shook her head. "I guess I should stay for a while, but thanks for the offer."

They finished their beer and stepped outside. The taxi, an ancient Cadillac the size of a parade float, showed up within five minutes. White smoke puffed from its tailpipe, but inside it blew cool air and the seats felt like velvet.

The driver looked about sixty and had white hair slicked back in duck tails.

"The woman that called said you want to go to Miami."

"That's right," Sam said from the back seat.

"It's gonna be expensive."

"How much?"

"Three hundred." The driver shrugged. "It'll knock me out of work for the rest of the day."

Sam handed the money over the seat, lay back, and dozed in the living-room comfort of the car from the past as the palms and motel signs flew by in a blur. They reached Florida City in about two hours. Sam woke and told the driver to take the road that led north to the Everglades instead of going downtown on US1. The driver glanced into the mirror but didn't say anything. He seemed to know the road and found Highway 997 with no problems, and pushed on north. It took another hour to reach the airstrip where they had left the rented car.

The trunk lid of the Chevy stood open. An old car sat inside the fence, but it didn't look like one La Salle might use, so Sam told the driver to turn in. They got out of the taxi and watched it roll away, exhaust climbing from under the rear bumper like an escaping stowaway.

Looking inside the open trunk, J.T. found the scattered contents of his overnight bag, his computer gone. Sam was relieved when he spotted the car keys in the trunk where the searcher had dropped them.

"What can they do with the computer?" Sam asked.

"Not much. I keep the good stuff on my web site, and it's locked down tight."

Sam looked inside the Chevy and saw the glove box open and the car rental agreement on the floor. A cell phone lay on the driver's seat.

They got inside and Sam picked up the cell phone. "This yours?"

"No," J.T. said, "I have mine in my pocket."

Sam laid it on the seat, reached under the carpet edge and found the bank box key. "At least they didn't find this." He put it into his pocket.

Sam started the engine and backed out of the parking spot. The side door of the hangar pushed open and a man in coveralls Sam didn't recognize stepped outside and watched them drive away.

They rode for a mile or so toward Miami before the cell phone chirped. It had to be La Salle. Sam glanced at J.T. and punched the answer button. "How's the leg?"

"It's better than you'll be when this is over."

"I take it you have Candi."

"Very astute of you, Mr. Mackenzie."

La Salle wanted his money, but he hadn't called because of that; in the scheme of things, that money was small potatoes.

"So, what's the deal?"

"The deal, as you put it, is this: I have Miss Moran and you and your friend can do something for me to get her back."

"Like what?"

"Come to the house on South Beach and we'll talk."

Sam wondered if it might be a trap. La Salle would blame him for what happened on the island. Had he and J.T. not intervened, Grimes might have stopped the men in the helicopter, and all the gold might still be there.

"I assume you remember the location." La Salle's tone dripped poison.

"No dice. We can talk in the bar at the Palma," Sam said.

La Salle paused, and then sighed on the other end. "All right, be there at six o'clock." The connection went dead and Sam closed the phone and laid it on the seat beside him.

"What did he want?" J.T. said.

"He wants us to do something, and he said he'll let Candi go if we do it."

"You don't believe him, do you?"

Sam glanced at him. "I don't know. If he wanted to kill us, he could have done it when we came for the car."

J.T. nodded. "So we're going to meet him at the Palma?"

"Yes, at six." Sam glanced at him. "And he never said anything about those guys letting us go."

Sam drove to the marina, and they went to his boat. It didn't look as if it had been disturbed since he'd left. They went aboard and Sam took a shower in the master bath while J.T. used the smaller one forward next to the guest quarters. After putting on a fresh shirt and a pair of slacks, Sam got a thousand dollars from his stash. He also pulled out a couple of spare handguns, leaving the holsters, and gave J.T. one. On the way to the Chevy, Sam glanced down the dock at Jack Craft's boat. He didn't see Jack outside, and a couple of newspapers lay on the gangway. *What are you up to, Jack?*

The trip to the Palma Hotel took less than five minutes. Sam parked the car and they went in the side door to the bar. They found a table in the corner next to an indoor palm and sat in rattan wing chairs. Only two other tables were occupied, each with a man and a woman. Three men and one woman sat at the bar. Sam didn't recognize anybody. Island music played from speakers somewhere close by, the volume low and easy on the ears, and a ceiling fan stirred the barroom air. The waiter arrived and they ordered beer. Sam looked at his watch: ten minutes early.

The beer came about the same time La Salle entered through the side door with Marcus. Both wore sunglasses and tailored suits.

La Salle spotted them and eased to the table, the limp in his gait barely noticeable. Pretty remarkable, because Sam knew he had injured the knee when he delivered the kick. They sat in the two empty chairs. Sam heard the clink of metal and wondered if La Salle might be wearing a leg brace. Marcus avoided Sam's eyes as if afraid he might bring up the business about double-crossing him, and what that conversation might lead to. The waiter came back a second later. La Salle ordered two glasses of mineral water, and the waiter rolled his eyes and hurried away.

La Salle looked at Sam and almost smiled.

"I suppose I underestimated you. I should have had you killed two days ago. Looking back, the money you stole from me seems like a small price to pay." His gaze turned cold.

"Where's Candi?"

"You'll find out soon enough. She's safe, for now."

"You better hope she stays that way," J.T. said.

Marcus reached for something inside his coat. La Salle raised his hand and Marcus stopped and gave J.T. a threatening look. No one spoke for several seconds. The piped-in island music played on, and the palm did a slow dance under the fan. The waiter brought the mineral water, noticed the tension in the air, and almost tripped getting away from the table.

Sam glanced at J.T., who had a smirk on his face, and then looked at La Salle. "So, what's this all about?"

La Salle removed his sunglasses and laid them on the table. "It should come as no surprise to you that my business partner has been detained."

"What does that have to do with us?"

"A small statue lies at the bottom of the sea and I want it. If you find it and bring it to me, I'll release Miss Moran."

"They brought back half a dozen crates of gold things this morning."

"Yes, but they never found this piece. Danilov called on his flight back and told me. It is an Aztec ruler, about twelve inches tall."

"You have a list of what's down there?" Sam said.

La Salle leaned back in his chair and said, "Something like that."

"Why us? There are other people you could hire to do this."

"Indeed, but you are the only one I can trust to return with the statue." La Salle glanced at J.T. and his look said he couldn't be so sure about him.

Sam nodded. "Who are those guys who took the gold?"

"They are not your concern."

"What if I happen to run into them out there in the Caribbean?"

"That would be most unfortunate, for all of us."

Yeah, but particularly for the person holding the statue.

La Salle told Sam his workmen had repaired the seaplane and Randy would pick them up at the outermost point in Sam's marina at midnight.

"You must land at the site in the Caribbean at precisely 3:00 AM. Otherwise our surveillance will mistake you for a poacher and you will be terminated."

Sam nodded, remembering the missiles J.T. had described at the surveillance facility on Grand Cayman. He hoped Randy would understand the importance of the schedule and lay off the booze until after their flight.

"Okay, we'll do it, but Candi better be okay when we get back, or you'll never see that statue."

La Salle looked at him for a second, then wrote a telephone number on a napkin and pushed it across the table. Sam put the napkin in his pocket and laid a bill on the table to cover the drinks.

All four men stood at once and Marcus pushed the table into J.T., causing him to fall backward into his chair. J.T. glanced at him, smiled and pressed back from the table. He stood up, still smiling, and when it looked as if no one would throw punches, the four men walked out the door.

Outside, the sun hit the side of La Salle's face, revealing tiny lines around the eyes and nose. He turned and said, "Okay, now here's *my* warning: drop the ball on this and you'll all die, Candi included. Do you understand?"

"Yes, perfectly."

La Salle put on his sunglasses, turned and stepped toward the passenger side of a Lexus parked next to the Chevy. It probably belonged to Marcus, purchased after Sam gave him the stack of money from La Salle's safe.

J.T. brushed close to the Lexus as Marcus slammed his door. Sam saw J.T. close his pocket knife with one hand and put it into his pocket. They got into the Chevy, and Sam started it and drove out of the parking lot into the traffic heading toward the causeway.

"That wasn't very nice," Sam said.

"What do you mean?"

"Scraping the paint on Marcus' new car."

"Yeah, well, he got off easy, for now."

Sam nodded. He hadn't decided yet what *he* might do about Marcus before this ended.

"Where're we going?"

"Carling Research."

"The butcher shop? Why do you want to go there?"

"Just something Carling said." He glanced at J.T. "I think she can tell us about La Salle."

TWENTY-ONE

SAM SAID HIS name into the microphone at Carling Research and smiled for the camera. A man's scratchy voice came from the speaker.

"What do you want?"

"I need to talk to Carling."

"Sorry, she isn't here."

Sam looked at J.T., then turned his back to him, leaned in close to the microphone, and said, "Tell her I said I'm sorry," his voice almost a whisper.

A pause stretched into several seconds, then Carling's voice came back. "That's a start. What else?"

"I'm a heel. How about that?"

J.T. snickered and Sam turned and stared at him until he stopped.

Carling sighed. "What do you want? Nobody looks hurt."

"I need to ask you something."

"This isn't an information service."

"Just let me in, okay? I'll make it worth your time."

Carling paused. "Okay, but this better be good."

One of the doors swung open and Carling looked beyond them down the driveway and then at Sam and nodded toward the inside. They followed her down the hall to her office and sat in the two chairs in front of her desk.

Sam glanced at J.T., who couldn't take his eyes off Carling.

"Have you two met?" Sam said.

Carling took a quick look at J.T. and said, "No. What's this all about?"

All business.

"You do cosmetic surgery, right?" Sam said.

Carling nodded. "Why, you want a facelift?"

Sam smiled. "There's this guy, and I think you might have done some work on him."

Carling raised an eyebrow. "Why do you say that?"

"Just a hunch."

Carling shrugged and leaned back in her chair. "Sorry, I don't keep records. I thought you would realize that."

"I think you'll remember this man."

"Why?"

"He's a big dude, about six-foot-eight."

Grabbing a pack of long cigarettes, she pulled one out and lit it. She drew the smoke into her lungs and cocked her head, squinted her eyes and blew a cloud across the desk toward J.T. "I don't remember anybody like that."

"You sure?"

"Yeah, I'm sure."

Sam nodded. "That's okay. Maybe Jack will remember."

"What does Jack have to do with anything?"

"When I came here before, you mentioned that he did some consulting for you. I wondered at the time what kind of consulting that might be. Then I learned that Jack is acquainted with this guy who had the plastic surgery. It seems like too much of a connection to be just coincidence. I figure you asked Jack to check him out before you did the work on him."

Carling took another drag on the cigarette, blew the smoke into the air and crushed the butt in a clean ashtray on the desk. "Trying to quit."

Sam leaned back and waited.

She smiled with her eyes and said, "Cosmetic surgery can be risky. After you finish, a guy might look in the mirror and say, 'Yeah, good job,' then turn around and pop you because you know what his new face looks like."

"So you did get Jack to look into this guy?"

"What are you going to do to him?"

Sam shrugged. "I don't know yet. He has the woman you patched up, and he said she won't live if we don't do something for him."

She nodded. "Still about the girl, huh?"

Sam smiled and said, "Yes, it is."

Carling took a deep breath and sighed. "Jack found out he'd been a Government agent of some kind working in Central America."

"How did he do that?"

"I gave him a fingerprint I took from a glass when the guy first visited."

"Did you get a name?"

"No, I didn't want the name. Jack had it, though."

"So, what did Jack say about him?"

"He said he didn't think the guy would be any trouble." Carling rolled her eyes.

"You look as if you wish you hadn't listened to him."

She smiled and showed her beautiful teeth, and Sam wondered how he could have left her the night they kissed on the sofa.

"Yeah, he threatened me when we finished his face."

She probably had decided then that she'd get even if she ever had the chance.

"When was that?" Sam said.

"Several months ago." She glanced at a clock on the wall and said, "Time for you to go. I have an appointment."

They stood and left the office, and Carling escorted them back to the door they'd entered.

"Nice meeting you," J.T. said as he opened the door and backed out, smiling.

"Sure, same here," Carling said. She squeezed Sam's upper arm and said to him, "Wait." He turned and almost bumped into her, their faces only an inch or so apart. "You don't look so good," she said. "Maybe you should think about another line of work."

"Yeah, maybe I'll do that."

Carling said, "You owe me," pushed him out the door, and closed it.

They got into the car and drove away, and Sam tried calling Jack Craft again. He punched both numbers into the cell phone and didn't get an answer on either.

"Other than a person in law enforcement, there probably aren't many people who could check out a print," Sam said.

"And I know most of them," J.T. said, then added, "Carling has a thing for you. It was written all over her face."

"Yeah? I didn't notice. Why don't you make some calls and see if you can find out who ran that print."

DARKNESS HAD FALLEN by the time they got back to Sam's boat. Sam left J.T. working his contacts on the phone, and strode down the dock to Jack's boat, *The Clipper*. It looked as abandoned as it had before. He crossed the gangway to the hatch, looked around to make sure no one watched, and worked the pick in the lock. It opened within a few minutes and he stepped inside.

Sam could see well enough without lights to navigate around the furniture in the lounge. He stepped to the chair by the telephone and turned on a wall lamp. A notepad lay next to the phone. Thumbing through it, he found notes about times for high and low tides on one page and something about a boat Jack sold to a man in Georgia on another page. Sam dowsed the light and stepped into the galley where a wall lamp lit the surface of a small desk. He opened the desk drawer and found a note dated about three weeks earlier that read, "Dave at the restaurant 7:00." The reference to Dave might be the man Jack occasionally employed for confidence schemes. His real name was Rutger Longstreet, but they had called him Uncle Dave when they ran a game on an English Duke a few years before, and the name stuck.

Candi had said a man approached La Salle about investing in the casino. La Salle's part in the deal would be a cool hundred million, and he would get to manage the whole deal. Candi didn't know the identity of the man, but said, "...who would try to swindle somebody like La Salle?" Who, indeed? Would Uncle Dave and Jackson Craft be up to that kind of con? Uncle Dave could convince someone he ran Harvard Business School if he needed to.

Sam put the note back into the drawer, closed it, and looked around another few minutes before giving up and leaving. He locked the hatch when he went out and wondered if Jack would know someone had been aboard, although he didn't really care. Jack should have answered his phone at least once the last five times Sam had called.

Sauntering toward the end of the dock, Sam watched a middle-aged man navigate a motorized yacht into a ninety-foot slip. A shapely woman in her twenties ran around the deck trying to get ropes ready to tie up while the man yelled at her.

Feeling sorry for the woman, Sam told her to toss him the lines and he would tie them off. She did as he asked and he waited while the engines revved and the sides of the big boat banged into the dock bumpers. Ten minutes passed before the man got it parked.

The yacht reminded Sam of the casino La Salle had built: big and flashy with an inexperienced captain at the helm. He secured the last line to the cleat and backed away. The man yelled some more and the woman told him what he could do with his fancy boat.

The marina lay silent after that, the air still and hot. Looking into the night sky, Sam saw only darkness. Cloud cover had moved in and he wondered if a storm might be brewing in the Caribbean where they would be in an hour or so.

He ambled toward *Slipstream* and tried to visualize how the pieces of the La Salle puzzle might fit together. Carling had said La Salle had come in for the surgery a few months ago, and she asked Jack to check him out. Jack called a connection or two and learned the owner of the fingerprint, and maybe more, and told Carling she could take the risk. After the surgery Jack probably followed the man who became La

Salle, maybe learned why he wanted to have his face changed, and watched him take over the business from Philly Moran. Jack knew Tommy Shoes, so he cozied up to him, maybe did him a favor or two, and listened to Tommy complain about La Salle horning in on his clients. Tommy probably mentioned La Salle's plan to build a gambling paradise in the Caribbean, and that crystallized the con for Jack. Uncle Dave came onto the scene and convinced La Salle that his investment group would put up most of the money to build the casino, if he would weigh in with a hundred million. La Salle didn't have the ready cash, but he knew about the treasure, and he started the salvage operation to pay his part. Then whatever he did that made him want to get his face changed came into play, and some bad men with guns and a helicopter came after the harvested gold.

It might have happened like that, but it really didn't matter. La Salle had Candi, and if Sam didn't find the statue and deliver it as requested, she might disappear. Jack liked this kind of con: everybody watching the game on the table, the shells moving round and round, back and forth, eyes tracking the one with the billion dollars underneath, and nobody noticing the one percent that slops over the edge onto the floor.

Inside the boat Sam entered the lounge. J.T. put down the phone and said, "Looks like La Salle used to be a man named Thomas Beeker. My contact didn't keep a record, so he couldn't be certain of the spelling. Beeker worked in Central America for a long time, but disappeared almost a year ago, and nobody has heard from him since."

"Who did he work for?"

J.T. shrugged. "That's all my contact had. If I could get another computer I might find out some more."

Sam looked at his watch and shook his head. "Maybe later, if we still need to know. We need to catch our plane."

They strode down the dock to the place where La Salle said Randy would be, and got there a few minutes before midnight. The seaplane sat at the tip of the dock normally reserved for over-sized boats. A man stood on the gangway of his houseboat several slips away, watching, and probably wondering what business an airplane had at the marina. He lost interest when he saw Sam and J.T. going to the plane, and disappeared inside.

The engines still ticked as they cooled down from the flight in from the Caribbean. Randy stood waiting, his eyes red and darting around the marina. "Get on the plane. I refueled before I got here, so we're ready to fly." Sam wondered how long Randy had been on the clock without a drink.

They climbed aboard and took a seat directly behind the cockpit close enough to see the instruments. A couple more seats sat empty behind them. The rest of the space was open deck with inset eyelets for tying down cargo. Coiled on the floor was a rope with an odd-looking anchor on one end and a float the size of a basketball on the other. Two diving tanks lay strapped down in the corner, and masks hung on the bulkhead. A spear gun also hung there, and Sam wondered if they had ever had occasion to use it.

Randy untied the lines, climbed inside, and secured the hatch. He glanced at Sam as he passed between the seats, and hesitated as if he might say something, but then sighed and made his way forward.

The lights went off in the cabin and the plane became dark except for the glow of the dash in the cockpit. Randy started the engines, taxied out of the marina, and gave the plane full throttle. They lifted above the water a few seconds later, and Randy banked south. A web of lightning lit the sky to the southeast and Sam saw the tops of boats in a neighboring marina. Thunder rumbled in the distance, barely audible over the hum of the engines.

A drop of perspiration rolled down Sam's cheek. "How about some air back here?"

Randy glanced back at them and nodded. A few minutes later the air got slightly cooler and Sam dozed in his seat. He dreamed about being at the bottom of the sea, sifting through the wreckage of a Spanish galleon. Gold coins lay everywhere, glittering in the light of the diving lamp. Sam reached for one and it disintegrated at his touch, as if made of paste. Then he swam around the bow of the ship, the ancient hull almost completely buried in the sand, and saw a gaping hole in the wood. He shone the light inside and saw the statue. It gleamed in the light and its eyes beckoned Sam. He reached in but couldn't quite touch it, then pushed through the hole and the rotted planks scraped against his sides. He got closer and saw a skeleton beside the statue, its bony hand wrapped around it as if protecting it even in death. When he reached for the statue, the skeleton rose up like a cobra and grabbed Sam by the wrist. Sam's pulse fired in his ears and he dropped the light. He pulled a flare from his belt and fired it into the skeleton's ribcage. The hull flooded with light and exploded, and the old ship began to turn over, collapsing against Sam's body. He tried to push his way out, but couldn't budge. His heart felt as if it might explode, and the air tasted like sour milk in his throat. Another light flashed, and he woke.

The plane rocked and jerked in the turbulence, its old joints groaning with every move. Rain pounded its metal skin like a bass drum. Lightning flashed through the windscreen and thunder exploded.

Randy bounced in his seat like a bronco rider, hanging onto the yoke with one hand and flipping switches with the other. Sam glanced at J.T. He looked as if he might have just awakened, too: eyes wide, hands gripping the armrests, knuckles white.

"We'll probably fly out of this in a little while." Sam hoped his voice sounded more confident than he felt.

"Yeah, I hope so," J.T. said. "This crate is too old to be flying in a storm like this."

The turbulence quieted to a tremor a few minutes later and the smell of alcohol bit into Sam's nostrils. He looked into the cockpit as Randy raised a pint bottle of rum to his mouth and chugged a third of it before stopping. Randy coughed and wiped his lips with the back of his hand, then turned around in his seat. His eyes shone in the glow of the instruments and seemed more assured than before. He held up the open bottle. "Would any of our first class passengers care for a complimentary beverage?"

TWENTY-TWO

"Hey, lay off the sauce until this is over," Sam said.

Randy gave him a dirty look and chugged the rest of the bottle. He didn't open another, and his flying didn't seem to suffer, but Sam decided to stay awake the rest of the trip.

They flew through a seemingly endless wall of wind and water for a couple more hours, and the old plane's engines groaned all the way.

Randy turned around and said, "We're getting close to the site." He cut back on the throttle and Sam felt the plane drop. The wind whipsawed them as they glided several hundred yards before touching down on the water.

The plane bounced and rocked, and when they slowed, Randy circled and taxied to their spot. Sam checked his watch: 3:05 AM. Even with the weather, they had made it on time. Randy turned off the engines, came back through the cabin and popped the hatch, and Sam saw black swells rolling outside.

Randy punched a button on the odd-looking anchor and turned on a light, a sealed unit about half the size of an automobile headlamp.

"This'll burn at the bottom for a couple of hours before it kills the battery."

He threw it into the water, and the coils of rope disappeared over the side. In a few seconds the rope jerked the float in and it sank below the surface.

"We're directly over the site. Look for the light when you start back up and you can't go wrong."

"How deep is it?" Sam said.

"About ninety feet. The air tanks contain a special mixture to allow you to stay down longer, enough for about an hour."

They got out of their seats and unstrapped the diving gear from the deck.

Sam eyed Randy. "What are you going to do while we're gone?"

"I'll have to leave so we don't draw any attention to this place."

J.T. shot Sam a look that said, *Are we going to let him do that?*

"Where are you going?" Sam said.

"Grand Cayman. I know a marina where I can gas up."

Sam didn't care much for the idea of Randy leaving, but he had already considered the possibility and he would have to live with it. Besides, it wouldn't be in Randy's best interest to leave them in the middle of the Caribbean and return empty-handed.

"How long will you be gone?"

"Exactly an hour. And when I get back I'll wait fifteen minutes." Randy shook his head. "You're not back by then I'll have to fly."

Sam nodded, but something in Randy's eyes bothered him.

They suited up, checked out their lights and breathing equipment, and Sam synchronized his watch with Randy's. Randy turned away for a second and Sam took the spear gun from its hook on the bulkhead and held it behind him so Randy wouldn't notice. They climbed into the water and swam toward the light.

It took several minutes to reach the bottom where a half-dozen curious fish swam around the lighted anchor. A few feet away lay several conch shells among tall tendrils of seaweed in the still water.

Sam turned on his light and scanned the area. He could see for twenty or thirty feet, the water clear. The glint of metal to the south reflected on the light. Sam laid the spear gun next to the anchor and motioned for J.T. to follow him.

After about fifty feet, the source of the reflection became clear. A wreck lay in the sand, not a Spanish galleon from the sixteenth century, but a twin engine jet airplane. It rested on its belly and faced Sam's left, tilted up on the closest side. The wing on the far side was jammed into the sand, broken in the middle, but still attached and twisted up at an odd angle. Bullet holes riddled the fuselage where the fuel tanks might be. It probably had lost fuel and went down, the wing grabbing the water first and rupturing on impact.

Sam turned and looked at J.T. who held his hand out, palm up. Turning back, Sam shook his head and made a mental note of the numbers painted beneath the cockpit. The emergency hatch over the wing had fallen away. He shone the light under the plane where the hatch cover had wedged between the sand and the fuselage.

La Salle and Danilov had robbed someone's collection of artifacts and flown away in a shower of bullets. When all the fuel leaked out, they made a belly landing on the water, kicked out the hatch, and got into an inflatable raft before the plane sank. They left the gold, thinking they would retrieve it later.

Sam motioned toward the open hatch. They swam over the wing and inside, and shone the lights up and down the cabin. The luggage compartments stood open above about fifty empty seats. One seat toward the front appeared to be occupied and they swam forward to get a better look. A man sat there buckled in. He had only one arm and it floated above the armrest, as if waiting for the seat belt warning light to go off so he could pop the belt and run for a connecting flight. Sam wondered if the man had figured out yet that he would wait at this stopover for a *long* time. The Grand Slam of all journeys. He probably had helped steal the gold and La Salle or Danilov killed him for his part of the take.

Sam shone the light on the man's decomposed face. Black hair swirled above a translucent scalp. Sea scavengers had been at work for several months and his eyes had been eaten away. Bloodless gouges covered his face, and a grin pinched at one corner of his mouth. Sam unbuckled the seat belt and checked the man's pocket for a wallet. Finding nothing, he re-buckled the belt and left the one-armed man where he found him.

Pieces of thick pasteboard mush floated throughout the cabin. Probably remnants of boxes used to load the gold onto the plane. Clumps of the soggy material also lay on the deck. Danilov probably had cursed at the sight of the rotting boxes when they came back for the gold, wishing they'd had more foresight in their theft.

Sam looked at his watch and saw that they'd been gone about twenty-five minutes. Time ticked away, and they hadn't begun their search. From the looks of things it would take a while. He motioned for J.T. to

follow him forward in the cabin and pushed his way
through the muck of wet pasteboard toward the cockpit.

They searched every compartment and in and under
every seat, working their way aft from the cockpit to
the lavatory, and even checked the pockets on the back
of each seat. J.T. found a gold mask in one of the seat
pockets that probably had been worn by an Aztec war-
rior in his death. No statue. While J.T. bagged the mask,
Sam looked at his watch: Randy would return in about
twenty minutes. He checked his air level and still had
enough for at least that long.

The second emergency hatch on the other side of
the plane also had fallen away. That could mean they
tried it first upon landing and saw the damage to the
wing, then went out the other one, worried that the
sharp, broken metal might cut the raft. Sam made his
way to the hatch, leaned out and shone his light down
below. A school of fish swam by, and pieces of trash
lay on the sandy bottom. He couldn't see underneath
the wing. Checking his watch again, he decided he had
enough time to go down and take a look, and motioned
for J.T. to follow him.

They swam to the bottom and Sam shone his light
into the dark space underneath the wing. Something
exploded from the crevice, moving so fast that Sam saw
only teeth flashing toward his face. He dug his heels
into the sand and pushed back, but not fast enough.
The creature hit him in the stomach and the air from
his lungs blew the breathing apparatus from his mouth.
Sam tumbled in the sand and grit scrubbed the side of
his face. He pushed up and the creature swam away. It
looked like a tiger shark, about eight feet long.

Sam's stomach felt like it had been ripped out and

his lungs ached for air. A second later J.T. swam around him, shone the beam toward his face and handed him the lost mouthpiece. Sam filled his lungs with air and waited a few seconds for his heart to slow down. The fish had knocked the light out of his hands, too, and he saw it glowing in the cloudy spot where he'd churned up the sand. After retrieving it, he went back to the place under the wing and hoped another shark didn't wait there. He found only the dead man's other arm.

Sam started around the plane, ready to call it quits, when he thought about something. Why had Danilov been unable to find the statue? They had to know its value and would put it somewhere they could easily remember. And yet, they hadn't found it. Had someone else discovered the plane and taken only the statue? Unlikely. All the other pieces had to be worth millions, too. What if something happened after the plane sank that La Salle couldn't have known about? Something like the plane hitting bottom on one side and some of the gold spilling out the hatch?

Sam swam back to the damaged wing and shone his light down its length to the point of the break. No gold glittered there, but sand covered part of the damaged area. He glided down and brushed away sand with his fingers. His fingers touched something slick and he laid the light down, reached in with both hands and pulled out an urn about the size of a sugar bowl.

The urn must have fallen out of the hatch when the plane sank, slid down the wing, and gotten covered up when the broken wing penetrated the sea bottom. Sam turned and handed it to J.T., who searched the sand a few feet behind him, then went back to work and uncovered a slightly taller gold piece, a bird of prey. After removing several more handfuls of sand, the face of the statue smiled up at him, as if happy to be rescued. Sam pulled it out of the sand and held it up. It stood about a foot tall. J.T. gave him a thumbs-up. Sam moved aside and J.T. combed through the sand and found a gold bar and a couple more items before Sam punched him on the arm and pointed at his watch.

They stuffed the smaller items into net bags clipped to their suits and started back to the lighted anchor. Sam carried the statue in his hand and should have been glad for their discovery, but had a feeling of dread that nothing good might come of it. He just wanted to get Candi back to safety…and then get as far away from this mess as he could.

Reaching the lighted anchor, Sam handed the statue to J.T. and picked up the spear gun. They swam up the rope, and when they neared the float at the top, Sam lagged behind. He saw the glow of the seaplane's cabin through the last foot or so of water and watched as J.T. broke the surface with the statue in his hand. Then he saw a man move to the edge of the hatch. The seaplane rocked up and down with the swells, distorting the view, but the man didn't look like Randy, unless Randy had bleached his hair almost white and lost one leg. Sam surfaced momentarily and went back under, but he had seen Grimes standing with a crutch, holding a gun in his outstretched hand pointed at J.T.'s head.

TWENTY-THREE

J.T. PUSHED AWAY from the plane and submerged. Grimes' gun exploded and Sam saw bubbly lines in the water that traced the trajectory of the rounds. Surely Grimes knew that if he hit J.T., the statue would be lost.

Sam held onto the spear gun, shed his diving gear and swam to the surface. Grimes saw him and jerked around with the gun. Sam squeezed the trigger and the spear sailed through the air and hit Grimes in the shoulder. His arm went slack and the gun slipped from his fingers and fell into the water.

Sam tossed the spear gun aside, climbed the ladder and stepped aboard the plane. Grimes seemed disoriented, eyes wide, face twitching, and he turned his head to look at the blood soaking the front of his shirt. He grasped the spear with his fingers and pulled, screaming as the barb ripped through the flesh. The crutch fell away as he dropped to the floor of the plane and passed out.

Sam looked into the cockpit and saw Randy slumped in the pilot's seat. An empty liquor bottle lay on the deck a few inches from his fingers.

J.T. climbed up the ladder and stepped aboard, his gear dripping water on the deck. Dropping his face mask, he said, "That idiot tried to kill me." He laid the statue on one of the seats. "I don't think he cared whether he got this baby or not."

"I think you're right."

Sam checked Grimes' pulse and the wound in his shoulder and decided he'd live, then tied his hands across his stomach and left him lying on his back.

"You'll have to fly," Sam said as he closed the hatch.

J.T. looked at Randy and said, "Yeah, I guess so."

They dragged Randy out of the cockpit and strapped him into a seat in the cabin. After they changed into dry clothes, J.T. went back into the cockpit.

Sam followed and sat in a jump seat behind him. "Let's get out of here."

"Okay, give me a minute. I've never flown anything this old."

He flipped switches and pressed buttons and Sam heard the starter turn over. Within a couple of minutes he had the engines running and the old airplane rocked and vibrated as it struggled across the swells and gained speed. After what seemed like an eternity, they finally lifted off and J.T. turned and grinned.

"Piece of cake. By the way, where are we going?"

"How much fuel do we have?" Sam said.

"It's full. Randy must have filled it up in Grand Cayman like he said he would."

"Okay, head toward Miami. I don't know what La Salle had in mind, but all that's off now."

"You mean because of Grimes?"

"Yeah, that, and seeing that jet and the dead body down there. It looks like they planned to take the statue when we came back with it, and turn us into shark food."

"What's your take on what happened with that airplane?"

Sam told his theory about La Salle and Danilov stealing the gold collection and ditching the plane at sea.

J.T. nodded and said, "Yeah, that would fit." He glanced at Sam. "What about Candi?"

Sam ran his fingers through his damp hair. "I think we need to put the statue in a safe place and talk to her before we make any plans for an exchange."

THE STORM GOT worse with every mile, as if it might be following them and gaining strength. They flew off course a couple of times and the fuel got low by the time they saw lights in the Upper Keys. The engines sputtered and coughed, draining the bottom of the fuel tanks, and J.T. glided the plane to the edge of an inlet and landed. He killed one engine and cut the throttle as low as he dared on the other. It ran for a couple of minutes before giving out.

Gray light shone through the windscreen. Rain beat against the side of the plane and the wind blew them toward the coast and into mangroves that hung over the water. The limbs scrubbed against the sheet metal, cracking and screeching until the plane came to a halt and rocked gently in the blowing rain.

"What about these guys?" J.T. said. Grimes seemed to be coming around, moaning with pain. Randy still snored in his seat.

"They'll be okay. Randy'll figure out how to get some fuel when he wakes up."

"No, I meant should we leave them here alive?"

Sam searched his face for any sign that he might be kidding, but already knew the answer.

"Yes, we leave them here alive."

J.T. shrugged. "Okay, fine with me."

Sam put the gold articles into his overnight bag and strapped it to his back. He popped the hatch and they slid down into waist-deep water and pushed toward land. Their shoes slipped on the slimy mangrove roots and they grabbed onto limbs to steady themselves. A small water snake swam toward Sam. He broke a branch, lifted the snake out of the water with it and tossed it several feet away. They reached the bank and slogged about twenty feet in swamp muck before the land became firm.

"How far to a road?" J.T. said, as if expecting Sam to be an expert on South Florida coastal geography.

"I don't know, I'm guessing maybe a hundred yards."

It turned out to be at least twice that far, and they took more than an hour to beat their way through the dense swamp growth. Both of them were breathing hard and soaked from the rain and wet foliage. They reached a muddy road and followed it in the rain to an old fish camp that had been closed for at least a decade. A weather-beaten sign indicated that the place had once operated as Captain Lamar's Boats and Charters. Old wooden boats, half submerged in the water with weeds growing out of the wood, lay in the shallows next to a rotted dock. A shack stood next to the dock, and Sam saw a light inside a dingy window. An old Buick sat next to the shack. The tires on the front looked new. They eased over, stepped onto a rickety porch, and Sam knocked on the screen door. Rain pounded a rhythm on the tin roof while they waited.

"Who is it?" The voice behind the door sounded old.

"Our boat broke down and we need a ride."

The door cracked a couple of inches and a man with

thick glasses peered out, his eyes rheumy, like eight-balls behind the magnified lenses. Wondering if this might be Captain Lamar, Sam smoothed back his wet hair and smiled, trying to look as unthreatening as possible.

The man said, "Go away," and slammed the door.

Sam looked at J.T., who grinned, and took two hundred-dollar-bills out of his wallet. He stuck his hand through a tear in the screen and slid one of the bills underneath the door, leaving a half inch or so outside. It disappeared in less than a second.

"I have another one for you if you'll give us a ride," he said through the door.

A couple of minutes passed and Sam thought they might have to travel on up the road. Then the door opened and the man swung it wide, leaving the screen door closed. Wearing a pair of old dress pants and a tee shirt, he had thinning hair and a drinker's nose splotched with red, and looked about seventy years old.

"Where do you want to go?" His accent sounded northeastern, maybe New York.

"Just up to the mainland," Sam said.

He shook his head. "Too far. I don't drive up there no more."

"We need to rent a car."

He narrowed his eyes for a couple of seconds, as if thinking, then nodded his head. "Okay, let me get dressed and I'll take you somewhere."

He closed the door and stayed gone for several minutes. When he came back, he wore a Hawaiian shirt and a sporty straw hat. They got into the car, and he took off the hat and shook rain from it and said, "I want the rest of the money before we go."

Sam looked at him and glanced up at the sign. "You Captain Lamar?"

The man smiled. "Yeah, I'm the Captain. What about it?"

Sam handed him the other hundred. "Just wondered."

The Captain started the Buick and gunned the engine, spinning the tires as they slid onto the muddy road. They reached US1 within a couple of minutes and he turned south. He drove a few miles and turned into a gravel driveway that led to large metal building with closed garage bays.

The car stopped in front of the building and he said, "You can rent a car in there."

A man wearing blue jeans and a hunter's vest opened the entry door of the building and stepped out under an awning. He waved at the Captain and motioned for Sam and J.T. to come inside.

Sam glanced at the Captain. "You called this guy?"

"I sure did," the Captain said. He smiled and patted his shirt pocket where he had put the hundred. "Pleasure doing business with you." Captain Lamar looked about twenty years younger than he had when Sam first saw him.

The man under the awning motioned again.

They got out and the Buick sped away, throwing gravel and sand on their feet. Sam noticed the Dade County license plate and wondered why the Captain would have a Miami tag. A shiver ran from between his shoulder blades to the nape of his neck. He glanced at J.T., who had an odd look on his face, and then reached into his bag and pulled out his 9mm.

"Hey, what's going on?" the man in the vest said.

Sam pointed the gun at his head and said, "Turn around and go inside."

Vest Man went in and Sam and J.T. followed him. Another man, with a shotgun in the firing position, as if ready for a round of skeet, stood there waiting. He smiled, flashing a mouthful of bad teeth. Then he saw Sam's gun and his eyes went wide. Sam kicked Vest Man in the back, and he fell into Bad Teeth.

The shotgun went off and Vest Man screamed and dropped to the floor. "My foot! I can't feel my foot!" His shoe lay on the floor covered in blood, and a glob of bloody tissue hung from the end of his pants leg.

Bad Teeth's mouth hung open. "Aw man, why'd you bump into me?"

"I think you shot my foot off!"

"It wasn't supposed to work this way."

Sam pointed the 9mm at Bad Teeth's head and said, "Hand me the gun, stock first."

Bad teeth glanced at his friend's ruined foot and handed Sam the gun.

Two cars sat inside the building, one a late model Acura and the other a vintage T-Bird.

"Give me the keys to the Acura," Sam said.

"It's his," Bad Teeth said, nodding toward the other man, who was sitting on the floor, staring at his foot, and sobbing.

"You can't take my car," Vest Man said from between clenched teeth.

J.T. pointed his gun at Bad Teeth and thumbed the hammer. "Get the keys, or I'm going to shoot *your* foot off, too."

He reached down and grabbed the keys from the

wounded man's vest pocket and handed them over to Sam.

Sam opened the bay door and J.T. eased the Acura outside. Vest Man and Bad Teeth argued about getting medical attention for the injured foot.

"You got to take me to the hospital."

Bad Teeth shook his head. "I'll call the old man."

"What? I'll die before he gets back."

"You're not gettin' blood on my leather seats."

Sam got in the car and they rode to US1 and turned north.

TWENTY-FOUR

J.T. RAN HIS hands over the steering wheel and grinned. "This is a pretty good car for two hundred dollars."

"Yeah," Sam said, "probably stolen." He opened the glove box and found it empty. "No registration."

"They planned to rob us, and would have hit the jackpot if they'd gotten those gold pieces. I think we should go back to the fish camp and teach that old man a lesson."

Sam glanced at him. "What would you do, beat him up?"

J.T. raised an eyebrow. "No, but we could shoot out his tires, or something."

"Forget it. We've got better things to do."

Sam tried calling Jack Craft and got no answer.

"We need to go to the marina," Sam said. "I want to talk to Jack before we do anything else."

They followed US1 through Florida City, for the second time in two days, staying on course toward Miami Beach. When they reached the marina, Jack's car was gone.

Sam looked at the clock on the dash: 2:35 PM. He couldn't remember the last meal they'd had and his stomach ached for food. "Let's get something to eat. We can come back and wait around, see if he shows up."

They went to a takeout shop for Cuban sandwiches,

came back, and parked a block away from the marina. Sam could see the parking lot and *The Clipper* below the street with his field glasses. After they ate the sandwiches, the hours dragged on while they listened to the rain drum on the top of the car. They took turns watching for Jack and dozed between shifts. Two Miami Beach PD cruisers drove by late in the afternoon, but neither seemed to notice them. The list of stolen vehicles in Miami was probably too long to memorize, and there were lots of Acuras on the street that looked exactly like theirs.

About an hour after dark, J.T. said, "Well, if it isn't the Casino King."

Sam picked up the glasses and watched La Salle's Jaguar turn into the marina. La Salle was driving and Gino sat in the passenger seat. They parked under the large flood lights and headed toward the docks, La Salle still walking with a limp. The rain had slackened, so Sam got out and peered over the roof of the car for a better view. No street lights burned close to the Acura, so La Salle would be unlikely to see him, even if he looked his way. La Salle wore a gray suit and held a large umbrella above his head. Gino wore an unbuttoned raincoat with his hands stuffed in the pockets. Rain washed over his forehead, colored a deep shade of blue, still swollen and resembling the front of a bicycle helmet.

They went directly to Sam's boat and tried the hatch. It wouldn't budge, and Gino glanced up and down the dock and then pulled a silenced handgun from inside his coat and fired three rounds into the lock. The hatch popped open and they went inside. Sam cringed, thinking it would take a couple of hours to fix that, if he could fix it at all. They stayed for a few minutes and came out, then went back to the Jaguar, sat there for a while, and drove away.

Sam got back into the Acura and wiped the rain from his face. He handed the glasses to J.T. and told him what La Salle and Gino had done. "They didn't come here for Jack. Didn't even glance toward his boat."

Sam and J.T. decided to get some more food, left their stakeout for about fifteen minutes, and returned with cups of hot chili and burgers. Nothing else happened until almost midnight. The rain had stopped and the streets looked like mirrors under the lights. Jack's Mercedes passed them and Sam watched as he turned into the parking lot, got out and hurried toward his boat.

"Let's go," Sam said.

J.T. started the Acura and they rode to the marina and parked. They got out and strode down the dock toward *The Clipper*.

Jack saw them as he opened the hatch, glanced beyond them to see if anyone else followed, and motioned with a nod to come inside. He closed the hatch behind them. "Does anyone know you're here?"

Sam shook his head and told about La Salle's visit. Jack made drinks and they sat in the soft chairs of the big lounge.

"I've been calling you for a couple of days," Sam said. "Where've you been?"

Jack sighed, loosened his tie and took a long drink from his gin and tonic. "You wouldn't believe it."

Sam waited for him to say more, but Jack just laid his head back and stared at the overhead.

"I know about your scheme and NeoWorld, and about Uncle Dave, too."

Jack raised his head, smiled and glanced at J.T. "He's a pretty smart guy, you know it?"

"Quit stalling," Sam said.

Jack took a deep breath and another long drink. "Yeah, okay... I went to Grand Cayman, to try to keep this thing from falling apart."

"How much did La Salle invest in NeoWorld?"

Jack looked at Sam for a few seconds before replying.

"It's probably better if you don't have any more information than you need, Samuel."

"How much?"

"About eighty million, and he's supposed to come up with twenty more."

J.T. whistled and Jack smiled.

"But he's already spent most of the money," Jack continued. "We were just in it for the escrow."

"Escrow?"

Jack nodded. "Dave told him he had to keep ten percent in escrow until the rest of his money came through. Of course, he'll never see the escrow again."

Sam knew La Salle had lost all the gold. "Did the money belong to his clients?"

Jack nodded, drained his drink and got up to make another round. "He planned to replace it with what he got out of the gold." Jack handed out the drinks and returned to his seat. "At least I think that's what he intended."

"You knew about the gold artifacts," Sam said, more a statement than a question.

Jack grinned. "Oh yes."

Sam sipped his drink. "So the rest of the NeoWorld assets are bogus, and when La Salle spends what he's put into the company, minus the escrow, everything is gone."

"That's the way this kind of thing works, Samuel."

"What about Danilov?"

"Our deal was just with La Salle. I suppose Danilov might have helped him with his share, but we never dealt with him."

Sam considered that for a few moments and decided Jack could be telling the truth. "Is Dave doing all the front work?"

"Sure. You know I never get involved any more than I have to."

"I saw you on La Salle's island," Sam said.

Jack nodded. "La Salle wanted to discuss some details with Dave, and I went along in case he had problems, but La Salle never knew I was there."

"What kind of details?"

"Well, it's pretty complicated, but he wanted to make sure he has clearance to run a gambling establishment."

"Does he?"

"He thinks he does."

Sam glanced at J.T. and grinned, then turned back to Jack. "When will he find out?"

Jack winked and said, "You know, that's the beauty of this business. By the time he finds out, it won't matter anymore."

They remained silent for several moments. Ice cubes clinked in their glasses and new rain pelted against the portholes. Sam felt the gin beginning to soothe the raw nerves and wondered how they would get Candi, and themselves, out of this alive. Jack had said little that he hadn't already guessed, and none of it would help Candi.

"Tell me about the gold, Jack."

"Why don't you tell *me*? You seem to know everything." Jack's voice had an edge to it.

Sam felt his forehead heat up and his pulse thump harder. He told himself to stay calm, even though Jack had caused him a lot of grief. "Okay," he said. "I think you got the idea for all this when Carling asked you to check on La Salle. You discovered he stole that collection of artifacts, and wanted the face surgery so he could change his identity."

Jack's eyes tightened into a smile.

Sam continued: "You knew he had this source of money, and found out from Tommy Shoes that he wanted to build a casino. So you cooked up a way to make him think he could pull it off. I think you also knew who La Salle stole the gold from, and maybe made a deal to recover it and deliver La Salle's head on a platter."

Jack's smile stayed in place, but something sparked in his eyes, and Sam wondered if he had tripped over something important.

"You know that isn't my style," Jack said. "I like to do the number and then slide out leaving the mark wondering what happened. And I could have done that here, too, except my inquiries got back to the man who lost the collection, and his thugs paid me a visit."

Jack took a drink and ran his fingers through his hair. He got up and fished a cigar out of a box, and asked if anyone else wanted a smoke. Sam declined and J.T. reached for a cigar. Jack sat down and they lit up.

"You were telling us about the men who paid you a visit," Sam said.

Jack drew in the smoke, squinted, and blew a ring in the air above his head.

"Oh, yeah, they visited, all right. Came in the middle of the night and boarded my boat. I didn't hear a thing until the guy thumbed the hammer of the gun and stuck it to my temple. They wanted the man who stole the collection."

"Thomas Beeker."

Jack nodded, a hint of surprise in his eyes. "They had tracked him back to Miami, but ran into a dead end. Of course, he had a new identity by then and left no trail that would lead anyone to him."

"Who did they work for?"

Jack frowned. "Well, they weren't exactly in a talking mood."

"You already knew, didn't you?" Sam said.

Jack leaned back in his chair and closed his eyes. The fingers of one hand wrapped around his drink glass and his other hand held the half-burned cigar, smoke drifting to the overhead. He looked as if he might be considering his options, and finally decided to say something.

"Yes, Gideon Barge."

"The oil man?" J.T. asked.

No one answered the question, and the silence hung in the air like stale breath. Gideon Barge, one of the richest men alive, in his sixties by now. To call him ruthless would be like saying Einstein had an interest in science. He had killed people to build his fortune, and got away with it every time. That someone had stolen something from him so valuable would make him furious. A rabid collector of anything rare, the gold artifacts had to be his most prized possessions. The rain started again and pounded the overhead.

Jack glanced at Sam. "You did some work for him, didn't you?"

Sam's eyes narrowed. "You know I did. As I remember, you did too."

Jack nodded and smiled sadly.

J.T. took a puff on the cigar, laid it in the ashtray, and looked from one to the other. "You guys are kidding, right?"

"So you made a deal with them," Sam said, ignoring J.T.'s question.

"Well, yeah, when someone is holding a gun to your head you tend to make a deal."

"What did you tell them?"

Jack shrugged. "I gave them La Salle's name and told them where to find him. I also told them he'd lost the gold on the bottom of the Caribbean, and if they would wait a while, he'd retrieve it for them."

"And that's how they knew when to swoop in and take it all back."

Jack sighed and said, "Yes, I'm afraid so."

"Who fed you the information about La Salle's activity down there?"

Jack smiled, drained his glass and crunched an ice cube between his teeth.

"Randy, the pilot." He glanced at Sam's bag. "You have the statue in there?"

Sam knew they eventually would get around to it. "I suppose you want it so you can give it back to Gideon?"

Jack nodded. "That would be the simplest solution."

Sam leaned forward in his chair. "What about

Candi? La Salle said he'll kill her if I don't give him the statue."

Jack closed his eyes for a long blink and shook his head. "He wouldn't do that."

"What makes you so sure?"

"They're working together. You're blind if you can't see that. She'll sell you out for a lot less than the value of that statue."

Sam had considered that possibility. Though difficult to read, Candi had been in a fix when she first came looking for Sam's help. She had a bullet hole in her side, said La Salle wanted to kill her, and had convinced Sam of it. Could she have patched it up with La Salle, maybe come to an agreement about splitting the gold? "Why do you care what happens to the statue now?" Sam asked.

"I got a call from Gideon himself when he didn't find the statue in the crates they got from La Salle."

"He threatened you?"

"Something like that."

Why would Gideon hold Jack responsible for getting the statue back? Sam thought he knew the answer. "Maybe you're right about Candi."

Jack smiled and glanced again at the bag. Sam stood up with it in his hand and turned toward the door. "Thanks for the drinks."

Jack's eyes narrowed. "Where are you going? We need to resolve this."

"I'll have to think about it," Sam said. "Who knows, I might find a buyer for this baby and head off to South America with the cash." Sam opened the hatch and he and J.T. stepped out into the rain.

Jack followed them, but stopped under the awning

and stood there with his hands in his pockets. "Don't make a stupid mistake, Samuel."

They strode to the car, quiet as they left the marina, J.T. probably thinking about his share of the take if they sold the statue, Sam trying to make some sense of it all. Jack had been right about one thing, Sam didn't want to make a stupid mistake.

"Did you mean what you said back there?" J.T. said.

"Which part?"

"The part about selling the statue and going to South America. Because if you did, I can find someone who'll pay top dollar."

Sam glanced at him and grinned.

"No, I didn't mean that. Just giving Jack something to worry about."

J.T. frowned and said, "But what about the stuff he said about Candi?"

"Jack wants the statue. He'll say anything to get it."

"Yeah, I guess it's his skin or Candi's, huh?"

"It might not be that simple."

"What do you mean?"

"I did the job for Gideon Barge that Jack mentioned about three years ago. I tracked down an accountant who cheated him out of a lot of money. When I turned in the accountant and went to collect my fee at Gideon's headquarters in Mexico City, I saw Jack. He and Gideon looked real chummy, and I'll bet Jack knew about Gideon's collection of artifacts back then."

"So, what are you saying?"

"I think Jack is behind the whole thing."

TWENTY-FIVE

THE PHONE WOKE SAM. He picked it up and mumbled a hello.

"You up yet?" J.T.

Sam looked at the clock by the bed: 6:35 AM. They had checked into the hotel only four hours earlier. He sat up on the side of the bed and rubbed his eyes.

"I am now."

They met in the restaurant twenty minutes later and had a breakfast of eggs, sausages and home fries. When they left for the car, J.T glanced at Sam, an awkward look on his face. "You decide what you're going to do with the statue?"

Sam raised an eyebrow. "I thought we covered that last night. We're going to spring Candi."

"Okay, just checking. You know, like, it was pretty late, and you were tired."

When they reached the car, Sam said, "Why don't you drive. I need to use the phone."

They got in and Sam dug into his bag and found the napkin La Salle had given him at the Palma bar. He punched the numbers into his cell phone and waited for three rings before La Salle answered.

"Find anything interesting on my boat?" Sam asked.

La Salle ignored the question. "You'd better still have that statue."

"I want to talk to Candi."

Pause. "You think you have some kind of bargaining position, Mackenzie?" La Salle's voice had an edge to it.

"That's right. Unless you want me to turn this statue into a sack full of commemorative coins."

Sam heard La Salle sigh, and then the phone went silent for several seconds, except for the sound of muffled voices.

"Sam?" Candi whispered.

"Yes. Are you all right?"

"I guess so. They've had me locked up the whole time." She sounded sleepy.

"Where are you?"

"I think we're still—"

Candi's voice stopped abruptly and La Salle came back on the line.

"Okay, so you know she's alive. Meet me on the airstrip ramp at noon and we'll make the exchange."

"I don't think so."

La Salle remained silent for several seconds, and Sam thought he heard teeth grinding.

"We had a deal."

"Yeah," Sam said, "but you sent Grimes to kill us. That raises the ante."

"What do you want?" La Salle's tone bordered on rage.

"Three million cash, in addition to Candi."

"Three million? You're insane. Why would I agree to that?"

"Because the statue is worth a *hundred* million, that's why."

"You still have the money you stole from me."

"Oh, yeah, I'm keeping that too."

After a couple of seconds, Sam wondered if they'd lost the connection, then La Salle said, "All right, but it will take a few hours to get it together."

They agreed to make the exchange at midnight.

"Only you and Candi at the airstrip," Sam said, "and don't bring any bills less than a hundred."

Sam ended the call and J.T. said, "I like the sound of that."

"I thought you might. But you won't like the next part; I'm giving Candi two million of it because that's what La Salle took from her dad."

J.T. frowned and said, "I figured it was too good to be true. You should've asked for four or five million if that's what you had in mind."

Sam ignored the comment and told J.T. to drive toward the airport. A half hour later, they turned in at a small commercial building with a sign that read "Custom Parts," a place owned by an engineer named Lenny Berne, who operated a business of manufacturing unusual parts for airplanes.

SAM SAT IN a threadbare chair and drank a soda from a refrigerator behind Lenny Berne's desk. J.T. waited in the car to make sure no one had followed.

"Where did you get this?" Lenny turned the statue in his hands and ran his fingers over the ancient workmanship.

"I found it."

Lenny looked up from the statue at Sam's face and nodded. He put on his glasses and held the statue closer.

"It's solid gold."

"That's right."

Lenny shook his head. "I don't know. I've never

done anything like this before. I guess I could cast it using something to match the weight, but I don't have anything for plating."

Sam pulled the gold bar from his bag and laid it on the desk.

"Use this."

Lenny glanced at Sam and picked up the bar. He left his desk, came back a couple minutes later with a scale, and set the bar on top of it. His eyes widened. "Yeah, that'll be plenty."

Lenny looked the statue over again. "Is this stuff hot?"

Sam leaned back in his chair and smiled. "The police aren't on my trail, if that's what you mean."

"What about anybody else? If I do this, is anybody going to come around here with a gun looking for the Real McCoy?"

"It's a possibility," Sam said, "but I don't think so."

Lenny ran his fingers through his hair and pushed away from the desk, as if distancing himself from the gold.

"I don't know. I need the money, but this kind of thing…"

"Ten thousand dollars, and you can keep what's left of the gold bar."

Lenny leaned forward. "You're serious?"

"Yes."

He considered that for several seconds, said, "Okay, I guess it's worth a shot," and then chuckled at his own joke.

"I need it by eleven tonight."

Lenny glanced at a clock on the wall and then at his

shop through a glass window next to the desk. One person stood out there, operating some type of machine.

"Yeah, I think I can manage that. I'll send my employee on some errands and tell him to go home from there."

"One other thing," Sam said. "You can't damage it in any way."

"There won't be a scratch."

They talked a couple more minutes and Sam went out the door.

"See anybody suspicious?" Sam said as he got into the car.

"No. Lots of cars went by, but nobody turned in or even slowed down. What did you give the guy to do the plating with?"

"The gold bar."

J.T. nodded, his face solemn in the glow of the morning sun. "That's worth, what, thirty thousand?"

"Maybe. It's a pretty small bar. Don't worry. We're going to get a lot more than that from La Salle if everything works out like it should."

"Yeah, I guess so. Let's just make sure it does."

"Swing by the bank," Sam said. "We need to get some money."

At the bank where Sam had rented the deposit box they removed enough cash to pay Lenny, plus some extra to cover expenses they knew they would have, and deposited the remaining gold pieces they'd found on their dive.

They got back into the car and Sam said, "We'll split what's left after we give Candi her part."

J.T. nodded, glanced out the windshield, then back at Sam. "What about the statue?"

"What about it?"

"If we're giving La Salle a fake, that means we're going to keep the real one. Like I said, I can find a buyer for it."

"Let's get this done and then we'll talk about it."

J.T. held Sam's gaze for a couple of seconds, as if Sam might be pulling a fast one, then nodded and said, "Okay, that's cool."

They drove to a computer store so J.T. could get another laptop. Sam got in the driver's seat when J.T. got out and said, "I'll be back in an hour."

He located a public library and went inside and asked a middle-aged woman behind the desk about using a computer for an Internet search. The woman entered his first name into a log and pointed to a work station. Sam immediately found references to Aztec artifacts, and a few minutes later a photograph of the statue he'd left with Lenny Berne popped up on the screen. It had been discovered outside Mexico City in 1882 by an English archaeologist named Branson. A reference in an archaeological journal said Branson deemed the statue an important symbol to the Aztec people that somehow had escaped the plundering of the Spaniards in the sixteenth century. The statue disappeared from public view a couple of years later. Rumored to have been traded by wealthy collectors around the world, at one time in the early twentieth century the value had been placed at more than ten million dollars. Finally, an anonymous person sent the statue home to a museum in Mexico City in 1951. It remained there for more than half a century, until stolen only a couple of years ago.

Sam found little relating to the current monetary

value of the statue, other than it being "priceless." He supposed that might mean the statue could actually fetch a hundred million dollars if offered to the right collector.

Sam thanked the librarian and left. He picked up J.T. at the computer store and they drove to a restaurant in Coconut Grove where they sat at an outside table, had beer and burgers, and planned how Sam would exchange the statue for Candi and the cash. Sam would call J.T. on his cell phone and leave the call open as they had done before, then go inside the fence at the airstrip with the fake statue and meet La Salle. J.T. would remain in the car until Sam returned with the money, unless Sam said the word "double-cross," and J.T. would come running.

"Sound okay to you?" Sam asked.

"Sure, fine with me."

Their plan worried Sam a little, since the real statue would be left in the car with J.T. Sam had known he could be faced with a situation like this since the time J.T. came onto the scene, but he felt as though he would be in control. Now, the way things had worked out, it didn't look as if he had any choice.

Candi also worried him. *She'll sell you out for a lot less than the value of that statue.* Jack's words. However, as Sam had told J.T., Jack would say anything to get what he wanted. Sam had promised to help Candi, so he would follow this mess through to the end. If she sold him out, he would deal with it.

They spent the rest of the day lining up an easy getaway in case things went badly. Sam knew a man with a fast boat that would transport them to anywhere in the Caribbean, no questions asked, no passport required.

They dropped off a retainer with the man in the late afternoon, with the agreement that they would show up at the meeting place by 2:00 AM. If they didn't show, he could keep the retainer.

LENNY COMPLETED THE work by eleven, as promised, and Sam came out of the shop with his bag in his hand and got into the car. He took out the two statues and J.T. clicked on the map light and took one of them. After examining it, he took the other one and grinned.

"I can't tell the difference."

"Let's hope La Salle can't, either."

"I don't see how he could. The gold looks so real."

"It is real. The only way anyone will know it isn't gold through and through is to cut into it. Or maybe X-ray it. I don't think they'll be doing either."

"Hey," J.T. said, "the important thing is *you* know which one is real."

Sam glanced at J.T. and clicked off the light.

"Don't worry, I know. Let's get going."

THEY TURNED INTO the airstrip parking lot at 11:45. A flood light illuminated the area. An old Honda Civic sat inside the fence next to the hangar. *Probably belongs to the night watchman.*

Sam took out his cell phone and punched in the number for J.T.'s phone. J.T. answered and Sam turned on the speaker, put the phone into his shirt pocket and buttoned the pocket to keep the phone from falling out. He took the fake statue from his bag and put the bag in the trunk, then eased to the gate and spoke to the air in front of his face: "Can you hear me?"

"Loud and clear," J.T. replied.

Closing the gate behind him, he gripped the gun in the pocket of his jacket and walked around the corner of the hangar. The doors stood open, the hangar empty. An old man with keys hanging from his belt stepped out of the office.

"Waiting for a flight to come in," Sam said.

The old man touched his index finger to his forehead and waved in a mock salute.

Floodlights radiated from the rim of the airstrip like a nighttime ballpark. Sam stood inside the edge of the hangar and waited. The heat, oppressive for that time of night, rose beads of perspiration inside his shirt. His pulse fired in his ears, and he wondered if the heat might be just his imagination.

Mosquitoes buzzed somewhere nearby. When the buzzing got louder, Sam realized it hadn't been mosquitoes at all; instead, a propeller driven airplane arrived from the east. He watched the small craft land and taxi back toward the hangar. It stopped about fifty feet away, and the pilot cut the engines.

Candi exited from the hatch on Sam's side and La Salle followed, carrying a large metal case in one hand. He still had the limp, and probably would for a long time. Candi, beautiful as ever, her eyes electric in the incandescent lights, didn't look like someone who had been mistreated. She wore a thin jacket and stretch pants, her hair pulled back in a pony tail.

Sam stepped over to meet them and nodded toward the metal case. "Is that the money?"

"Yes." La Salle curled back his upper lip in a sneer and glanced at the airplane. "I had to sell my jets."

Sam looked at a man still in the airplane. "I told you to come alone."

"He's just the pilot."

Candi stepped over to Sam's side and looked back at La Salle. She had her hands in the pockets of the jacket.

"Okay," Sam said, "turn over the case and I'll hand you this little guy."

La Salle looked at the statue for what seemed like a couple of seconds too long, then glanced at Sam. "All right, but it had better be authentic."

They made the exchange. Sam set the heavy case down next to Candi and asked her to check out the cash.

La Salle held the statue up to the light and ran his fingers over the gold surfaces. He turned it over and examined the base, scratching it with his fingernail, and glanced at Sam. Sam tightened his fingers around the stock of the gun in his pocket.

"It's quite exquisite," La Salle said, almost smiling.

"Yes, it is."

Candi laid the case flat and opened it, and Sam heard her thumb through several of the stacks. "It looks like it's all here." She snapped the lid shut and stepped away.

"Then our business is concluded," La Salle said. He turned toward the plane and took a step, then turned back and said, "Take the case, Candi, and let's go."

Sam glanced at Candi. She held a small caliber gun in her hand pointed at Sam's chest.

"I halfway expected a double-cross from him," Sam said, "but not you."

"Nothing personal, Sam. This is strictly business."

Then she turned and shot La Salle in the head. The gun popped like a toy, its sound lost in the vastness of the airstrip. Blood spurted from La Salle's hair, his eyes full of surprise as he crashed to the tarmac.

Candi stood in the same position for several seconds. Sam had his gun out and pointed at her, and wondered if J.T. had heard the signal. Then Candi looked at Sam and put the gun back in her pocket.

"Sorry about that. I didn't have any way to let you know."

Sam took a deep breath and hung the gun by his side.

She stepped close and kissed him on the lips for what seemed like a long time, and her eyes glistened when she pulled away. "Call me in a couple of days. I have to go back to the island and pick up a few things that belong to Philly." Then she smiled and sauntered toward the airplane.

"Don't you want the money?"

"No, you keep it. It's a lot less than its supposed to be."

She got onto the plane and the pilot started the engines, taxied to the runway and took off. They flew east, leaving La Salle lying there in the same condition he had left Candi's father months before.

"You look pretty bummed out," J.T. said from behind Sam.

"Where have you been?"

"I heard you say the magic word, but by the time I got to the hangar Candi had shot La Salle. You had your gun out and looked like you had things under control. I stayed around the corner of the hangar, figuring I might get you killed if I came out there."

That seem pretty logical, the only problem being that Sam had been ready to believe J.T. would make a run for it. The fact that he hadn't made Sam feel a little guilty.

"Yeah, okay, let's get out of here." He stepped over to the body and pulled the statue from La Salle's fingers.

The sound of a helicopter sputtered in the distance and Sam said, "I hope that isn't the cops."

"I don't see how it could be. That gunshot couldn't have been heard more than a quarter mile from here."

J.T. picked up the metal case and they hurried back to the car. The satellite phone Sam had taken from the man on La Salle's island lay on the top of the Acura. Sam vaguely remembered putting it in his bag, and hadn't thought about it again until now.

Sam laid the statue on the driver's seat and picked up the phone. "Did you use this?"

"Yeah. Mine was tied up with your call, and I wanted to check on some things while I waited. Why?"

Sam glanced up at the helicopter closing in fast.

TWENTY-SIX

THE THUMPING OF helicopter blades filled the night sky, and a spotlight swept the area around the hangar. A black van screamed down the highway and slid to a stop, blocking the entrance of the parking lot. Sam and J.T. watched with their guns in their hands, standing next to the Acura. There was no place to run, and within seconds four men armed with automatic weapons surrounded them. Sam recognized them as the same ones who had taken the gold artifacts from La Salle's island.

Renaldo, the tall leader with graying hair, said to the man with the scar on his face, "Take their guns."

Sam saw no future in resisting; he would see how it played out. The last time this happened, they had let them go free after they got what they wanted. This time he was pretty sure they wanted the statue.

Sam glanced at J.T., hoping he wouldn't do anything stupid, and said, "Give it up."

J.T. nodded.

Scarface stepped forward and took their weapons.

The helicopter landed in the parking lot, and its blades slowed to a stop. A man with a familiar face exited and sauntered toward them. His white hair stood up a couple of inches on top, and he had a thin black mustache. He wore safari khakis, as if out for a hunt, and reminded Sam of an aging movie actor, still waiting for the big role. He held up his hand and the men with guns moved back.

"So, we meet again," the man said when the noise of the helicopter quieted. "You *do* remember me, don't you?"

"Yes," Sam said, "Gideon Barge."

Barge looked at J.T. "And this is your partner, I presume." It didn't seem to be a question and no one said anything. "He doesn't look all that dangerous."

Sam tried to stay cool. He knew this guy as a businessman. Maybe he'd listen to reason. He glanced at J.T. "That's the way people look when surrounded by other people with automatic weapons."

Barge snorted a laugh and said to Sam, "You have something that belongs to me, and I hope you will turn it over without a fuss."

Sam nodded, reached into the car and picked up the statue. He handed it to Barge. "No fuss."

Barge motioned for one of the men who held a flashlight to come closer. In the light he examined it. Satisfied that he had the real thing, he said, "You do know it was stolen from me by Mr. La Salle."

"And before that, you stole it from a museum in Mexico City."

Barge's face stretched into a smile. "Why, yes, indeed I did. You must be smarter than you look."

"You'll find La Salle lying on the flight line with a bullet in his head."

"Really? How disappointing. I planned to do that myself. But I must say, it will be a lot less trouble. I understood you were going to trade him the statue for the freedom of your girlfriend."

"That's right."

Barge leaned down and looked inside the Acura. "What happened to your girlfriend?"

Sam sighed. "I'm afraid she ran away with the pilot."

Barge made a clicking noise with his tongue and shook his head, then turned to the man with a tattoo on his neck and told him to go check out Sam's story. Tattoo trotted off toward the airstrip. The other three men kept their guns trained on Sam and J.T. while Barge took the statue to the helicopter and handed it to someone inside. He came back and stood in front of Sam.

"Now, what should I do with you?"

"I did return your statue."

Barge grinned. "I suppose you were on your way to give it to me."

"That's right."

Barge crossed his hands behind his back and looked around as if studying the situation. Tattoo returned from the airstrip and nodded to Barge.

Barge looked at Sam and narrowed his eyes. "Kill them, but do it somewhere else and get rid of the bodies." He turned, ambled toward the helicopter, and said over his shoulder, "Get rid of La Salle, too." The helicopter spun its blades as he boarded and took off a few seconds later.

"Barge got what he wanted," Sam said to Renaldo, "and La Salle is dead. Just let us go and you won't ever hear from us again."

Renaldo smiled. "Sorry. You would already be dead if Mr. Barge hadn't thought you would get the statue for him."

J.T. spoke up. "You do everything he says, even kill people?"

Renaldo shrugged. "He pays us well. Now, shut up or I'll shoot you right here."

Two of the men went out, got La Salle, and tossed him onto the floor in the rear of the van. Renaldo told Sam and J.T. to get in with the body. Climbing over La Salle, they sat on the floor in a cargo area separated from the rest of the vehicle by reinforced glass. Sam turned and peered through the glass. Two captain's chairs sat behind the driver and front passenger seat, facing the front. The space where Sam and J.T. sat, the body just inches from their feet, would measure about five feet between the glass and the rear double doors. There were no handles on the inside, meaning the rear doors could be locked and unlocked only from the outside. A vehicle for carrying prisoners. After securing Sam and J.T. inside, Renaldo got into the driver's seat and the others got into the remaining seats. Renaldo turned the van around in the road and headed toward Miami.

Sam's pulse thumped in his ears and his skin felt clammy. He didn't know where they would go, but he knew it would be bad, no matter the place. He wished he had a weapon so they could have some kind of chance. Maybe he and J.T. could kick the doors when they opened and knock the men down. But what if all four men stood outside the doors? They couldn't knock all of them down. Still, it might be their only chance. He whispered the plan to J.T. and J.T. nodded.

They rode for a half hour and slowed down. Sam had been following their route and knew they were headed toward the loading docks for cargo ships. He turned and peered through the glass. A security station and a sign that read "Barge World Freight" came into view.

A guard stepped out and waved them through. They probably planned to take them out on a boat, shoot them, and drop them in the ocean. Sam glanced at La Salle, who lay on his side, his legs bent to fit inside the van. Something nagged at Sam. A moment later it crystallized and he glanced at J.T.

"He never drew his gun," Sam whispered.

"What?"

"La Salle never drew his gun."

"So?"

Sam pulled open La Salle's coat and saw the butt of a 9mm sticking out of an inside pocket. They hadn't searched the dead man. Sam reached for the gun, and a hand clamped on his wrist. He jerked it away and saw La Salle's eyes pop open.

La Salle took the gun from the pocket and thumbed the hammer. He winced from the sudden movement and touched the side of his head where his hair was wet with blood. The bullet must have just grazed his scalp, and he probably had the grandmother of all headaches. He pushed back so he could prop his head against the side of the van and peered at Sam and J.T. "Where are we?"

"Better keep it down," Sam said, whispering. "We're at the docks, a place owned by Gideon Barge. They're going to kill us and drop us in the ocean. Of course, they think you're already dead."

Sam glanced at the men in front who faced the other way, comfortable that Sam and J.T. were no danger behind the thick glass.

La Salle touched his head again. "Candi did this to me." He took a deep breath and sighed.

"Well, you did kill Philly Moran, who happened to be her father."

La Salle rubbed his eyes. "He didn't give me any choice." Then he said, "Where's the statue?"

"Long gone. Barge took it away in a helicopter."

La Salle's eyes narrowed and he pointed the gun at Sam. "I should kill you both where you sit."

Sam shrugged. "It'd save them the trouble." He glanced through the glass and saw that the men still looked the other way. "Better stay still, though. If they see you're alive, you won't get a chance to use that gun."

La Salle closed his eyes, his breathing shallow and his face covered with sweat, then opened them wide, as if fighting unconsciousness. "How many are there?"

"Four, with automatic weapons."

La Salle nodded and dozed off again. Sam leaned forward, but La Salle snapped his eyes open and glared at him.

The van stopped and backed up, and the engine went dead. La Salle stuck the gun inside his coat and closed his eyes. Tattoo and the man with gold teeth opened the rear doors, illuminating the van from flood lights outside, and reached in for him. Their weapons hung from their shoulders on straps. Renaldo and Scarface stood several feet behind them with their guns pointed at Sam and J.T.

Tattoo and Gold Teeth lifted La Salle's hulk out of the van, walked sideways a few steps and dropped him on the ground. He hit, rolled onto his side and fired at the men holding the guns. Renaldo's eyes grew wide and his mouth opened as if to scream. He grabbed his stomach and stared at the blood running between his fingers, his face went slack, and he dropped to the ground. The other man, Scarface, stumbled on a wounded leg, yelled a string of words in Spanish, and brought his weapon up to fire. La Salle shot him again, this time in the head, and the man fell backward, firing a burst of rounds into the night sky.

One of the men who had carried La Salle, Gold Teeth, struggled to get his weapon unstrapped from his shoulder. La Salle shot him in the chest and Gold Teeth dropped his hands and fell to the ground. Sam hit the other man, Tattoo, in a tackle. As they descended, the gun fired wild next to Sam's head, and the heat from the barrel singed his ear. Sam straddled the man, ripped the gun away and back-fisted his temple. The man's eyes rolled up and he passed out. Sam stood up and turned around.

"I'll take that gun," La Salle said.

La Salle had gotten to his feet and pointed his gun at Sam. Sam wished he'd had his finger on the trigger, ready to fire, but La Salle would certainly get a shot off before Sam could. He handed over the weapon and looked around. Four men lay on the ground, three of them dead and holding silenced weapons. The smell of exploded gun powder bit into Sam's nostrils like an ammonia cap. Although grateful to be alive, Sam knew La Salle wouldn't have raised a finger to save them had his own life not been in danger. It angered Sam that he might have bought only a little more time.

"You need to let us go," J.T. said. "After all, we did help you."

"Forget it," La Salle said. He put his hand to his head, staggered slightly, as if dizzy, and glanced at Sam, probably wondering if Sam had seen him falter.

"What did you do with the case of money I gave you at the airstrip?"

Sam thought the big man might have a concussion. The longer they strung him along, the better their chances would be of staying alive. "I hid it before Barge came in and took the statue."

"Where?" La Salle put his hand to his head again and closed his eyes for a long blink, but held the gun steady.

"I'll take you to it."

La Salle seemed to consider the offer for a couple of beats, then said, "Okay get in the van."

They closed the rear doors.

"You're driving," La Salle said, prodding J.T. with his gun. "And you sit up front with him," he said to Sam.

La Salle got in the seat behind J.T. and said to Sam, "I'll have the gun on you the whole time, so don't try any funny stuff or you'll die."

They rode out the gate, and Sam wondered where the security guard had gone. Probably took a break when the van came in; what he didn't see he couldn't talk about. Too bad; Sam had thought he might do something to help them after hearing the shots.

Sam glanced at La Salle, hoping he would drop off to sleep in the back seat, but he seemed better now that he sat down. He would kill them after he got the cash, so if he didn't pass out before getting to the airstrip, Sam would have no choice but to try to take him and hope for the best.

La Salle made several calls on his phone, keeping his eyes and the gun trained on Sam. He didn't seem to get any answers to his calls and finally closed the phone and put it in his pocket.

Sirens screamed in the distance, but that seemed normal, like any other night in the city. The noise faded away as they rode toward the Everglades.

Sam turned to La Salle. "Can I ask you something?"

"Quiet. I'm trying to think."

"How were you able steal all that gold from Barge? He had to have tight security around it."

Several seconds passed, and Sam wondered if his appeal to La Salle's ego might have failed.

"Danilov and I worked for him. We engineered the theft of the statue from the museum, and Barge had agreed to pay us five million each. He kept putting us off so we finally just took everything."

"What about Barge's security?"

"We *were* the security, but one of Barge's men drove in as we took off and fired several rounds into the side of the plane. If not for him, we would have flown out of there without a scratch."

"What about the dead guy on the plane? Was he in on it?"

"Yes, but when the plane started losing fuel, he freaked out and pulled a gun. We had to kill him."

"So you escaped in a raft?"

La Salle glanced out the window and the gun dipped slightly. Sam thought it might be his chance to grab it, but La Salle looked back and said, "That's right. Danilov had friends in Cuba who helped us get back to Miami."

"What part did Miro play?"

"Who?"

"Miro, the dead antiquities expert."

"Ah, him. Danilov knew the man. After a month or so, Danilov dived the wrecked plane and brought up some of the items to help finance a salvage operation. Miro examined them and found a buyer, but he got greedy."

"I thought you were a Government agent of some kind."

La Salle hesitated, shook the tip of the gun at Sam, and in a loud voice said, "That's none of your business."

End of conversation. Sam didn't want to provoke him, since La Salle probably realized he could kill Sam and still force J.T. to take him to the cash.

So La Salle did work for the Government, maybe investigating Barge, the possibility of getting rich a little too tempting to pass up. Sam wondered if La Salle regretted what he had done, and decided that he probably just regretted failing at it.

They rode the rest of the way in silence.

The Acura sat where they had left it. They got out of the van and Sam saw the metal case lying underneath the edge of the Acura. J.T. probably had pushed it there when the van showed up the first time. La Salle saw it, too. He told J.T. to get it and hand it to him. J.T. did as he was told and La Salle laid it on the hood of the car and opened it. It looked exactly the same as when he had given it to Sam.

La Salle nodded toward the rear of the Acura. "Open the trunk."

"You have your money," Sam said.

"Open it. I want the money you stole from my safe."

They walked around the car and La Salle staggered, but regained his footing and followed them to the trunk.

J.T. pulled the key from his pocket and popped the trunk lid.

La Salle saw the bag and told them to step away. When they were several feet from the car, he laid the case on the floor of the trunk and opened the bag. Seeing the statue inside, he glanced at Sam and smiled. "Ah, what have we here?" He grabbed the statue and examined it, remaining careful to keep a watch on Sam and J.T. "I suppose you told Barge that Candi took this."

Sam glanced at J.T. "Actually, it's a fake. Barge got the real one."

La Salle's eyes narrowed. "I don't believe you. It looks just like the one I saw earlier."

Sam shrugged. "It's good quality, gold plated."

La Salle looked at it for a few seconds, still keeping a watch on Sam and J.T., then closed the trunk and said, "Whatever you say. I'm taking it anyway." He pointed the gun at Sam, as if ready to shoot, but then staggered and leaned against the side of the car. Sam started to step toward him to grab the gun, but hesitated, thinking there might be a safer way out.

"That's a pretty bad head injury," Sam said. "You might die if you don't go to a hospital. We'll take you. You're in no condition to drive. You'll never make it."

"You're just trying to stall for time. This is no big deal. I've been hit on the head worse than this." La Salle tried to sound confident, but his eyes said something different.

"You probably made things worse when you fell on the ground and shot those guys back there. You probably have a blood clot traveling to your brain. You'll have a stroke, and even if you live, you'll be paralyzed."

La Salle pushed away from the car, but staggered

again and leaned back against it. "A hospital will ask too many questions."

"You can tell them you fell down and hit your head."

After what seemed like an eternity, he narrowed his eyes and said, "Okay, put the statue in the case with the money and give it to me."

They got into the car, Sam and J.T. in front, La Salle in back. J.T. searched his computer for the nearest medical center while Sam drove. Sam felt a surge of relief as he realized that this part of the nightmare might be over. Even La Salle wouldn't kill them in a public place and risk being caught.

Within a couple of minutes J.T. located a hospital on the outskirts of town, and they rode the rest of the way in silence. They found the place, and Sam steered into the driveway designated for ambulances and stopped a few feet from the entrance.

La Salle opened the door and said, "We'll finish this later." He got out of the car, holding his gun hand behind the case, and staggered toward the door.

Sam drove away, watching in the rearview mirror as La Salle dropped his free hand by his side and went into the building.

"He didn't have the gun," Sam said. "Check the back seat."

J.T. reached into the floor behind Sam's seat and came back with La Salle's gun. "Yeah, here it is. His head must have been working okay. He knew it wouldn't be a good idea to go into the ER carrying a gun that had just been used to kill three men."

J.T. wiped down the gun, and twenty minutes later he tossed it out the window as they crossed the Miami River.

The clock on the dash read 3:00 AM, so the man with the boat had already taken their retainer and gone home. They drove to a hotel on Miami Beach, and after checking in Sam went to his room and called Candi's cell phone. She answered after several rings, sounding sleepy.

"Where are you?" Sam asked.

"I just got back to the island. Why?"

"La Salle is still alive."

"What do you mean?" Sleep left her voice and alarm took its place. "I saw him fall and he looked dead."

"Yes, he did. But we just dropped him off at the hospital ER and he walked in the door. You need to get out of there as soon as you can."

Candi was silent for a moment and said, "He won't be able to get back to the island before morning. I'll leave at first light."

They said their goodbyes and Sam hung up. His phone chirped before he dropped it on the nightstand. It was J.T.

"Hey, I just wanted to let you know about something. You know when you called me from your cell phone before you went out on the airstrip to meet La Salle?"

"Yeah?"

"Well, I connected the phone to my computer and started a recording. I didn't get a chance to break the connection until we got in the car to take La Salle to the ER."

"Why would you record the conversation?"

J.T. hesitated before saying, "I guess I wanted something I could pinch La Salle with, in case he flew in there, and, you know...took the statue and blew you away."

Silence. A couple of seconds passed. Sam knew J.T.'s reason had to be a self-serving one.

J.T. continued, "I checked out the recording, and it picked up everything. Barge admitted stealing the statue from the museum and gave the order to execute us. La Salle admitted killing Philly Moran and the man on the plane, and as much as admitted killing Miro. I'm not sure what it's worth, now that you're okay, but it seems like it could come in handy."

Maybe it could.

"Can you clean it up, take out the parts we don't want in there?"

"Sure."

They hung up and Sam went to bed and slept until 10:00 AM. Sun shone through the window and a gull stood on the patio ledge, squawking. Vacationers probably fed the gulls regularly, and this one had come by for his snack. Sam got up, showered and called J.T. They met in the restaurant at 10:45 and had breakfast.

J.T. remained quiet for most of the meal, probably thinking about the fortune he almost had. Finally, he said, "There's something I wish you'd explain to me."

"Sure." Sam poured a second cup of coffee and stirred in cream and sugar.

"Why'd you tell La Salle the statue's a fake?"

"I was hoping he wouldn't take it."

J.T. raised an eyebrow. "That's the only reason?"

"What other reason would there be?"

J.T. nodded. "Okay, that's what I thought."

"You get a chance to work on the recording?"

J.T. nodded. "The quality's almost perfect. I enhanced the voices and eliminated most of the background noise."

They paid for breakfast and left the hotel. Sam called Jack Craft on his boat line and told him they would drop by.

"Sure," Jack said, "I heard from Gideon. Sounds like we should celebrate."

"Yeah, maybe, but you might hold the beer for later."

"What do you mean?"

"I'll tell you when we get there."

They drove to the marina and parked, and went straight to *The Clipper*. Jack stood on the deck, waiting, and asked them inside. He offered them something to drink and they both declined. They sat in the chairs in the lounge and Jack raised an eyebrow.

"So, what's the problem?"

"No problem. I just wanted to let you in on something."

Jack leaned back and crossed his legs. "Tell me."

"I want to ask you something first," Sam said.

"Go ahead."

"Why did Barge hold you responsible for La Salle stealing his collection?"

Jack looked at them and smiled. "I suppose it doesn't matter now. I met Thomas Beeker—the guy who became La Salle—in Mexico City several years ago. He worked for the Government, investigating a company that did business with Gideon Barge. The man who owned the company asked me to talk with Beeker and try to get him to back off. Beeker was pretty ruthless, even back then, and I sensed that he could be paid off. I negotiated a settlement, so to speak. Beeker wanted me to recommend him for a job as a security consultant with Gideon Barge. I think you can figure out the rest."

Sam shook his head, wondering how Jack had lived as long as he had.

Jack raised an eyebrow. "What?"

Sam smiled and said, "Nothing," then nodded at J.T. "Play the recording."

J.T. opened his computer and played the part to do with Gideon Barge. The voices came to life; J.T. had altered his own voice and Sam's to sound like those of other people, and had taken out any references to their names.

The recording finished and Jack's eyes tightened at the corners, as if he might smile. "Pretty damaging stuff for someone like Gideon Barge. There are probably a dozen people who would love to have that recording."

"I'd say."

"Why did you play it for me?"

"We gave Barge a fake statue."

Jack's eyes widened and he stood up and stepped to the bar. "I see," he said over his shoulder. "Sure I can't get you something?"

"Yeah, we'll take whatever you're having," J.T. said.

Jack came back with the glasses and handed them out. He sat back down, took a long drink, and sighed.

"Barge certainly thought it was real from the way he sounded when he called."

"It's a good fake."

Jack shrugged. "Then he might never know the difference, unless someone tells him."

"That's right."

"What are you going to do with the recording?"

Sam smiled. "I'm going to give it to you."

TWENTY-SEVEN

THEY RODE TO the bank and cleaned out the safe deposit box. Back in the car, Sam counted the money, gave J.T. half, and said, "You can have all the gold pieces we found, too."

J.T. glanced at him, one eyebrow raised. "You sure?"

"Yeah, I'm sure." Sam started the car. "What are you going to do now?"

"I'll probably hang around and soak up some rays. I can find a buyer for these things better in Miami than up north."

Sam drove to the car rental agency and picked up his own car. J.T. took the Chevy and said he would turn it in before he left town. They agreed to meet back at Sam's boat in a couple of hours and have a celebration drink.

SAM PARKED HIS car next to the Custom Parts building and went inside. Lenny Berne heard the bell on the door and came into the office.

"I hoped you would forget about coming back."

"Yeah, I bet," Sam said.

Lenny opened his safe and took out the package wrapped in newspaper.

Sam peeled away the paper and looked at the statue. It looked exactly as it had when he'd left it there. "Are we square on the bill?"

"Sure, the rest of that gold is going to get me out of debt. I wasn't so sure when you called back and asked for two copies, but there was plenty left. What are you going to do now that you're a rich man?"

Sam glanced at Lenny. "What makes you say that?"

Lenny leaned back in his chair and grinned. "I checked it out on the Internet. That thing has to be worth at least seventy or eighty million dollars."

Sam smiled. *Yes, at least.*

"Thanks, for holding it for me," Sam said, ignoring Lenny's question.

He rewrapped the statue and put it inside a bag Lenny gave him.

"Let me know if anything else like this comes along," Lenny said.

"I'll do that." They shook hands and Sam left.

J.T. SHOWED UP at two o'clock with a bottle of champagne. He also had a girl with him, and Prince Alfred followed them down the dock. The dog saw Sam standing on the boat and trotted across the gangway. Sam reached down and scratched his ears. Whatever injuries Grimes had inflicted on him seemed to be gone.

"I thought you'd want to see him," J.T. said, nodding toward Prince Alfred. "This is Amy. She patched him up after Grimes hit him with the crutch. He had a small gash on his jaw and she took a couple of stitches."

Prince Alfred turned and saw a pelican squatted on a dock timber. He licked his lips and lay down on his stomach on the deck, his eyes glued to the bird.

Amy had long dark hair, blue eyes, and a blushing smile. Very attractive. She leaned against J.T. and caressed the back of his neck. J.T.'s face turned red and he pulled her toward a chair under the awning.

"Amy worked for a vet, but Grimes shot him and now she's out of a job. I'm going to help her set up a pet grooming business. She's really good with animals."

Sam wondered why Grimes would shoot a veterinarian, and decided he didn't want to ask. He didn't want to be reminded of Grimes any more than he had to.

J.T. popped the cork on the champagne and filled glasses from the galley. He passed them out and clinked his with Sam's and Amy's.

Prince Alfred got tired of watching the bird, saw some fish jump, and dived into the water. He looked like an otter swimming toward the school of skipjack.

"Amy and I are going down to Grand Cayman for a while. Why don't you and Candi tag along?"

Sam nodded absently. He'd spoken with her right after visiting Lenny Berne. "Candi wants the recording. She gave me an e-mail address you can use."

"Yeah, okay. What about Grand Cayman?"

"I'll check with her."

They drank the entire bottle, then went to the marina restaurant and had several more drinks and dinner while Prince Alfred guarded the boat. After that, they brought a piece of steak back for the dog and J.T. and Amy left with him for parts unknown. Sam went inside and tried to sleep, but his mind wouldn't shut down. He still had questions, like what Gideon Barge might do if he found out about the fake statue, and how Jack would take him down. He also wondered about Grimes. They hadn't seen him since they left him unconscious inside the seaplane in the Keys. And Sam contemplated what he would do with the real statue that now rested in the secret storage spot in his closet. If he sold it he'd never have to work again. Maybe buy an island of his own, get a bigger boat, sail around the world. He wondered if the statue could be sold without Gideon Barge getting wind of it. Finally, after a few minutes, he fell asleep, and a dream vision of Candi climbed into his bed.

TWO WEEKS LATER, J.T. sat in the shade of the hotel cabana on Grand Cayman, watching Amy sunbathe by the pool.

"She's beautiful, don't you think?"

"Yes, she is," Sam said. He found himself marveling at J.T.'s good fortune, meeting someone like her at the airstrip while Grimes did his dirty work inside the hangar.

They had been at the hotel for two days.

"When will Candi get here?"

"Tomorrow," Sam said. "She had to wrap up a few things."

J.T. nodded, eyes behind the sunglasses still on Amy. "You know, I think we might find a few more gold pieces on that wrecked plane if we dive it."

Sam took a sip of his beer and put it on the table next to his lounge chair.

"What about La Salle's set-up? We might be killed by one of his missiles."

J.T. shook his head. "I went out there last night and La Salle's men had left. The computer was still running, so I disabled the program, shut down the system, and pulled the plug."

"They've abandoned the place?"

"Looks that way, but if they come back, it'll take them weeks to fix what I did, if they can do it at all."

Sam nodded, not too sure he wanted to go back down to that plane. At night when he dozed off, he still could see the man belted in the seat, hair swirling above his dead face.

"Let me think about it."

"I rented a fast boat and some diving gear. We pick it up tonight at ten."

"How long will it take us to get there?"

J.T. shrugged. "Couple hours, maybe, no more."

J.T. HAD RENTED a thirty-foot boat.

"You sure this is big enough?" Sam said. "We have to go sixty or seventy miles. It could get rough out there."

J.T. looked up at the night sky. "It's clear as a bell. This should do it."

They would be a long way from anything when they reached their destination, and thirty feet of boat seemed pretty small in all that water. Sam had the satellite phone he'd taken from the thug who worked for Barge, but he wasn't sure who he would call if they had a problem.

They left the dock at 10:15 and ran the engine full throttle for almost three hours before reaching the co-ordinates. Sam had looked at his watch several times in the last half hour while glancing at the GPS unit. The water remained smooth, with almost no chop. They dropped anchor, suited up and checked out their gear and lights. Everything seemed to work, so they went into the water about 1:30 AM.

The plane and its surroundings looked the same as

they had left it. They went straight to the broken wing and sifted through the sand around it, finding nothing for almost an hour. Then J.T. uncovered another bird of prey, larger than the last, and another small cup.

The air gauge indicated Sam had little left when J.T. pointed to the plane and swam into the hatch. Sam followed and they scanned the deck and seats again. The dead man still sat there, awaiting his final destination. They found nothing else. Sam motioned to J.T.'s air supply and pointed to the surface. They went back to the rope and swam to the top.

"That was worth the trip," J.T. said, taking off his fins. He sounded disappointed.

"Yeah, that bird is probably worth a hundred thousand."

J.T. nodded. "You never asked what I got for the other pieces. You want to know?"

"Sure, but let's get started, we have a lot of hard riding ahead of us."

"The mask brought the most," J.T. said, as he started the engine. "I got two-fifty for it. But I got only a hundred out of the rest. Still, that's a lot of money."

"Sure is. Get this deathtrap going."

"I'm still puzzled why you didn't want any of the money."

Sam knew what J.T. had on his mind. "Yeah, well, you earned it."

J.T. paused, then said, "You sure there isn't something you want to say about that statue?"

Sam shook his head. "Nothing I can think of."

J.T. sighed and started the engine. The boat rumbled for several seconds before he put it into gear and rammed the throttle forward.

The sun lay on the horizon by the time they threw the lines to the man on the dock. He looked relieved that they had made it back with his boat and gear. J.T. tipped him a large bill and then remained quiet as they ambled to the rented car and rode back to the hotel.

"How about breakfast?" Sam asked when they entered the lobby.

"Nah. I'm going to catch the first plane out. I'll settle up with you later on these things we found." He had an edge in his voice.

The elevator door opened and J.T. stepped inside. Sam shrugged, went into the restaurant and ordered eggs and bacon. J.T. had obviously followed Sam when he got the real statue from Lenny, and thought he deserved part of it. Sam hadn't asked him to come along on this project to begin with; J.T. had invited himself. He'd helped, no doubt about that, but Sam had compensated him well, including the extra gold pieces they'd just found. He had made no promises concerning the statue.

The waiter poured coffee and the satellite phone chirped. Sam took it out of his pocket and answered.

"That creep blindsided me," J.T. said, his voice labored.

"What creep?"

"Grimes. He hit me with something and knocked me out when I opened the door to the room. I just came around and he's taken Amy and those gold pieces we found."

Sam got up, hurried from the restaurant to the lobby, and looked outside at the parking area. He caught a glimpse of Grimes driving a white Taurus out of the lot in the opposite direction from the airport. Amy sat in the passenger seat.

J.T. had the keys to the rental car, so Sam caught the elevator and headed for J.T.'s room.

"Are you okay?" Sam said into the phone.

"Yeah, I think so. I have a cut on the side of my head, but the bleeding is almost stopped."

"Grimes just drove out of the parking lot. I'll be at the door in a few seconds for the car keys."

The elevator opened and J.T. stepped inside, his hair matted in a bloody spot on the side of his head. He pressed a damp washcloth to the spot and looked at the blood.

"I'm going with you," J.T. said. His pupils had dilated, and Sam wondered if he had a concussion.

They reached the car and Sam drove. Grimes couldn't be too far ahead, but he could have gone anywhere. Since he hadn't turned toward the airport, that might mean he arrived by boat or seaplane.

"Don't you have a brochure with a map of the island? We need to know where the marinas are located."

J.T. opened the glove box and found a map.

"There's a big marina a few miles up ahead."

Sam drove as fast as he could without running them off the road, and they reached the place in about five minutes. A couple of white vehicles sat in the parking lot, neither one a Taurus. They parked at the marina office and went inside. A slim man with skin that looked like old leather sat behind a desk. Sam asked about Grimes and Amy. The man spoke with an English accent and said about a dozen cars had come through that morning, but none fit Sam's description. They started to walk out when Sam thought about something else and turned around.

"Have you seen an old seaplane in the last day or so?"

The man with leather skin said, "Yes, a seaplane did come here last night, but we had no space, so I just sold them some fuel."

"Do you know where they went?"

The man shook his head. "I called the marina up the road, and they didn't have a spot either, so the pilot taxied the plane down the coast."

"What's down there?" J.T. said.

The man shrugged. "Just vacation homes."

"Any of them have docks?"

"Certainly, some of them do."

They got back in the car and rode further down the road. J.T. mopped his temple with the cloth and tossed it on the floor mat.

"How's your head?" Sam said.

"I think I'll live." J.T. turned in the seat and looked at Sam. "You think he's going to hurt her?"

"No. You said he brought her to the airstrip with him that day, so I'd say he just wants her back."

"Yeah, but I don't think she would have gone with him willingly. She screamed something when I entered the door, I guess trying to warn me."

They drove for several minutes before spotting the Taurus. It sat behind a coral-colored house with only the rear of the car sticking out. The lawn, going to seed, had a For Rent sign stuck in the ground close to the street. Sam kept driving past and turned into a driveway a few doors down.

They didn't have any weapons because they'd flown

to the island on a commercial airline. Besides, Sam hadn't expected to run into any trouble on Grand Cayman. They got out of the car and Sam retrieved the lug wrench from the trunk. Walking back along the street, they entered the yard with the sign and eased around the house to the Taurus, which sat empty. Sam looked through the driver side window and saw the key in the ignition. He heard the rumble of the seaplane and they eased through a thicket of palmetto and pines toward the noise, staying behind the cover of the trees where possible. The landscape cleared when they got close to the water and the seaplane came into view, tied at a dock about thirty feet away, engines idling, ready for takeoff.

"It took you long enough."

Sam and J.T. turned around. Grimes stood next to a tree with a crutch under one arm and holding an Uzi pointed at Sam, looking better than the last time Sam had seen him. He still had some scars, but the dog bites on his face had healed, and he looked as if he might have had a recent bath.

"I don't think you'll be using that lug wrench. Drop it."

Sam tossed the wrench in the grass, cursing himself for thinking Grimes would just slink away.

"Where's Amy?" J.T. said.

Grimes waved the gun. "Forget about Amy. She's going with me. Get on the plane. We're going for a ride."

"Where to?" Sam said.

"You caused me a lot of trouble, Mackenzie. Not to mention this." He glanced down at the missing leg.

"You two thought you'd seen the last of me when you left me to die down there in the Keys."

"This is about revenge?"

"That's right, I always pay my debts. Now, get on the plane like I said or I'll shoot you right here."

Sam and J.T. took their time getting to the dock and boarded, Sam wondering what Grimes had done with Amy. Randy stepped out of the cockpit and nodded to Sam. Smelling of rum and looking as if he might still be drunk from the night before, he helped Grimes through the hatch.

"Where is Amy?" J.T. said.

Randy shrugged. "Who's Amy?"

"Shut up, Randy," Grimes said, "and check them for guns."

Randy started to say something, but looked as if he changed his mind when Grimes narrowed his eyes. He asked Sam and J.T. to empty their pockets. Sam had only the GPS unit and the satellite phone, both of which Randy let him keep.

Grimes closed the hatch, and Randy taxied the plane out of the harbor and took off. They seemed to be heading west toward Jamaica and flew for about an hour before Grimes spoke.

"Okay, this is where you two get off."

Sam looked out the porthole and saw nothing but water down below. His heart raced and a bead of perspiration rolled down his cheek. He knew Grimes would stand them in front of the hatch and shoot them. They would fall out of the plane to the water below, and if they didn't die from the bullets, the impact with the surface would kill them. He had to do something! How could he disable Grimes?

Grimes stood up next to his seat with the crutch under one arm and waved the Uzi toward the hatch. "Open the door," he said to Sam.

He had to shoot them in the doorway so he wouldn't damage the plane with stray bullets. Sam thought he would take a chance, maybe upset Grimes and buy some extra time. "Shoot us right here," he said, keeping his voice steady and defiant.

J.T. had a worried look on his face.

Grimes thumped the deck with the crutch and moved closer to Sam's seat. He stuck the tip of the Uzi to the side of Sam's head.

"You think I won't do it?" His eyes narrowed and his face reddened, as if he might pop a gasket. Then he sighed and turned his head toward the cockpit.

"Randy, put it on auto, and get back here and open the door."

Randy turned around and grimaced. He unbuckled his seat belt and stood up, grabbing a bottle of rum as he did. He opened it, took a long drink and staggered down the passageway.

Grimes moved back, so Randy could get to the hatch. Randy passed between Sam and Grimes, and Sam sprang out of his seat. He grabbed the open rum bottle from Randy's fingers, threw the contents at Grimes face and at the same time pushed Randy into him. Grimes screamed when the rum hit his eyes and he and Randy, already unsteady on his feet, toppled to the deck.

Sam grabbed for the Uzi, but Grimes, his eyes streaming tears, raised up and fired a burst of rounds. One of the slugs hit Sam in the upper arm and his arm felt as if it might drop off. Sam wrested the weapon away and hit Grimes in the face with the stock. Grimes fell back to the deck, unconscious.

The bullet had gone straight through Sam's arm. Blood ran down and dripped from his fingers. Randy staggered to his feet. Sam pointed the Uzi at him and told him to get in the cockpit and take them back to Grand Cayman.

Sam turned to say something to J.T. and saw him looking down at a red spot blossoming on the front of his shirt. A bullet had gone through the back of the seat and exited through his chest.

"Hang in there, you'll be okay," Sam said and gingerly touched his shoulder.

"He shot me in the chest," J.T. mumbled. Raising his head, he stared at Sam and said, "Am I going to die?"

"No, you're not. I'm going to get you back."

It would take an hour to return to Grand Cayman, and that might be too long for J.T. He turned toward the cockpit to ask Randy if they could get to Jamaica any quicker. Randy yelled something Sam couldn't understand and came racing from the cockpit.

"The starboard engine's on fire! We're all going to die if we don't jump!" Although he'd had several drinks too many, he stumbled to the rear of the cabin, snatched open a storage compartment on the bulkhead, and pulled parachutes out.

Sam glanced out the porthole. Sure enough, the engine was ablaze, and flames ran down the wing toward the fuselage.

Sam opened an overhead compartment with a red cross on it and found a first-aid kit with tape, gauze and a small knife. He put gauze compresses over J.T.'s wounds and piled on extra tape since they would be in the water. The color had drained from J.T.'s face, and his eyelids looked heavy as Sam put the shirt on him over the bandages. J.T. winced from the effort and said, "I'm not going to make it, Sam, I just know it. Tell Amy goodbye for me. Okay?"

"You can tell her yourself. But right now we have to get out of this plane."

Blood streamed down Sam's arm, and he cut a piece of the tape and wrapped it around his own wound. He dropped the knife into his pocket in case he needed it later.

Randy came back with two parachutes and life vests and handed them to Sam.

"What about him?" Randy nodded toward Grimes.

Sam glanced at the unconscious man on the deck. "Yeah, might as well take him, too."

Sam helped J.T. with his vest and parachute and then strapped on his own. He opened the hatch and Randy asked for help with Grimes. Sam sighed and helped Randy put the parachute on him. They lifted him and dropped him next to the hatch.

"You'll need to open his 'chute for him," Sam said.

Randy nodded and put his arms through the straps of his own parachute. "I've done this before. I am a pilot, you know."

Sam turned to J.T. His eyes had glazed over and his face was pale.

"Can you stand up?"

"I think so," he mumbled.

Sam glanced at the starboard porthole and saw only flames. It would be too late when the tanks caught fire. He popped the canisters that filled their life vests with air, helped J.T. to the hatch, and shoved him out the opening. Jumping out behind him, Sam saw J.T. tumbling in the air. Probably unconscious. Sam dived and tried to grab him, but J.T. careened away, still tumbling. *Got to get his parachute open. I can't let him die.* Sam dived again and caught onto a strap. He held on for a few seconds, until they both stabilized, and pulled J.T.'s rip cord. The air caught the parachute and yanked J.T. away.

Sam saw the water coming up fast. He pulled his own cord and the straps jerked against him. Then his descent seemed to stop as he hung in a lazy panorama of sky and water, nearly impossible to discern where one stopped and the other began. His head felt light as a balloon, as if it might go into a spin. He looked up and saw only one parachute other than J.T.'s, and wondered if Grimes had made it. The seaplane, now more than a mile away, resembled a fiery kite with a black tail on the otherwise flawless sky. Then it exploded and became an expanding blob of smoke.

They drifted in the sky, alone in the middle of nowhere. Only the hiss of sea air passed Sam's ears. Nothing waited beneath them but desolation. He remembered the phone and took it out and punched in a number he had committed to memory several weeks before. A computer voice answered and Sam yelled at it until he hit the water.

He submerged, and the vest popped him out of the water a couple of seconds later. Then his parachute glided to the surface and lay down like a dying swan. He released the straps and let it drift away. J.T. had dropped into the water about thirty feet away, submerged, and came up coughing. Sam swam over to him and released the parachute. Then he cut one of its shroud lines with the knife in his pocket and tied it between him and J.T.

J.T. lost consciousness after his coughing fit, leaving Sam alone to worry about what might happen to them. They could be here for days, or until they died, so far away from anything it would be unlikely for even a small craft to fly over. The jets flew so high they'd never see them, but he hoped the 'chutes stayed afloat for a while just in case. He wondered if he'd completely sealed off the bleeding from their wounds with the tape. If he hadn't, they'd soon have company they didn't want.

TWENTY-EIGHT

THEY FLOATED IN the Caribbean for almost four hours before the helicopter flew over from the east. It looked like a Vietnam-era Huey, the big chopper used for personnel transport and rescue. Sam waved his arms and it circled and set down on pontoons a few feet away, its blades still turning, churning up the water around them.

J.T. opened his eyes without seeing anything and said, "What's that?" His teeth chattered when he spoke.

"It's our ride home," Sam said over the noise of the chopper engine. "How do you feel?"

"Cold. The water is so cold." He dozed off again.

Sam didn't feel so great himself. His arm hurt and he felt weak, dehydrated. He had covered their heads for most of the time with J.T.'s parachute, but they still got sunburned, and Sam felt as if he could drink a gallon of fresh water.

Two men stood inside the chopper door. One of them, a man with a shaved head and a green beard, threw a life preserver to Sam and he grabbed it. Green Beard pulled them over to the pontoon and lifted them out of the water. The other man, who had gold rings in his eyebrows, closed the door and nodded toward J.T. "What happened to him?"

"He took a round in the back and it came out his chest."

Sam sat down next to the bulkhead and took off his vest while they put J.T. on a gurney and strapped him down. Although large enough to carry several gurneys, this Huey had only two, leaving plenty of room for the medical men to work while in the air. Green Beard tossed Sam a blanket and went back and told the pilot they were ready for takeoff. Sam could see only the back of the pilot's head and his right arm inside the cockpit as he accelerated the engines and they lifted off the water. The man looked older than the other two. He was thin and had long, graying hair. Maybe a Vietnam veteran.

An ice chest sat on the floor a few feet away from Sam. He took a large bottle of water from it and drank it down.

Rings tossed a jumpsuit to Sam. "Here, get out of those wet clothes."

Once they got airborne and the ride stabilized, the two men started working on J.T. They removed his vest, cut off his shirt and peeled away the tape.

"Doesn't look too good," Green Beard said.

Rings nodded. "Probably has some internal bleeding."

Green Beard studied J.T.'s wounds. "Think we should open him up?"

"Are you doctors?" Sam said.

Rings glanced at Sam and smiled. "Sure, you can call us that if you want. You got any injuries?"

"Just the arm." Sam pushed up the baggy sleeve of the jumpsuit.

Rings stepped over, removed the tape and looked at the wound.

"You'll be okay. We'll put a couple of sutures in after we work on your friend."

He got a syringe and went back to Sam.

Sam didn't care much for needles. "What's that?"

"Don't worry. This is good for anything wrong with you."

"You work for Carling?"

Rings shrugged. "Who else would come out here and get you? I thought she was joking."

He gave Sam the injection, and after a few seconds the inside of the helicopter became a blur of colors. Sam heard music, a familiar tune from an old cartoon show long ago. It went faster and faster. Then the music faded and he floated away on a cloud.

Sam woke when they landed. He looked outside and saw only a portable building and a white van. J.T. still lay on the gurney, his face the color of granite. A couple of IVs hung above him, one of them red.

"How's he doing?" Sam said.

Green Beard shrugged. "Hard to say. He lost a lot of blood."

The rotor blades slowed to a stop and the two men who might be doctors got out, pulled a ramp from underneath the helicopter, and dropped it on the ground. They came back and rolled J.T.'s gurney down to the van.

Sam staggered behind them. His arm had a fresh bandage and he felt no pain. A man came out of the building, glanced at J.T. and winced.

"He going to make it?" the new man said to Rings.

"Don't know. Your guess is as good as mine. Carling's expecting him."

The man nodded and got in the driver's seat of the

van. Sam got in the back with J.T., and Rings and Green Beard stayed with the helicopter. The trip to Carling Research took about twenty minutes. Two men in hospital greens met them at the door and rolled J.T. inside.

Sam walked in behind them and took a seat in the waiting room. He saw Carling coming down the hall and stood up. She wore a short white dress, and looked as if she might be going to a party.

"So, you made it back alive," she said.

A hint of perfume reached Sam's nostrils and the room suddenly felt warmer than it had.

"Yeah, thanks to you."

She looked beautiful, and she might have read his mind because her face flushed.

Taking his hand, she said, "You look like you could use a drink. I need to go to a fund-raiser, but I have a few minutes before I leave."

Sam nodded and strolled with her down the hall, her hand warm, pleasant, inside his. She passed the office where he'd been before, and led him in another door further down.

Letting go of his hand, she said, "This is where I sleep when I have to stay here overnight."

Sam looked around the small, furnished apartment and took a seat on a leather sofa.

"How about a brandy?"

"Sounds good if you're having one."

"Why not. I could be a little late."

She went to the bar, came back with two drinks, and handed one to him. Sitting on the sofa a couple of feet away, she held her glass up for a toast.

Sam took a drink and felt the burn at the back of

his throat. He took another and set the glass on the coffee table.

"Thanks for coming to get us. J.T. would be dead by now, and I might be too."

Carling smiled and crossed her legs.

"Don't mention it."

Sam thought he had reached a wrong number when he called from the satellite phone, but now knew they must have heard everything he said, GPS coordinates and all.

"I'll take care of the bill, of course."

"Forget it, it's already covered."

"Oh, yeah? By who?"

"Jack Craft. I checked with him when we got your call, and he said you went to the Caribbean on vacation."

"Yeah, some vacation."

Sam made a mental note to call Candi later and let her know what had happened, in case she still planned to show up on Grand Cayman. He glanced back at Carling and could tell from her smile that he'd been drifting.

Several seconds passed before either of them said anything else. Finally, Carling took a sip of her drink and stood up.

"Well, I have to go. Can I drop you somewhere?"

Sam stood, too. "I'll wait around awhile, if that's okay, to see what the doctors say about J.T."

"Sure, you can wait right here. I'll tell the staff to give you a ride when you're ready to go."

Carling turned to leave and Sam said, "What kind of fund-raiser?"

She turned. "What? Oh, one of the local hospitals

has a program to help people who need expensive treatment and can't afford it."

"What do you do, to raise funds, I mean?" Sam wondered if he might be talking too much. And it didn't even sound much like his own voice. Probably the effects of the brandy on top of the medication. Or Carling's perfume. Or Carling.

"You know, the usual; I talk rich people out of their money."

"Hmmm. I didn't know you would be into that sort of thing."

Smiling with her eyes, she said, "There's a lot more you don't know about me." She picked up her handbag from the coffee table and left.

Sam drank another brandy and went back to the waiting room. He looked at magazines for a few minutes before one of the doctors came out, the same man who had worked on Candi Moran the night she showed up on Sam's boat with a bullet hole in her side.

"The jury is still out on your friend. He lost a lot of blood, but the good news is, the bullet only nicked his lung. Actually, he's very lucky to be alive at all."

The doctor told Sam to leave a number and they would call if J.T.'s condition changed. Sam nodded and gave him the telephone number on his boat, since he'd left his cell phone in the hotel room on Grand Cayman. Sam asked if he could get a ride, and a minute or so later a man came down the hall and took him to the airport where he'd left his car.

He drove to the marina and went to his boat. After a cool shower, he put on fresh clothes and sat down to call Candi Moran's cell phone.

"I'm glad you called," Candi said. "I've been try-ing to reach you."

"Where are you?"

"Still on the island. I need a few more days to fin-ish what I'm doing."

Sam told her what had happened and that he had returned to Miami.

"So, you okay?" Candi asked, sounding distracted.

"Sure, I'll be fine, but J.T.'s in pretty bad shape. The doctor said he lost a lot of blood."

"That's too bad. I hope he pulls through." She didn't sound very concerned. Sam wondered why she needed so much time on the island.

"What's happened with La Salle's operation?"

"He pulled it out of the fire after he got a bundle from selling that fake statue, and he also talked his cli-ents into investing more money."

"These are the same clients who lost their money when La Salle invested it without their consent?"

"Well, yes, but their investment didn't get lost. He showed them where all of it went, and made quite a presentation."

This casino business excited her. A feeling of dread settled into the pit of Sam's stomach.

"Why are you still down there?"

"Well, that's what I wanted to tell you. With that… uh…information you gave me, I convinced him to give me an equal share of the company."

Sam couldn't believe his ears. "You're partners?"

"Something like that. We actually work pretty well together."

"Are you crazy? He killed your father and put out a hit on you."

"Yeah…but he knows I have him now, with the recording, and this casino is just too good to pass up."

Sam didn't know what to say. He had expected her to use the recording for protection, or to send La Salle to jail, but not this. Well, they should make swell partners.

A silence stretched into a few seconds before Candi spoke: "Are you still there?"

"Yeah," Sam said, "I'm still here. That's great; I hope you're very successful."

"Thanks. I couldn't have done it without you."

Ready to hang up, Sam said, "Glad I could help."

"I'm going to send you a check for your work as soon as I get everything straightened out."

"Sure, that's fine."

"Okay, I'll call you as soon as I get free and we'll have a night on the town."

"Why don't I call *you*. I'm going to be busy for the next few days, and you might not be able to reach me."

Candi paused, maybe getting the message, and said, "That'll work. Don't forget me, though."

"Don't worry, I won't." Sam closed the phone.

Fat chance forgetting one of the most beautiful women he had ever known. Just two little problems: she's greedy and happens to be partners with a crime lord, who also is her former lover. *Serves you right, Mackenzie, for getting involved in this mess in the first place*. He might not forget her, but he wouldn't be calling back, either.

Sam leaned his head back on the chair and closed his eyes. Something nagged at the back of his mind, but he felt so tired he could barely think. Going over the last 24 hours, he remembered J.T.'s call from his hotel room saying Grimes had taken Amy. *Amy!* With all that had happened, he'd completely forgotten about her. She might still be at the house where Grimes had parked the car, but it would take hours to get back to Grand Cayman. Sam didn't know anyone there who could check on her. Then he remembered the man he'd met on the flight. What was his name? Harold something, and very nervous. Yes: Shakes, Harold Shakes.

Sam called Long Distance Information and got the number for the hotel where Harold said he had a job. Within a couple of minutes he had Harold on the line.

"Harold, this Sam Mackenzie. I met you on the plane a few weeks ago."

"Sam who?"

"Mackenzie, I sat next you and you told me all about your new job at the hotel. You said your girlfriend works there, too."

Pause. "Oh, yeah, I remember. She's not my girlfriend anymore, though..." Harold's voice trailed off.

"Sorry to hear that, Harold. I wonder if you'd do me a favor."

Harold remained silent for a couple of seconds, probably wondering what kind of con this might be. "Well, I don't know—"

"Harold, this is really important. A woman's life is at stake. You'll be a hero."

Sam told him what had happened to Amy and why he couldn't help her himself. He described the house and the location, and mentioned the For Sale sign.

"Shouldn't I call the police?" Harold had panic in his voice.

"No, no, don't do that. The guy who did it is long gone. You can handle this. I promise, I'll make it worth your time."

"What do you want me to do if I find her?"

"Just get her out of there and call me."

"My shift doesn't end for another half hour." Harold lowered his voice and continued, "But I can leave now, and nobody'll notice."

Sam gave him his telephone number and hung up. He made a sandwich in the galley and ate it leaning against the sink, then went to the lounge and dozed in a chair until the phone rang. Harold Shakes.

"I found her where you said, tied to a chair."

"Is she okay?"

"Yeah, she seems okay, other than being starved and dehydrated." Harold's voice trembled. "You sure I shouldn't call the police."

"No, that won't help anything. You rescued Amy and everything's going to be fine. Put her on the phone."

The phone clattered, as if dropped, and Amy came onto the line. "Where's J.T., Sam?"

Sam told her what had happened and could hear her crying.

"He'll be okay, though. It'll just take a while." Sam had his fingers crossed when he said it. "I'll come down there tomorrow and we'll get J.T.'s things and fly back together."

She sobbed, said, "Okay," and put Harold back on the line.

Sam asked Harold if Amy could stay with him for the night, just in case Grimes had escaped getting on the shark menu. Harold said he would be glad to take Amy to his place, and seemed a little more pleased than he should have been.

SAM THOUGHT ABOUT Prince Alfred; they had left him with Jack Craft when they went to Grand Cayman. He telephoned Jack, brought him up-to-date on J.T., and asked about the dog.

"You know, it was the funniest thing. I took him to the beach with me a couple of times when I went fishing, and the last time I did, a teenage girl ran up and claimed he belonged to her. She said he'd gotten lost when they moved across town."

"You let her take him?" Sam felt a knot in his stomach.

"Well...yeah. I could tell he knew her, and when she left, Prince Alfred looked up at me, as if to say good-bye, and then followed her away."

"Huh."

"You don't sound too happy. I thought you'd be glad we found his owner."

"Yeah, I guess that's the best thing."

Sam hung up the phone. *A lot of grief to digest in one day.* He got up and poured a large brandy.

TWENTY-NINE

SAM CAUGHT THE first flight out to Grand Cayman the next morning. He took a taxi directly from the airport to the hotel and collected his things, and then called Harold and asked him to bring Amy over. When they arrived, Sam gave Harold several large bills for his gallantry. Harold made noises about not wanting the money, but Sam knew he probably needed it and insisted.

They went to J.T.'s room and packed his and Amy's things. Harold followed Amy around as if he might be in love, but she didn't seem to notice. When they had almost finished packing, Amy asked him if he would go ahead and carry some of the bags to the lobby.

Harold hustled the bags out the door and Amy said to Sam, "Grimes left the gold items he stole from J.T. in the house where he tied me up." She winked. "I have them in one of my bags."

They checked out of the hotel and Harold took them to the airport. He parked the car and walked them into the terminal where they said their goodbyes.

Harold had a forlorn look when they ambled to the counter, and Amy stopped and said to Sam, "Wait here, I'll be right back."

She hurried away and called to Harold. He hadn't gotten to the door. Sam couldn't hear what she said, but saw Harold's face light up, and then Amy hugged him and gave him a quick kiss on the lips. She returned to the counter while Harold stood there with a smile on his face, his fingers touching his lips.

When they arrived in Miami, Sam took Amy to Carling Research. He tried to prepare her for what she would see, but it didn't help much. Tears streamed down her face as she stared at J.T. lying there like a corpse, tubes running from his arm and side, the machines making industrial noises by his bed. Sam took her home, and she stopped crying by the time they reached her apartment. She said she would pack a bag and go stay with J.T. in case he woke up.

Three days later, as Sam finished breakfast in his galley and poured another cup of coffee, he felt someone step onto the boat outside. He glanced through the peep hole, saw Jack Craft with a newspaper under his arm, and opened the door.

"Good morning," Jack said. "How's J.T. doing?"

"Not much change. I spoke with Amy last night and she said he's still under."

Jack sighed. "That's too bad. J.T.'s a good man."

Sam didn't think Jack had come by to ask about J.T.

"I was just about to have a cup of coffee outside. How about joining me?"

"Sure, I could use another cup."

Sam poured the coffee and they went onto the deck and took a seat under the awning near the stern.

Jack laid the newspaper on a table between their chairs and pointed to a story.

"You might like this."

Jack had a twinkle in his eye, and Sam looked down at the headline: Gideon Barge Missing. He picked up the paper and read the story about how Barge had merged his holding company with another international conglomerate, and now had neither a controlling interest nor a prominent position in either company. The business world wondered why he would do such a thing, but no one had been able to reach him since the merger. Reported missing a couple of days later, none of the executives in his former company seemed to know where he might have gone.

"What do you think happened?" Sam said.

Jack shrugged and took a sip of his coffee. "Hard to say."

A woman on the boat in the next slip over came out and threw bread crumbs in the air. Several gulls appeared, grabbed the bread, and squawked at each other. Jack shook his head.

"You know, she really shouldn't do that."

"Everybody does," Sam said. "The gulls love it."

Jack nodded and smiled. "Yes, they do."

"Do you think they'll find Barge?"

Jack took another sip of coffee and looked at the birds. "No, they probably won't."

SAM WENT TO see J.T. every day, but the situation stayed the same. He stopped by Carling's office a couple of times, too, but missed her. Then, eight days after J.T. had been shot, at 7:00 in the evening, Carling called Sam on his boat and said J.T. regained consciousness and asked for some food.

"Is Amy there?" Sam asked.

"She went home to shower before he awoke, but said she'll be right back."

Sam arrived a half hour later. J.T. sat in his bed having a meal from a tray. Although thinner than he had been, he didn't look too bad.

"Hey, you're awake," Sam said, smiling. "How're you feeling?"

J.T. laid down his fork and grinned. "I think I'll live." The grin faded and he said, "I remember most of what happened, and I really appreciate you saving my life."

Sam shrugged. "You would've done the same for me. I'm just glad we both made it."

J.T. nodded. "Still, I won't forget it." He picked up his fork. "You know, this is pretty good food for a hospital." It looked like filet mignon. "They said I've been here over a week. It seems like just yesterday that Grimes took us on that seaplane."

Sam told him about Harold rescuing Amy. "She's been staying here with you most of the time."

J.T.'s face lit up and he put the plate aside. "No kidding?"

"No kidding. Carling said she went home a few minutes ago, but she'll be right back."

The door opened and Amy came in, smiling. She eased to the bed, leaned over the plastic tubes and kissed J.T.

Sam stepped out the door and met Carling in the hall.

"You saw him?" she said.

"Sure did. How long before he can leave?"

"Maybe a day or two. He's out of danger now."

A long silence lay between them while they looked into each other's eyes. Finally, Carling glanced down the hall and said, "Well, if there's nothing else…"

"Wait… I…"

A suave man wearing a navy blazer came around the corner. He looked at Carling, glanced at his watch and said, "We're going to be late."

Carling smiled. "Give me a minute."

Suave Man glanced at Sam, then back at Carling.

"Okay, but they won't hold the reservation." He paced in the hallway.

Carling turned back to Sam and squeezed his arm. "What is it?"

Sam glanced toward the man. "Uh…nothing. You're busy, I'll talk to you later."

Carling stared at him for a couple of beats and said, "Wait here."

She went and said something to Suave Man. He stepped back, gave her a stern look, turned, and hurried around the corner.

Carling came back and said, "Okay, now, tell me."

"I just wondered if we could start over, maybe go out sometime."

"Sure, how about right now?"

"I thought you had a date?"

She shrugged. "I told him I'm going out with you."

AMY PICKED UP J.T. the next day and took him to her apartment. Two days after that, they met Sam and Carling at the marina restaurant. They had drinks and dinner, and then talked about Amy's plans for a pet grooming business.

"By the way," Amy said, "whatever happened to Prince Alfred?"

Sam relayed the conversation he'd had with Jack, about the dog's owner showing up on the beach.

Tears in Amy's eyes glistened in the restaurant lights. "So I guess we won't ever see him again, huh?"

"Guess not," Sam said.

That seemed to cast a pall over the conversation, and after a period of silence Sam asked J.T. to go out to the dock with him.

J.T. held his gaze for a couple of seconds and nodded. He winced as he got up from his chair and touched his chest where the bandages still covered his injuries.

Outside, a school of skipjack bounced across the water. A pelican perched on one of the timbers and looked down at the fish.

J.T. leaned on the rail, squinting at the sun on the horizon. Sam pulled a piece of paper from his pocket, unfolded it and handed it to J.T.

"I wanted you to see this."

J.T. looked at the paper, a courier receipt dated the day after Sam retrieved the genuine statue from Lenny Berne.

"This says you sent something to a museum in Mexico City." He glanced at Sam. "The statue?"

Sam nodded and J.T.'s eyes narrowed.

He handed the paper back to Sam, looked down at the schooling skipjack, and shook his head.

"Man, I knew you'd do something like that. I just knew it."

"I decided the legitimate owner should have it back."

J.T. drew in a breath and sighed. "You know what you remind me of?"

"What's that?"

"That bird over there, looking down his nose at those fish, like he's better than they are."

Sam knew the pelican just had his sights on a meal,

but thought it might not be a good idea to argue with J.T. right then.

"And I'll tell you something else," J.T. said, his face red and his voiced pitched higher than normal. "You know that night on the flight line when Candi shot La Salle?"

"That's a picture I won't forget for a long time."

"The reason I didn't come out there right away is, when I heard the shot, I had driven a mile up the road with the other statue."

Sam had suspected something like that, but it still surprised him to hear J.T. say it.

The pelican flapped its wings, lunged into the water, and came up with a fish in its beak.

J.T. looked at Sam, shook his head, and turned and walked back into the restaurant. Sam followed him in and J.T. told Amy they had to leave. Amy gave Sam a questioning glance, picked up her purse and hurried away with J.T.

J.T.'s angry, but he'll get over it, and if he doesn't, that's his problem.

THIRTY

SAM WENT TO the marina office on a hot Thursday the first week in June and checked his mailbox. Although he had several envelopes addressed to Occupant, one had Candi's name handwritten in the upper left corner. He opened it and found an invitation to a party the following month to celebrate the grand opening of The Casino on New Miami. Sam remembered what Jack Craft had said about not actually having a gambling license, and wondered how La Salle had gotten around that.

The invitation indicated that the attendees would be a small group of close friends and associates. Candi had also sent a check for more than Sam had expected. There was no note, and Sam was disappointed for a moment, but realized none of her words would have made anything any better. He put the invitation on the table by the phone and stood there for a minute, wondering what might happen to her.

La Salle might have given her an equal share in the company, but she had already shot him once, and might try it again some day. He would never trust her, and as soon as he found that recording, Candi would be history. She would take the long way down, maybe join the one-armed man at the bottom waiting for a connecting flight. Sam wished it had turned out differently, but he didn't know anything else he could do for Candi Moran. He got a beer from the reefer, stepped out on deck and took a seat in the shade.

Jack dropped by a little later to talk about a new scheme he had in mind. "You've heard of Archibald Schmidt, haven't you?"

Sam nodded. "It was in the news. The Feds went after his company and he disappeared with a few million in cash. You want a beer?"

"Yeah, that'd be great."

Sam got two fresh beers, came back and handed Jack one of them.

Jack opened the bottle and took a long drink. "About this Schmidt guy, one of my contacts told me he's hiding in the Cayman Islands. I've got his location and some details about the money he stole."

Sam glanced at him. "You're going after the money?"

Jack beamed and drank more beer. "Yes, I feel it's my duty. I've got a role for you, too. Could be very lucrative."

Sam shook his head. "I think I'm going to retire."

"Retire? You're twenty years younger than I am."

Maybe more than that, but he didn't want to get into that discussion. "Yeah, well, I guess I'm tired of being shot at and looking over my shoulder."

"What are you going to do for money?"

"I have some packed away. It should last awhile."

Jack grinned. "Okay, fine. It'll be at least a month before I do this, so just think about it."

"Sure, but don't count on me changing my mind."

Jack nodded and blinked a couple of times. "Yeah, well, you mind if I ask J.T. about it?"

"Not at all."

Jack left and called back a few minutes later. He said he'd spoken with J.T., and J.T. wouldn't do it unless Sam would.

J.T. CALLED THE next day to tell Sam about selling the gold.

"I did better than I thought. You can still have your share if you want."

"No, that's okay, you keep it."

"You sure?"

"Yeah, I'm sure."

"Okay…well, I also wanted to apologize about the other day. You know, the stuff I said."

"Hey, don't worry about it."

"I guess I felt guilty about running out on you like that."

"Yeah, well, everybody makes mistakes."

An awkward silence stretched on for several seconds before Sam said, "Why don't you stop by and we'll have a six-pack and catch some fish."

"Yeah, that sounds good. How about this afternoon?"

A FEW DAYS LATER, Sam and Carling flew to Cancun and stayed three weeks. The sun was hot, the beer and margaritas were cold, and the nights were steamy. Worries about gold on a ditched airplane and a crook named La Salle slowly faded into the tropical sunset. Candi Moran still slow-danced across Sam's subconscious, but even that happened less and less as the days passed and the surf lapped at their feet.

They returned to Miami the day before the grand opening of the casino. Carling had to get back to the

medical business, and Sam wanted to do some work
on his boat. He would replace a couple of boards on
the rear deck that had gone soft and put on another
coat of varnish.

Sam unlocked the hatch, went into the lounge and
looked around. Nothing had changed. The place had
a musty smell until he turned on the air conditioner
and ran it for a few minutes. The invitation lay where
he had left it by the phone. He opened it and read it
again. Visions of Candi and La Salle hosting the event
together caused his stomach to ache. He tossed the invitation in the trash, got a cold beer from the reefer and
sauntered out onto the deck in the shade of the awning.
The repairs could wait another day.

Sam heard a scream somewhere down the dock,
then a rumbling sound that seemed to get closer by the
second. He looked around just in time to see Prince
Alfred run across the gangway. The dog leapt into the
chair next to Sam and barked at him.

Sam grinned. "Hello, little buddy. Where have you
been?" He scratched behind Prince Alfred's ears and
the dog barked again.

A teenage girl ran across the gangway and yelled,
"Beamer!"

The dog raised an ear.

Sam stood up and the girl gave him an uneasy look.

"Did you see my dog?" She took a couple of deep
breaths, winded. "He just ran this way." Then she noticed the dog sitting in the chair and walked over to
him. "There you are. What are you doing here?" She
patted him on the head. "I don't know what's wrong
with him. This is the second time he's run away toward this marina."

"We're old friends," Sam said. "I found him in the parking lot of a restaurant a few weeks ago. Jack told me you saw him on the beach and took him home."

A pelican flew down and perched on a timber nearby. Prince Alfred jumped down from the chair, skipped over to the rail, and sat, so he could get a closer look.

The girl looked past Sam toward the dock. "Mom. Over here," she called.

Sam turned and saw a woman standing next to the gangway. She was very attractive, with long black hair and lips like ripe plums.

"This is the man who found Beamer."

The woman smiled, stepped aboard, and reached out her hand. "Hello, I'm Natalie."

Sam shook her hand and said, "Sam Mackenzie."

"I can't thank you enough for watching Beamer. He looked very well-fed."

"You're welcome; I'm glad I could help." Sam glanced at Prince Alfred, smiled, and considered telling them how the dog had saved his life, maybe twice, but decided that might be too much of a story to tell.

They talked for a couple of minutes and Sam offered them drinks, but Natalie said they had to be going.

"I could use a soda," the girl said and stepped over and sat down on the deck next to the dog.

Sam told Natalie to have a seat, went inside, and brought back two colas. "I brought two, in case you change your mind."

"Okay, why not."

They sat in silence for several seconds, and Natalie said, "Well, I'm glad to know why he's been moping around. He just wanted to see you."

Sam thought about Amy's misty eyes when he had told her about Jack letting the girl take the dog from the beach.

"I know someone else who would like to see him, too, if you don't mind leaving a number."

She looked at Sam and smiled, like it might be a come-on line, but also like she might not mind him calling her.

"Sure. Beamer's a good judge of character."

She pulled a card from her purse and handed it to Sam. The card indicated she worked for a local law firm as an attorney.

"This is my cell number. When I'm not at work, I spend a lot of time taking Christi to her swim class and other activities. I'm a single parent."

Sam glanced at the card again and wondered how it might be, dating an attorney. His lifestyle might scare her off, but maybe not, and she might even help him out of a legal jam someday. Then the image of Carling floated behind his eyes and the dream faded.

Natalie and Christi left a couple minutes later and Sam went with them to the dock and watched them walk away. Prince Alfred seemed to be perfectly happy to go with them, investigating a skipping mullet along the way. Christi stood on tiptoes to whisper something in her mother's ear and then turned and grinned at Sam. Natalie seemed embarrassed, but smiled and waved. Prince Alfred turned for one last look and barked.

Sam sauntered back to the deck and leaned on the rail. He called J.T. and told him about Prince Alfred.

"No kidding. Man, that's great news. That'll make Amy's day. She's mentioned that dog about ten times since the night you told us what happened."

They talked another minute or so, and Sam ended the call and looked out over the water. The pelican had flown away some time after the dog left. Clouds, like white castles, floated in the sky, and a jet glided overhead on its approach to Miami International. Gulls squawked nearby, fighting over crumbs of bread. Notes from an old rock song drifted on a warm breeze.

He wondered if he could get used to this sort of thing all the time. No more guns, no more close calls, and no more stress. That sounded pretty good. Of course, someone from his past might show up occasionally, and he might have to deal with them. But he could manage that.

If careful with his money, he could live several years on what he had stashed away. Just piddle around the boat, drink some beer, do some fishing, and watch the sunsets. He might start it off by taking a cruise. Maybe go over to Freeport, then down to Nassau, and swing back by the Keys. What could be bad about that? People worked thirty or forty years to get there, and he had a front-row seat.

Just watching those sunsets.

Day after day.

Sam thought about it a few more minutes, got another beer and ambled down the dock to see Jack Craft about that job.

* * * * *